DEAD END

IN NORVELT

Also by Jack Gantos

Joey Pigza Swallowed the Key
Joey Pigza Loses Control
What Would Joey Do?
I Am Not Joey Pigza

For Older Readers

Desire Lines
Hole in My Life

JACK GANTOS

DEAD END

IN NORVELT

CORGI YEARLING

DEAD END IN NORVELT
A CORGI YEARLING BOOK 978 0 440 87004 3

Originally published in the United States by Farrar, Straus and Giroux, 2011

First published in Great Britain by Corgi Yearling,
an imprint of Random House Children's Publishers UK
A Random House Group Company

This edition published 2012

3 5 7 9 10 8 6 4 2

The Random House Group Limited supports The Forest Stewardship Council® (FSC®), the leading international forest-certification organisation. Our books carrying the FSC label are printed on FSC®-certified paper. FSC is the only forest-certification scheme supported by the leading environmental organisations, including Greenpeace. Our paper procurement policy can be found at www.randomhouse.co.uk/environment

Set in Sabon

Corgi Yearling Books are published by Random House Children's Publishers UK, 61–63 Uxbridge Road, London W5 5SA

www.randomhousechildrens.co.uk
www.totallyrandombooks.co.uk
www.randomhouse.co.uk

Addresses for companies within The Random House Group Limited can be found at: www.randomhouse.co.uk/offices.htm

THE RANDOM HOUSE GROUP Limited Reg. No. 954009

A CIP catalogue record for this book is available from the British Library.

Printed and bound by CPI Group (UK) Ltd, Croydon, CR0 4YY

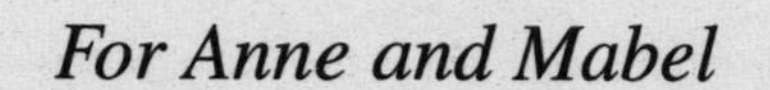

For Anne and Mabel

DEAD END

IN NORVELT

1

School was finally out and I was standing on a picnic table in our backyard getting ready for a great summer vacation when my mother walked up to me and ruined it. I was holding a pair of camouflage Japanese WWII binoculars to my eyes and focusing across her newly planted vegetable garden, and her cornfield, and over ancient Miss Volker's roof, and then up the Norvelt road, and past the brick bell tower on my school, and beyond the Community Center, and the tall silver whistle on top of the volunteer fire department to the most distant dark blue hill, which is where the screen for the Viking drive-in movie theater had recently been erected.

Down by my feet I had laid out all the Japanese army souvenirs Dad had shipped home from the war. He had been in the navy, and after a Pacific island invasion in the Solomons he and some other sailor buddies had blindly crawled around at night and found a bunker of dead Japanese soldiers half buried in the sand. They stripped everything military off of them and dragged the loot back to their camp. Dad had an officer's sword with what he said was real dried blood along the razor-sharp edge of the long blade. He had a Japanese flag, a sniper's rifle with a full ammo clip, a dented canteen, a pair of dirty white gloves with a scorched hole shot right through the bloody palm of the left hand, and a color-tinted photo of an elegant Japanese woman in a kimono. Of course he also had the powerful binoculars I was using.

I knew Mom had come to ruin my fun, so I thought I would distract her and maybe she'd forget what was on her mind.

"Hey, Mom," I said matter-of-factly with the binoculars still pressed against my face, "how come blood on a sword dries red, and blood on cloth dries brown? How come?"

"Honey," Mom replied, sticking with what was on her mind, "does your dad know you have all this dangerous war stuff out?"

"He always lets me play with it as long as I'm careful," I said, which wasn't true. In fact, he never let me play with it, because as he put it, "This swag will be worth a bundle of money someday, so keep your grubby hands off it."

"Well, don't hurt yourself," Mom warned. "And if there is blood on some of that stuff, don't touch it. You might *catch* something, like Japanese polio."

"Don't you mean Japanese *beetles*?" I asked. She had an invasion of those in her garden that were winning the plant war.

She didn't answer my question. Instead, she switched back to why she came to speak to me in the first place. "I just got a call from Miss Volker. She needs a few minutes of your time in the morning, so I told her I'd send you down."

I gazed at my mom through the binoculars but she was too close to bring into focus. Her face was just a hazy pink cupcake with strawberry icing.

"And," she continued, "Miss Volker said she would give you a little *something* for your help, but I don't want you to take any money. You can take a slice of pie but no money. We never help neighbors for cash."

"Pie? That's all I get?" I asked. "Pie? But what if it makes her feel good to give me money?"

"It won't make *me* feel good if she gives you money," she stressed. "And it shouldn't make you feel good either. Helping others is a far greater reward than doing it for money."

"Okay," I said, giving in to her before she pushed me in. "What time?"

Mom looked away from me for a moment and stared over at War Chief, my uncle Will's Indian pony, who was grinding his chunky yellow teeth. He was working up a sweat from scratching his itchy side back and forth against the rough bark on a prickly oak. About a month ago my uncle visited us when he got a pass from the army. He used to work for the county road department and for kicks he had painted big orange and white circles with reflective paint all over War Chief's hair. He said it made War Chief look like he was getting ready to battle General Custer. But War Chief was only battling the paint which wouldn't wash off, and it had been driving him crazy. Mom said the army had turned her younger brother Will from being a "nice kid" to being a "confused jerk."

Earlier, the pony had been rubbing himself against the barbed wire around the turkey coop, but the long-necked turkeys got all riled up and pecked his legs. It had been so long since a farrier had trimmed War Chief's hooves that he hobbled painfully around the yard like a crippled ballerina. It was sad. If my uncle gave me the pony I'd take really good care of him, but he wouldn't give him up.

"Miss Volker will need you there at six in the morning," Mom said casually, "but she said you were welcome to come earlier if you wanted."

"Six!" I cried. "I don't even have to get up that early for school, and now that I'm on my summer vacation I want to sleep in. Why does she need me so early?"

"She said she has an important project with a deadline and she'll need you as early as she can get you."

I lifted my binoculars back toward the movie. The Japanese were snaking through the low palmettos toward the last few marines on Wake Island. One of the young marines was holding a prayer book and looking toward heaven, which was a sure Hollywood sign he was about to die with a slug to a vital organ. Then the scene cut to a young Japanese soldier aiming his sniper rifle, which looked just like mine. Then the film cut back to the young marine, and just as he crossed himself with the "Father, Son, and Holy—" *BANG!* He clutched his heart and slumped over.

"Yikes!" I called out. "They plugged him!"

"Is that a war movie?" Mom asked sharply, pointing toward the screen and squinting as if she were looking directly into the flickering projector.

"Not entirely," I replied. "It's more of a *love* war movie." I lied. It was *totally* a war movie except for when the soon-to-be-dead marines talked about their girlfriends, but I threw in the word *love* because I thought she wouldn't say what she said next.

"You know I don't like you watching war movies," she scolded me with her hands on her hips. "All that violence is bad for you—plus it gets you *worked up*."

"I *know*, Mom," I replied with as much huffiness in my voice as I thought I could get away with. "I know."

"Do I need to remind you of your *little* problem?" she asked.

How could I forget? I was a *nosebleeder*. The moment something startled me or whenever I got overexcited or spooked about any little thing blood would spray out of my nose holes like dragon flames.

"I *know*," I said to her, and instinctively swiped a finger under my nose to check for blood. "You remind me of my *little* problem all day long."

"You know the doctor thinks it's the sign of a *bigger* problem," she said seriously. "If you have iron-poor blood you may not be getting enough oxygen to your brain."

"Can you just leave, please?"

"Don't be disrespectful," she said, reminding me of my manners, but I was already obsessing about my bleeding-nose problem. When Dad's old Chevy truck backfired I showered blood across the sidewalk. When I fell off the pony and landed on my butt my nose spewed blood down over my chest. At night, if I had a disturbing dream then my nose leaked through the pillow. I swear, with the blood I was losing I needed a transfusion about every other day. Something had to be wrong with me, but one really good advantage about being dirt-poor is that you can't afford to go to the doctor and get bad news.

"Jack!" my mom called, and reached forward to poke my kneecap. "Jack! Are you listening? Come into the house soon. You'll have to get to bed early now that you have morning plans."

"Okay," I said, and felt my fun evening leap off a cliff as she walked back toward the kitchen door. I knew she was still soaking the dishes in the sink so I had a little more time. Once she was out of sight I turned back to what I had been planning all along. I lifted the binoculars and focused in on the movie screen. The Japanese hadn't quite finished off all the marines and I figured I'd be a marine too and help defend them. I knew we wouldn't be fighting the Japanese anymore because they were now our friends, but it was good to use movie enemies for target practice because Dad said I had to get ready to fight off the Russian Commies who had already sneaked into the country and were planning to launch a surprise attack. I put down the binoculars and removed the ammo clip on the sniper rifle then aimed it toward the screen where I could just make out the small images. There was no scope on the rifle so I had to use the regular sight—the kind where you lined up a little metal ball on the far end of the barrel with the V-notch above the trigger where you pressed your cheek and eye to the cool wooden stock. The rifle weighed a ton. I hoisted it up and tried to aim at the movie screen, but the barrel shook back and forth so wildly I couldn't get the ball to line up inside the V. I lowered the rifle and took a deep breath. I knew I didn't have all night to play because of Mom, so I gave it another try as the Japanese made their final "Banzai!" assault.

I lifted the rifle again and swung the tip of the barrel straight up into the air. I figured I could gradually lower the barrel at the screen, aim, and pick off one of the Japanese troops. With all my strength I slowly lowered the barrel and held it steady enough to finally get the ball centered inside the V, and when I saw a tiny Japanese soldier leap out of a bush I quickly pulled the trigger and let him have it.

BLAM! The rifle fired off and violently kicked out of my grip. It flipped into the air before clattering down across the picnic table and sliding onto the ground. "Oh sweet cheeze-us!" I wailed, and dropped butt-first onto the table. "Ohhh! Cheeze-us-crust!" I didn't know the rifle was loaded. I hadn't put a shell in the chamber. My ears were ringing like air raid warnings. I tried to stand but was too dizzy and flopped over. "This is bad. This is bad," I whispered over and over as I desperately gripped the tabletop.

"Jaaaack!" I heard my mother shriek and then the screen door slammed behind her.

"If I'm not already dead I soon will be," I said to myself.

She sprinted across the grass and mashed through a bed of peonies and lunged toward me like a crazed animal. Before I could drop down and hide under the picnic table she pounced on me. "Oh . . . my . . . God!" she panted, and grabbed at my body as I tried to wiggle away. "Oh dear Lord! There's blood! You've been shot! Where?" Then she gasped and pointed directly at my face. Her eyes bugged out and her scream was so high-pitched it was silent.

I tasted blood. "Oh cheeze!" I shouted. "I've been shot in the mouth!"

With the dish towel still clutched in her hand she pressed it against my forehead.

"Am I dying?" I blubbered. "Is there a hole in my head? Am I breathing?"

I felt her roughly wiping my face while trying to get a clear look at my wound. "Oh, good grief," she suddenly groaned, and flung her bloodied arms down to her side.

"What?" I asked desperately. "Am I too hurt to be fixed?"

"It's just your *nose problem*!" she said, exasperated. "Your dang bloody nose!" Then she pressed the towel to my face again. "Hold it there tightly," she instructed, "I'll go get another one."

She stomped back toward the house, and I sat there for a few torturous minutes with one hand pressing the towel against my nose and breathed deeply through my mouth. Even through the blood I could smell the flinty gunpowder from the bullet. Dad is going to kill me, I thought. He'll court-martial me and sentence me to death by firing squad. Before I could fully imagine the tragic end of my life I heard an ambulance wailing up the Norvelt road. It took a turn directly into Miss Volker's driveway and stopped. The driver jumped out and sprinted toward her house and jerked open the porch door.

That's not good, I thought and turned cold all over. If I shot Miss Volker through the head Mom will never believe it was an accident. She'll think I was just trying to get out of going to her house in the morning.

I lowered myself down onto the picnic bench and then onto the grass which was slippery from my blood.

I trotted across the yard to our screen door. I was still bleeding so I stood outside and dripped on the doormat. Please, please, please, don't let me have shot her, I thought over and over. I knew I had to say something to Mom, so I gathered up a little courage and as casually as possible said, "Um, there happens to be an ambulance at Miss Volker's house."

But Mom was a step ahead of me. "Don't worry," she said right back. "I just now called down there. She's fine. You didn't shoot her if that is what you are thinking."

"I was," I admitted. "I thought I shot her dead!"

"It wasn't that," she said, now frowning at me from the other side of the door. "The shock from hearing the rifle go off caused her to drop her hearing aid down the toilet—I guess she had it turned up too high."

"So why'd she call an ambulance? Did she get her arm stuck going after it?"

"No. She called the plumber, but he's also the ambulance driver so he made an emergency call. Really," she said with some admiration, "it's good that people around this town know how to help out in different ways."

"Hey, Mom," I said quietly before going to wash my face at the outside work sink, "please don't tell Dad about the gun accident." He was out of town but you never knew when he'd finish a construction job and suddenly show up.

"I'll consider it," she said without much promise. "But until he returns you are grounded—and if you do something this stupid again you'll barely live to regret it. Understand?"

I understood. I really didn't want Dad knowing what had happened because he would blow a fuse. On top of him not wanting me to touch his stuff he was always trying to teach me about gun safety, and I figured after this gun episode he might give up on me and I didn't want him to.

"Here," she said, and handed me a wad of tissues so I could roll them into pointy cones to plug up my nose holes. "And before bed I want you to take a double dose of your iron drops," she stressed. "The doctor doesn't want you to become anemic."

"It's just a nosebleed," I said glumly.

"There may be more to it," she replied. "Besides, given that stunt you just pulled, it's in your best interest to do exactly what I say."

I did exactly what she said and cleaned all my blood off and took my medicine and went to bed, but firing that rifle had me all wound up. How could that bullet have gotten into the chamber? The ammo clip was off. I thought about it as I tossed back and forth, but couldn't come up with an answer. Plus, it was hard to fall asleep with my nose stuffed with massive wads of bloody tissue while breathing through my dry mouth. I turned on my bedside lamp and picked a book from one of the tall stacks Mom had given me. She did some charity auction work for the old elementary school over in Hecla which was closing, and in return they gave her a bunch of books including their beat-up Landmark history series, which had dozens of titles about famous explorers. I was a little too drifty in school so she thought it was a good idea that I read more books, and she knew I liked history and adventure stories.

I started reading about Francisco Pizarro's hard-to-believe conquest of the Incas in Peru. In 1532 Pizarro and fewer than two hundred men captured Atahualpa, the Inca chief, who had an army of fifty thousand soldiers. Pizarro's men fired off an old flintlock blunderbuss and the noise and smoke scared the Inca army and Pizarro jumped on Atahualpa and held a sword to his neck and in that very instant the entire Inca empire was defeated. Amazing!

Pizarro then held Atahualpa hostage for a ransom of gold so the Incas brought Pizarro piles of golden life-size people and animals and plants—all sculpted from solid gold as if the Incas had the Midas touch while they strolled through their fantastic cities and farms and jungles and everything they even gently brushed up against turned into pure gold. But no one will ever again see that life-size golden world because once the conquistadors got their greedy hands on the gold they melted it down. They turned all those beautiful golden sculptures into boring Spanish coins and shipped boat-loads of them back to the king and queen of Spain, who loved the gold but wanted even more.

Pizarro then raided all the temples and palaces and melted down the gold he found and sent that back. Still, it wasn't enough for the king and queen. Pizarro even dug up the dead when it was discovered that they were buried with gold. He had their jewelry melted down and sent back to Spain. But it still wasn't enough. So Pizarro's men forced the Inca people to work harder in the gold mines. They melted the gold ore and sent that back to Spain, and when there was no more gold Pizarro broke his promise and strangled the Inca king. He turned the Inca people into slaves and they died by the thousands from harsh work and disease.

Finally, one of Pizarro's own men sneaked up and stabbed him to death because he thought Pizarro was cheating him out of his share of gold for helping to conquer the Incas. Gold had driven the conquistadors crazy and they ended up killing themselves and all of those poor Incas. It was a really tragic story. I just wished I had been with Atahualpa and his army when the conquistadors fired off that blunderbuss. I could have told Atahualpa that I had fired off a rifle too and that it was scary, but not to panic. Then we could have ordered the Inca army to capture the gold-crazed conquistadors and saved the Inca civilization, and history would have been different. If only . . .

2

I must have fallen asleep because I was dreaming of Pizarro's crazed men melting down the golden statues of people into a big pot like when you melt a plastic army man over a burner on the stove when your mother isn't looking. That's when my alarm clock went off. It was five in the morning. I knew I had set it for six, but after I fell asleep Mom must have reset it. I was just going to roll over and go back to sleep when she tapped my shoulder and whispered, "Jack, are you awake?"

"I'm dreaming of gold," I moaned. "Lots of gold."

"Stop dreaming," she ordered, and pinched my toe. "And hurry up. Miss Volker has probably made your breakfast already. She's been up for hours."

"I thought I was grounded," I said nasally, and plucked out my bloodied nose plugs.

"I'm just loaning you to her for a while," she explained. "When you finish with her come straight back home. Understand?"

I understood.

When she left I pulled on the same sweaty clothes I had peeled off the night before. I didn't care that there were bloodstains spattered down the front of my shirt because every shirt I owned was decorated with bloodstains. I glanced at my hair in the mirror. My brown curls stood up on my head like a field planted with question marks. There was no reason to brush it. The question marks would just stand up into exclamation points and then wilt back over into question marks. Besides, I was a boy. It is okay to be a boy slob because moms think they still have time to cure you of your bad habits before you grow up and become an annoying adult slob for someone else.

"Change that nasty shirt," Mom ordered when she spotted the crusty bib of dried blood across my chest.

I looked down at my shirt. "Hey, how come this blood is brown?" I asked. "Last night it was red."

"It is too early in the morning to mess with me," she replied. "Just change the shirt and get moving. I'm going back to bed."

I didn't change the shirt. Only a few spots of blood had soaked through, so I just turned it inside out as I walked down the narrow hall, past my small room, through the airless living room, and out the front door and down the three porch steps. All the Norvelt houses were built to look the same. It was like I was stepping out of one of those little green houses in a Monopoly game.

The dark grass was wet with morning dew and a little squeaky under my sneakers. It was tall enough for me to cut. I might be a slob but I kept the yard looking tidy because Dad allowed me to drive our big garden tractor with a mower attachment on the back. I'd love to drive a car, and just thinking of that word, *drive*, made me look toward the drive-in on the hill and wonder if the bullet I fired had passed cleanly over Norvelt and punctured the screen. From where I paused, the screen was a solid black square and I'd never know if I had hit that tiny Japanese soldier and put a hole in the screen unless I got up close to it, which I promised myself I would do before the summer was over.

Above the screen the western sky was still dark and the stars looked like holes from missed shots. It was a good thing John Glenn had orbited the earth back in February. If he'd still been up there last night I might have shot his Friendship 7 space capsule out of the air and started a world war. That would be just my luck. My uncle who had painted the pony claimed he had seen a UFO come down over that very same hill before the drive-in was built. He was in the newspaper and said he had "touched" the UFO and that it was "covered in a strange Martian language that looked like chicken feet." My dad called my uncle a nut, but it wasn't so nutty when the army sent troops and a big truck to take the mysterious UFO away and afterward military police went door-to-door to all the little towns around here, warning people not to talk about "the *fallen* object" with any strangers as they might be Russian spies.

Because my mind wanders in the morning my feet are always a few steps ahead of me and suddenly I found myself on Miss Volker's back porch. There was a large heart-shaped box of chocolates covered in red foil leaning against her door. I bent down and picked up the box. A small note card was tucked under the decorative red lace ribbon. I knew I shouldn't read it, but I couldn't help myself. I loved to know other people's personal business. Mom called me a *gossip lover*. But I called it *whisper history*, so as quickly as I could I pulled out the card and flipped it over. It was from Mr. Spizz. The handwriting was all chunky printing that leaned forward just like words blasting out of his mouth. It read, *I'm still ready, willing and wait ing. Your swain since 1912 with the patience of Job. —Edwin Spizz.*

He *was* patient—1912 was fifty years ago. Waiting for what, I wondered. I didn't know what a "swain" was. I put the card back into the envelope and slipped it under the ribbon. Mr. Spizz was with my uncle the night they found the UFO. Dad called him the town busybody. Mr. Spizz was an original Norvelter and worked for the Norvelt Association for the Public Good. He thought he was a big deal around town, but he was kind of sinister and lived and worked out of a tiny office in the moldy basement of the Community Center.

I rapped on Miss Volker's door with my knuckles. "Miss Volker!" I called out loudly because her hearing aid might still be waterlogged from the toilet. "It's Jack Gantos. I'm here to help you."

"Come in!" she cawed like a pirate parrot.

I pushed the door to and stuck my head inside. "Hello?"

"In the kitchen," she squawked.

I followed the smell of bacon and entered the kitchen where I was surprised to see her leaning over the gas stove with her hands inside a wide, tall pot and her face all screwed up in agony. I could tell by the leaf-size flames under the pot that it had to be scalding hot, and right away I was wondering if she was melting herself down. Mom had always said she was worth her weight in gold to our little town. But before I could start a conversation about Inca gold she said, "Sit and eat," and nodded her stiff bush of bluish cotton-candy hair toward a chair at the kitchen table where a plate had been set with bacon, eggs, and toast.

"I found these chocolates on the porch," I said, and offered her the box.

"Put them on the table!" she ordered without removing her hands from the pot.

"There is a card too," I pointed out.

"You can just throw that in the *trash*!" she snapped.

"Trash?" I asked. "Don't you want to know who it's from?"

"It's from the same hopeless case as always!" she said. "Now *trash it*!"

I tossed the card in the trash like she said. I put the chocolates on the table and when I sat down she began to talk as if someone were sticking her with sharp pins. "Thank you for coming!" she cried out, and did a spastic tippy-toe dance. "Today," she squeaked, "we are about to embark on a great experiment!" Then she took a deep breath, shifted her hips around, and grimaced.

"What kind of experiment?" I asked fearfully, and stared at the pot where I was sure her hands were melting.

"Oh, gosh," she said in a strained voice, and jerked her head back and stamped her thick old-lady shoe heels on the kitchen linoleum. "This is really, really scalding hot but let's still keep talking and pretend like nothing at all is wrong."

"Miss Volker," I asked quietly, trying to be ridiculously calm like when doctors talk to insane people in the movies. I didn't want her to snap and try and kill me like some psychotic lunatic. "You do realize that you are cooking your hands down in that big pot?"

"Of . . . course . . . I . . . do . . . dear," she sputtered, and bit down on her lip and hissed as if her words were driven by steam. "Now . . . please . . . turn . . . it . . . off."

I sprang out of my chair and twisted the knob on the stove and the flames doubled in size.

"Jeez Louise!" she shouted crossly. "I said *off*!"

"Whoops, sorry," I apologized, and quickly turned the knob the other way.

"Agrhhh!" she cried out. "I think I may have really melted them this time."

She lifted her hands out of the pot and they *were* melting. Lumps of glowing yellow flesh oozed down her forearms and spattered onto the floor.

"Oh mercy!" I cried, and fidgeted up and down like a terrified squirrel. "Miss Volker, what have you done to yourself?"

"Turn the cold water on over the sink!" she ordered. "I think I may have done permanent damage."

I nearly flew to the sink and turned the spigot handle. "Give me your hands," I said. "Quick."

She stumbled toward me, then held out the sagging stumps of her melted arms. I hesitated, but there was nothing else to do except run away screaming, so I grabbed what I thought were her wrists. Oh cheeze! The warm, lifeless flesh squished between my fingers as I tugged her forward and held her ruined hands under the water.

She stamped the floor and groaned in horsey agony as her eyes rolled back into her head.

"You'll be fine," I jabbered about five jittery times in a row, and each time my mind echoed back, "You won't be fine . . . you won't ever be fine because you *just melted your hands off*!"

"Ahhh," she sighed with a relaxed shudder, and after a moment her eyes leveled out. "That feels better," she said calmly. "Now turn off the water."

I did and she held her arms up. "Now peel it off," she ordered.

"Peel what off?" I asked.

"The sticky stuff on my arms," she said impatiently, and then she held a rounded stump up to her mouth, bit off a cooked chunk, and spit it into the trash.

I felt faint. I staggered back a few steps and by then my nose was spewing like an elephant bathing himself. "Please . . . Miss Volker," I said with my voice quavering. "Please don't eat your own flesh." Oh cheeze-us-crust. Mom didn't know Miss Volker had gone insane, and I knew I would go insane too if I had to watch her cannibalize her own body down to the white boiled bones.

"You're bleeding all over the floor," she said, turning her attention toward me as if she wanted to wash her flesh meal down with my blood. "Let me have a look at you." Then she reached toward me with her deformed stumps and touched my face and at that moment I yelped out loud and dropped over dead.

When I came to I was alive and stretched out on Miss Volker's kitchen floor. I was covered with blood but I didn't know if it was nose blood or blood from after she started eating me. I lifted my head and turned it left and right to check if she had eaten through my neck. I was fine but she was standing above me and pulling long, rotten strips of flesh off her arms and hands as if peeling a rotten banana. She wadded them all up, leaned to one side, and dropped a ball into the large pot on the stove.

"Am I dead?" I asked. I felt dead.

"You fainted," she replied. "And I fixed your nose."

"You touched me?" I asked fearfully, and reached for my nose to see if it was still on my face.

"Yes," she said. "After I got the wax off my fingers they were working okay so I folded some tissues into a wad and shoved them up between your upper lip and gum. That's what stops a nosebleed."

"You have fingers?" I asked, confused. I had seen them melt off like the Inca gold being melted down.

"Yes," she said. "I'm human and I have fingers. They don't work well because of my arthritis so I have to heat them up in a pot of hot paraffin in order to get them working for about fifteen minutes."

"Hot what?"

"Hot *wax*," she repeated impatiently. "You saw me doing it when you came in. Did that smack on your head when you hit the floor give you amnesia?"

I sat up and rubbed the lump on the back of my head. "I thought you were melting your fingers into gold," I said. "I thought you had gone crazy."

"I think you've gone crazy," she replied. "You're delusional. Now let's not waste any more time. I have a deadline."

"What are we doing?" I asked.

"Writing an obituary," she revealed.

"Mine?"

"No! You are fine—you're a spineless jellyfish, but not dead enough to bury. Now take a look at these hands," she ordered, and thrust them in front of me. They were still bright red from the hot wax and curled over like the talons of a hawk perched on a fence. "I can't write with them anymore," she explained, "or do anything that requires fine motor skills. My twin sister used to write out the obituaries for me but her jug-headed idiot husband moved her to Florida last month. I was hoping he'd just have a spasm and drop dead and she would move in with me—but it didn't work out that way. So you are now my official scribe. I got the idea from reading about President John Quincy Adams. He had arthritis too and when his hands gave out he had a young scribe who wrote for him. I'll talk and you'll write. You got that?"

"Sure," I said, and then she caught me sneaking a peek at the glowing kitchen clock which was in the shape of a giant Bayer aspirin. It was six-thirty in the morning.

"That," she said proudly, and aimed her chin at the clock, "was given to me by the Bayer Pharmaceutical Company after I gave out over a quarter million of their aspirin tablets to coal miners here in western Pennsylvania who suffered with back pain and splitting headaches."

"That is a lot of pills," I remarked, not knowing what else to say but the obvious.

"In nursing school," she said, "I was taught by the doctors that the role of medical science is to relieve human suffering, and I've lived by that motto all my life."

"What about your hands?" I said, pointing up at them.

"Someday science will solve that. But for now, get up off the floor," she ordered. "We've got to get this obit to the newspaper in an hour so Mr. Greene can print it for tomorrow morning's edition."

I stood all the way up and staggered into the living room.

"There's your office," she said, and pointed a shiny red hand toward an old school desk and matching chair. "Lift the top."

I did. There were several pads of lined paper and a bundle of sharpened pencils held together with a rubber band.

"I'll talk, and you write," she explained, setting the rules. "If I talk too quickly then you just tell me and I'll slow down. You got it?"

"Yeah," I said. I was really ready to do anything that would clear my head from thinking about this old lady melting her flesh in a kitchen pot.

Miss Volker stood by the fireplace mantel and took a breath so deep it straightened out her curved spine.

"Emma Devers Slater," she started, and sharply enunciated each flinty syllable as if she were using a hammer and chisel to phonetically carve the dead woman's name onto a stone crypt, "was born on Christmas day, 1878, and died on June 15, 1962, while attending to her prize honeybees, which were once essential for pollinating crops at Norvelt's community farm. She and her husband were original members of the two hundred and fifty families that started the Homestead of Norvelt in 1934, occupying house A-38, a two-bedroom model.

"The Slater family, which she married into, is an old name in these parts and famous for offspring with extremely hard heads. I remind the reader of the true story of the Slater 'girl' who was captured by Indians in the 1830s, knocked unconscious with a war club and scalped with a knife, but still managed to abscond with her life and survive hairlessly to live to a ripe old age beneath a wig made of curly hamster fur.

"And who can forget Emma Slater's brother-in-law, Frederick, who was tamping an explosive charge into a coal vein with a metal rod when the charge accidentally exploded and propelled the rod up through his cheek and clean out the top of his head? He survived and lived a long life as a traveling medical-miracle circus attraction and made money by charging people a dime to stick their finger into the damp hole in his head. Frederick married another circus attraction who when she was a girl had a piece of white picket fence driven through her upper torso during the great Johnstown Flood of 1889.

"Emma Slater is survived by four loving children who grew up in Norvelt, but none of them live in town any longer, having left to find jobs. Her husband, Herbert Mark Slater, passed away twenty-three years prior from black lung disease after working in the mines at Mutual Shaft all his life except during his military service in World War I and the Great Depression years when the mines were closed. Mrs. Slater belonged to the Mothers' Club of Norvelt, the Fancy Hat Club, and the Lutheran Church.

"We are grateful for her community service, especially her years as a school crossing guard where she was much loved by children. An open viewing and memorial service will be held at the Oscar Huffer Funeral Parlor next Friday from six until nine in the evening followed by a potluck buffet at the Community Center, where her exceptional needlepoint portrait of our town's esteemed founder, Eleanor Roosevelt, will be on display."

Then she bowed her head, closed her eyes, and quietly said a little prayer for Mrs. Slater.

By the time she opened her eyes I had put my pencil down. "Is that it?" I asked, and caught myself panting as if I'd run a marathon. My hand was feeling as cramped as hers looked.

"No," she replied, "but you can take a break. That's just the family part I *have* to write. I've done the best I can for Mrs. Slater. Writing obits is doing my duty for Mrs. Roosevelt, but it also allows me to write things that people wouldn't normally read around here. I guess you could say the obits are the honey to attract readers. Now here is the part I *want* to write, so stretch your fingers and get your pencil revved up—people may die but we've got some important *ideas* to keep alive."

Then she awkwardly palmed a small history book with one hand and raised it into the air. Her twisted fingers looked like the rough old roots of a tree that had grown around a clay brick. She puffed herself up like a tent preacher and began to belt out the other half of the story.

"For those of you interested in the history of hard-working people, Mrs. Slater died on the same day as

Wat Tyler in 1381. Wat Tyler, who was the heroic leader of the English Peasants' Revolt, was killed for wanting equality between peasants, who owned no land, and the Royalty and the Church, who owned all the land.

"All Wat Tyler was asking for was that the land be equally divided so that every peasant family could farm and feed themselves. The peasants fought hard with Wat against the king's army and finally Wat and his force of common people entered London and were poised to take over the city.

"At that time King Richard II was only fourteen years old, but he was surrounded by rich and powerful lords. Wat Tyler was invited to have a private talk with King Richard to solve the land problem. But he was tricked! At the meeting the Lord Mayor of London stepped forward and stabbed Wat in the neck, then had his head chopped off and spiked onto a tall pole as a gory lesson to all who would defy the king and revolt for equal rights.

"After their leader was beheaded the peasant army fled. But for those of us who live in Norvelt—a town of common people who own our own land—we should never forget Wat Tyler and his revolt to make life better for his own people!"

She was really worked up as she paced back and forth and swung her arms around like a windmill. I wrote as fast as humanly possible and did a pretty good job getting it down considering it was my first job as a scribe.

"Any questions?" she asked once she had concluded. "Anything seem unclear to you?"

"Why did you add the part about Wat Tyler?" I asked. "It's not like Mrs. Slater was alive in 1381."

"Connect the dots," she answered impatiently. "Our dear little Norvelt was founded by Eleanor Roosevelt, who knew common people like us wanted equality just like Wat and his people. Our hunger is related to their hunger. Our desire to work hard is related to their desire to work hard. Working people always share the same history of being kicked around by the rich."

"Okay," I said, "I get that part. So what is A-38? I never heard of that."

"Look at the map," she said, pointing above my head with a finger that was like a bent nail. "See house number A-38?"

I stood up and turned. Mounted behind me was a large needlepoint map of Norvelt which spread across the entire wall. On it were hand-stitched all the streets and houses and gardens and yard animals and businesses and municipal buildings and creeks. There were five sections: A, B, C, D, and E. Beneath each house a number was sewn in next to a last name.

"Take a red-topped map pin from the corner and stick it into house number A-38," she said. "Emma was the last of the Slater family in Norvelt."

"What's this map?" I asked.

"It's the town you were born in," she said irritably. "Don't tell me you are too ignorant to know where you are from?"

"It just doesn't look like this anymore," I said. "It's changed. Like, the Huffer Funeral Parlor isn't on here. Or the baseball field. Or the hardware store. Or Fenton's gas station and bar. And you have a Chicken Farm and Community Farm on here that I've never seen."

"You're looking at the original Norvelt," she said. "There are two hundred and fifty houses in five sections on this map with the names of the original owners. If you count up the red pins you'll see that all but nine—eight now that Mrs. Slater has passed—of the original owners have died or left since 1934."

"That's a long time ago," I said.

"Not for me," she replied. "Now, I don't have time to give you a Norvelt history lesson today because you have to type that obituary up and run it down to the *News*."

"I don't know how to type," I said, wilting a bit.

"A trained monkey can type," she snapped, and nearly popped her eyes right out of their sockets with exasperation. "Now bring your notebook and sit over here."

I did as she told me and sat in front of a tall black Royal typewriter that was sitting on an unused sewing table.

"This is really old," I remarked, and gently touched the chrome-rimmed keys.

"The government gave it to me," she said proudly. "When Mrs. Roosevelt hired me to be the chief nurse and medical examiner of this town I was given a typewriter so I could keep health records on the original two hundred and fifty families. Now it's my closing tribute to Mrs. Roosevelt that I write their final health report—which, in this case, would be their obituary. So put a sheet of paper in the roller and turn the wheel on the end."

"Miss Volker," I said about as politely as I knew how, "do you think you will outlast the rest of these original people?"

"I have to," she said. "I made a promise to Eleanor Roosevelt to see them to their graves, and I can't drop dead on the job—so let's get going."

She stood behind me and told me where the Shift key was for making capital letters, and where the punctuation keys were, and the space bar, and when I made a mistake she showed me how to back up the carriage and type a slash through the bad letter and then keep on going. It was slow work but I liked the machine. It smelled of oil and made a sharp clacking noise like a train running down a track as the keys snapped against the carriage.

While I typed she sat down and slid a book off a tabletop and muttered that her hands had cooled back down and were so bad she couldn't use her fingers to turn the pages. I offered to help her but instead she just held the book up to her lips and blew on the bottom edge of the page and flipped it over with the strength of her breath. She caught me watching her. "I'm full of tricks," she said proudly. "Now back to work!"

After I rolled the obituary out of the typewriter she pointed to her overstuffed bookshelf and to the piles of books stacked up against the opposite wall as if she were building a farmer's fence out of fieldstone. "Take one as a gift," she instructed. "I'm too old to read anything twice."

"Mom said I can only take food stuff," I explained.

"This stuff is *brain* food," she replied. "Now pick a book and get moving so we don't miss the deadline. And if someone else drops dead I'll call your mother and have her send you down and I'll teach you a few more things," she continued. "You need to know the history of this town because if it dies out someone will have to be around to write the obit."

"How does a town die?" I asked.

"One old person at a time," she said deliberately. "Now, what kind of books do you like?"

"History or real-life adventure books, mostly," I replied.

"Take that one," she suggested, and pointed the scuffed tip of her hard black shoe at a large book that was decorated with Egyptian hieroglyphics. It was titled *Lost Worlds*. "When Mrs. Roosevelt spoke at the opening of the school she told the students to learn their history or they'd be 'doomed to dust' like one of the Lost Worlds."

I bent over and picked the book up off the floor with both hands. "Tha-anks," I groaned as I stood up.

She smiled and waved her ruined hand toward the door. "Now scat," she ordered. "Beat it!"

I did. I held the big book against my chest and ran all the way down to the *Norvelt News* where Mr. Greene, the publisher, was inking up the printing press.

"Another dead one?" he remarked as he put on his ink-smeared reading glasses and sorrowfully shook his head back and forth mumbling through the obituary except to pause here and there to decipher what I had written.

"Be careful with the spelling," I warned him in a voice that was wormy with shame because I didn't do well in that subject at school.

He nodded. "And tell Miss Volker you got it to me on time," he replied.

"Will do," I said, then turned and staggered back home with my new book which was as tall, wide, thick, and heavy as a tombstone.

3

Life in Norvelt was pretty quiet but I could still never get any sleep. Even though it was a Sunday Mr. Spizz stopped by the house and rapped his chunky monkey knuckles crazily on the front door at about seven o'clock in the morning. "Anybody home!" he hollered. The volume on his raspy voice was stuck on maximum and he nearly blew you down like the Big Bad Wolf when he talked. He was a heavy breather on account of his asthma, which was why he didn't fight in the war even though he had a military flattop haircut that looked like an airport for paper airplanes.

He told my mom that the weeds in the public gutter along the front of our property had grown too high. He pulled out a tape measure and showed her what twenty-eight inches looked like. "Regulation weed size is only six inches high," he informed her. "Yours are twenty-two inches too tall."

If I was Mom I would have swatted him with a cast-iron skillet and left him conked out in the gutter until the weeds grew up through him.

"I'm a deputy of the volunteer police and fire department, and next time I come by if those weeds are not cut down to proper size I'll write you a ticket for intentional gutter clogging," he added.

"Yes, sir," Mom said politely, and closed the door, and when she walked down the hall past my room I heard her sing, "You're not the boss of me, no you are not the boss of me, you might be the boss of you but you're not the boss of me."

That must have made her feel a lot better.

In a few minutes Mom called me into the kitchen for breakfast. She always used the newspaper for place mats because she didn't like to waste anything. So as I ate I read through the local news. The volunteer police reported that escaped turkeys had attacked a passing Amish buggy and driver, so we all needed to keep an eye on our turkey pens. There was a warning that honeybees had taken over the post office mail drop box, "so don't open it unless you want to get stung." The Question of the Day was: *Which president is on the two-dollar bill?* I didn't know. I had never seen a two-dollar bill.

My favorite article was always a column of two or three facts called This Day In History, which was written by Miss Volker. I may have been bad with my spelling but Mr. Greene was equally bad with his dates. Today was June 17 but he had the history for the next day.

> ***June 18, 1812:*** **War declared on Britain. The British took it badly and burned down the White House which caused First Lady Dolley Madison to save the famous portrait of George Washington. Her slave, Paul Jennings, said he was really the one who saved the portrait, but slaves were not allowed to contradict white people. Years later, after President Madison had died and Paul Jennings had won his freedom, the ex-president's wife was broke and living in poverty. There was only one person kind enough to help Dolley Madison out—her ex-slave, Paul Jennings.**
>
> ***June 18, 1873:*** **Susan B. Anthony fined $100 for attempting to vote.**
>
> ***June 18, 1928:*** **Amelia Earhart became the first woman to fly across the Atlantic. Everyone said a**

woman could never do it, but she proved them wrong.

I loved proving people wrong about me. Somehow I was going to have to prove to Mom that I didn't know there was a bullet in that Japanese sniper rifle.

"Hey, Mom," I asked, "how come Miss Volker can't write the obituaries anymore but she can write the 'This Day In History' column?"

"Because she wrote it ages ago when she was younger and could use her hands. The newspaper just repeats the column from year to year. I read the same column when I was your age. It's history, so it really doesn't change."

"Unless you get the date wrong," I pointed out.

Mom shrugged. "Time moves so slowly in this town it doesn't much matter," she replied. "Yesterday, today, and tomorrow are all about the same to me."

But when it came to my chores she wanted me to move quickly. After breakfast she sent me out to the barn for the hedge shears and told me to hurry up and go cut down the gutter weeds before Mr. Spizz gave us a ticket for not following the community rules. I moseyed out front and was cutting them down when he furiously pedaled by on his new giant adult-size tricycle that towed a little red wagon full of what looked like shoe boxes. "Mr. Spizz," I hollered as he bounced past, "are these weeds short enough for you?"

"Not now, Gantos boy," he shouted over his right shoulder, and rang the shiny new bell on the chrome handlebars. "I'm delivering Sunday dinners to the elderly. I'll check on the weeds later."

I had seen him on the tricycle a couple of weeks ago and mentioned it to Dad.

"There must be something wrong with him *upstairs*," Dad remarked, and tapped himself on his noggin as if to say that Mr. Spizz was nuts.

"How can you tell if he's cracked?" I asked.

"How many adults do you know who ride around on a giant kindergarten tricycle?" he replied.

I didn't have to think about that for long. "None," I replied. I had never seen a giant adult tricycle before.

"That UFO must have zapped him with a ray gun," Dad said. "He's a freak! One of these days he'll flip his lid and hurt someone, so stay out of his way."

I definitely didn't want to get in the way of Mr. Spizz's whizzing tricycle.

4

A couple days later I woke up early and hungry and staggered out to the front porch to see if the milk had been delivered. I didn't find the milk. The *Norvelt News* had arrived and as I picked it up I saw that on this day in history, General Mills had introduced Cheerios in 1941. "Great," I griped out loud. "And I don't have milk!"

Then when I turned around to go back into the house my eyes bugged out. "Oh, no," I said angrily. Taped to the door was a three-dollar ticket for WEED OBSTRUCTION OF GUTTER WATER. I knew what it meant—more trouble. Sunday, after I had cut all the weeds, I piled them up in a big stack in the gutter. I was going to get a bag to haul them away and chop them up for our compost heap, but first I took a break and drank all the milk and then Mom caught me making a mess in the kitchen and chased me back to my room and I started reading about the Revolutionary War's Battle of Bunker Hill and General Prescott's order to his men: "Don't fire until you see the whites of their eyes!"

His troops obeyed. When the first line of British Redcoats got real close, the patriots aimed their muskets and started blasting the eyes out of the Redcoats at point-blank range, which must have been a bloody mess, especially for the Redcoats standing just behind the ones having their brains blown out. And then I wondered why the British soldiers would allow themselves to die so easily just because their king told them to go march up a hill and fight. I was thinking that I would tell the king to go fight his own war and then I started singing Mom's "you are not the boss of me" song to the king and I forgot about cleaning up the big stack of weeds, but Mr. Spizz must have whizzed by on his super kindergarten tricycle and spotted the pile and evilly given us the nasty ticket.

"What a creep!" I said, and looked down the road but he must have been off bugging other people. I ripped the ticket from the door and folded it over and stuck it in the waistband of my pajamas and made sure no one could see as I quickly ran into my room and hid it deep under my mattress. I knew it was going to have to be a secret I'd pay for myself. If Mom saw it she would never let me out of my room again. Dad had returned during the night from an out-of-town job and if he saw the ticket he'd go ape. But I didn't have any money. None. I'd have to figure it out on my own.

Since I was so worried about the ticket I couldn't lie in bed and read, so I just got dressed and went outside and started mowing the lawn with the tractor. I liked to mow patterns or pictures in the grass and had just finished the outline of something that looked like the Sphinx from the *Lost Worlds* book when Dad strolled out toward me. I could tell by his squinty eyes and tucked-in chin that whatever he was thinking about was more important than my next chore.

He cupped his hands around his mouth. "See that new corn?" he shouted over the tractor's engine.

I looked beyond his shoulder. There was a half acre of green corn that Mom had planted. She was going to sell it, then use the money to buy food for the charity dinners she cooked. The stalks were about a foot high.

"Yeah, I see it," I replied. "It's doing great." Yesterday Mom had made me weed it.

"Mow it down," he ordered. "Then later we'll put the heavy rake on your tractor and dig up all the roots."

"Why?" I asked, then quickly added, "Mom's not going to like this."

"Just hurry up and do what I say," he said, and glanced toward the kitchen. He wasn't angry. He was nervous because he knew Mom was going to erupt when she saw her corn cut down.

I didn't argue with him because I wanted to stay on his good side. Since he returned, Mom hadn't said anything to him about me firing off the sniper rifle, but she was a ticking time bomb and sooner or later she would blow up and tell Dad what I had done. I wanted to put that off for as long as I could, plus I had another reason too. I really wanted a car. A few older boys I knew were allowed to have a car once they learned how to drive a tractor. And now that I did all the tractor work around the house Dad said that if I could get a car for free he would help me fix it. I had found an old junker while snooping around in the woods behind Bob Fenton's gas station. It was a rusty brown 1936 Ford coupe with big bug-eyed headlights mounted on the fenders. The old tires were flat and the horsehair upholstery was ripped up inside but I loved it the moment I discovered it stored in a mossy old garage whose sagging roof beams were about to collapse. I had asked Mr. Fenton about it and he said he wanted a hundred bucks because it had historic value. "Eleanor Roosevelt was driven around

Norvelt in it," he crowed proudly, hooking his thumbs behind the straps on his farmer overalls. "It will be in a museum someday once she dies. She's sick so it won't be long before I cash in."

Every time her name was mentioned everything went up in price, which was so backward because she wanted everything to go *down* in price.

"Yep, I was even thinking of starting a museum right here in Norvelt . . ." Mr. Fenton trailed off as he scratched a part of his body that made me look away.

If it was a museum of human freaks, I thought, he could be the first display. He looked like a human corn grub with crusty wire-rimmed glasses over his bugged-out snow-globe eyes. On his flabby shoulders he had wispy blond hairs that flowed in the wind like corn silk. He reeked of gasoline and altogether he was pretty weird, but he wasn't dangerous. As Mom said, "He just doesn't know better. He's never lived with a woman so he's like a dog that has gone feral and returned to its wild state. In his case he has turned back into a worm." She was probably right, but he still wanted a hundred bucks for the car.

Before I drove the tractor over to the cornfield I adjusted the blade on the mower to cut a half inch above dirt level. Then, once I climbed back onto the tractor, I revved the engine, jammed it into gear, and hit the gas. The tractor tires spun and I hung on to the wheel. As I reached the first row of corn I pushed the lever that lowered the mower blade, and right away bits and pieces of cornstalk and chunks of dried dirt went flying out behind me in a thick cloud. From a distance I must have looked like a tornado tearing up the rows of corn. But I didn't look like a tornado to my mom. I was about halfway through when she must have spotted me from the kitchen window. She ran out to the porch and waved her hands over her head as if she were chasing off an attack of mud wasps. Her mouth was moving but I couldn't hear her since the tractor was so loud, but I knew why I was in trouble and I could already feel a little blood gathering under my nose. In no time at all she ran across the field and planted herself in front of the tractor to keep me from going forward. I put in the clutch, lifted my foot off the gas, and wiped my nose on the shoulder of my shirt.

"Have you lost your mind?" she yelled, and made a "turn the key off" hand gesture.

I twisted the key and the pistons coughed, then stopped, but she instantly filled the silence.

"What are you doing?" she asked angrily, and pointed wildly at the cornstalks as if they were little half-formed bodies. She picked up a piece of one and held it in her arms.

"Looking for Inca gold," I said weakly because that's all that was on my mind. "I want to buy a car."

"Then you better buy a hearse," she snapped back, and threw the piece of cornstalk at me.

I ducked and covered my face. "Dad made me do it," I cried out from behind my hands. "It wasn't my idea."

Just then he opened the side door on the garage, which was shaped like a little red barn. Dad called it his office because that was where he kept all his secret stuff.

"Did you tell him to mow the new corn down?" Mom shouted. She was pretty upset.

"Yes," he replied calmly with his hands fiddling with the tools in his trouser pockets. "I'm going to need this space for a major project."

"What kind of project," she asked hotly, "could be more important than growing food for the needy?"

"A bomb shelter," he said out of the blue, and gazed aimlessly into the glossy sky. "Yep, we need a bomb shelter. The Russian Commies say they are planning to bury us, but I've got news for them—we are going to survive whatever atom bomb attack they throw our way."

The sudden news of building a bomb shelter threw her off. "Well," she stumbled. "Well, can't we grow the corn first? Then you can build it?"

"Nope," Dad declared grandly, "this corn is growing in the way of progress."

"Well, what about these rows he hasn't mowed down?" She pointed to what I hadn't harmed. "Can we keep that? You know I always use the corn crop to fund my meals for the elderly."

Dad held his hand over his eyes to shade them from the sun as he surveyed the unmowed corn. "I'll have to measure and see," he said thoughtfully. "I can't promise you anything."

"Well, I keep my promises," she said firmly. "Especially to the old folks who depend on this food." Then she turned her anger toward me. "Don't you dare mow this, mister," she ordered, and aimed her pointer finger at my throbbing nose. "Don't you dare!" Then she marched back toward the house.

In my mind I heard her say, *"Don't you dare mow this or I'll tell your father you fired that sniper rifle."* This was going to be bad. I looked at Dad. He bent over to tie his bootlace. As soon as she was out of earshot he peeked up at me through his eyebrows and said, "Once she goes into the house wait about ten minutes, then I want you to mow down the rest of the corn and meet me in the garage."

"Are you sure?" I asked.

"Sure I'm sure. When you see what I have stashed

inside the garage you'll know why," he replied as he stood up and walked away. When I heard the porch door slap shut I knew she had gone inside. For a moment I sat there thinking I could drive the tractor off our property and down the Norvelt road until I got to the river, where I could build a raft and drift away and find a treasure from a Lost World and start my own life. But that thought was useless because I knew the only thing to find around western Pennsylvania was a lump of coal. Instead, I leaned my forehead against the steering wheel and closed my eyes. She'll kill me, I thought, as I got a head start on dying. The blood was already flowing from my nose and spattering on my blue jeans.

When Dad had returned home the night before, I heard his truck roll up the gravel driveway. I left my bedroom and crossed the hall into the bathroom where I could peek out the tiny vent window. I saw he was towing a trailer with a tarp roped over it. Once he stopped his truck he hopped out quickly and opened the wide garage doors. He then unhitched the trailer and with a lot of grunting effort he pulled it into the garage. Quickly he closed the doors and snapped the lock through the hasp. We rarely locked the doors so whatever was on that trailer must have been top secret.

By the time he came inside Mom was up to fix him a midnight snack. "How'd the work go?" she asked, and I could hear the *ping* of her setting a fork on the metal-topped table.

"Good," he replied. "Real good." The refrigerator opened and closed and he opened a can of beer. "I believe," he continued, "if we keep saving money we can think about moving within a year and buying a place in Florida."

I knew what was coming next. It was the same argument they always had. I don't know why it didn't change much, but I guess they each figured the other one was going to give in. Still, they were both pretty stubborn, so giving in wasn't in them.

"Wouldn't buying a new house in Florida just put us in debt?" she said. "Maybe we should use the money to make our lives better right here. We could fix up this house—modernize it and stay put."

"I've told you a hundred times," he said evenly, "that there is nothing for me here in Norvelt and never will be. A thousand years from now it will be just the same as it is now—a dirt-poor Commie town that is dying out."

"No, it's not a Commie town," my mother countered, sounding frustrated. "Stop calling it that. It's a town set up to give hardworking poor people a helping hand."

"It was started by that rich Commie Roosevelt

woman," he replied with contempt. "It was built by Commies with Commie money, and is rigged by Commies so that no real man can get ahead in life. If I wanted to live like a Commie, I'd move to Russia!"

"I bet all the Russians wish they could move to Norvelt," she replied, defending her town. This was where she grew up, and where her parents had built the Norvelt house we moved into once they passed away. She knew and loved everyone in our little town and they loved her too. I never thought we would move away because we all had so much in common.

But Dad wasn't focused on what we had in common. He was always thinking about all the things he didn't have, and all the things he wanted. "Well, if that rich Commie woman wanted to help poor people, she should have just given them a big fat check," Dad suggested. "That would have been a real helping hand."

"You don't mean that," Mom said, shaming him with the tone of her voice. "You always say people should work for what they have so they will appreciate it better. People want a hand *up*—not a hand*out*."

He did always say that and I guess hearing his own words thrown back at him settled him down. "You're right," he agreed. "I just want to get ahead in the world and this town is a dead end—basically it's the same do-nothing day here over and over."

"Well, I'd rather everyone have the same basic food on their plate," Mom said, "instead of some rich people eating steak and some poor people eating beans."

"Or leftover macaroni," Dad grumbled, and I heard his fork peck at his plate like the turkeys pecking at feed in their tin bowls.

I waited for Mom to say something more but she didn't. It was so odd how they never really ended a conversation. They just seemed to stop talking at some awkward, cliff-hanging moment and then Mom would attend to washing the dishes and Dad would silently read the newspaper.

I knew Dad wasn't planning to move us to Russia because they were poorer than we were. He wanted to move to Florida, where a hardworking man could make big money building houses for rich people. But first he had to convince Mom to uproot herself and that was not going to be easy.

Now as I rested my head against the tractor steering wheel while pinching my nose closed I knew Dad was waiting to hear the engine crank up and for me to do what I was told. As soon as I mow that corn, I said to myself, it will be like lighting the fuse on a stick of dynamite. But I had no choice. I turned the key and got down to business. There were three rows left. I gripped the steering wheel, hit the gas, and mowed down the first row, turned sharply and mowed up the second row, then gunned it down the third row like I was headed for the checkered flag. I glanced over my shoulder and didn't see Mom as I parked the tractor over by the pony pen. War Chief was rubbing himself against the rough cinder-block wall and snapping his big teeth at the turkeys, who stared back at him with their heads turned sideways as if they were ready for the chopping block. "You better watch yourself," I warned War Chief as I ran toward the garage. "Mom's gonna be on the warpath at any moment."

When I got to the garage I pounded on the door. "Hey, Dad!" I hollered desperately. "Let me in." I knew he was up to something Mom wouldn't like, but he knew I could mostly keep a secret except for the times my nose would betray me. All Mom had to do to get the truth out of me was hold me by the chin, look me in the eye, and ask her question. If my nose stayed dry, I was telling the truth. If I leaked one little drop of blood, then she knew I was lying.

I kept pounding on the garage door until he pulled it open. "Get in," he ordered, and grabbed the front of my T-shirt and yanked me inside. As he closed the door and relocked it my eyes adjusted to the dim garage light, and that's when I saw the green fuselage of a small airplane on the trailer, with the wings and wheels and other parts carefully laid out on the floor.

"Wow," I said, staring at it from prop to tail. "What is it?"

"It's an army surplus J-3," he said, smiling proudly. "The same as a Piper Cub. We used them during the war as training planes and for spotting enemy subs and all kinds of things."

"Can you put it together?" I asked, pointing at all the pieces.

"Sure," he said with confidence. "I took it apart so I suppose I'll just reverse the process."

"Do you know how to fly it?"

"Somewhat," he said loosely, "but I'll take a few lessons just to keep your mom happy—then I can teach you too."

"This is why you wanted me to mow the corn, right?" I asked.

He grinned widely. "Yep," he said. "You and I are building a runway out back and we need that field so we can fly anywhere we want at any time."

"Cool," I said. "What about the bomb shelter?"

"We'll get to that later," he said dismissively. "We'll start the runway at the cornfield and that leads to the dirt road out to the long pasture so we'll get about enough distance to take off."

"Does Mom know you have the J-3?" I leaned forward and looked into the spare wood-and-canvas cockpit. There were only a few basic instruments, like a big toy.

Just then her voice put a chill in me. "Jackie!" she called out furiously. "Jackie?" She called me Jack when Dad was gone and Jackie when he was home. She rattled the barn door.

"Not a sound out of you," Dad whispered.

Mom pulled on the door even harder. "Jackie, if you are in there playing with your dad's Japanese stuff again I'm going to tell him about the other night."

I looked up at Dad in horror.

"Have you been messing with my Jap stuff?" he whispered, and got a grip on my forearm. "I told you never to touch it."

I felt the blood run over my upper lip and then I could taste it.

"What happened the other night?" he asked.

I pulled my T-shirt up over my face with my free arm.

Mom rattled the door. "Jackie! If you are hiding in there I'm going to kick this door down and punish you for the rest of your very short life."

Dad pointed to the closed half-high door on the other side of the garage which years ago led to an outside pen for goats and sheep.

"Can I borrow your baseball glove?" I quickly asked as I pointed to where it hung by a nail. "I've got a practice and Bunny and the team are waiting for me."

"Grab it and run," he said as Mom kicked the door and a weathered piece of the bottom board cracked off. "Now scat!" he said. "I'll cover your butt, but you better tell me about the Jap stuff when you get back."

I grabbed the glove, then pulled open the short door. I ran up through the thick woods behind the garage. A few deer bolted when they saw me. I veered off and passed beyond Fenton's gas station and around the town dump where hundreds of rats were picking through the trash before I circled back down to the baseball fields beside the Roosevelt Community Center to meet my friend, Bunny Huffer.

5

Maybe since there were so few kids in our town we did things differently, because even though Bunny was a girl the size of one of Santa's little helpers she was still my best friend. She was so short she could run full speed under her dining room table without ducking. I tried it once and nearly decapitated myself. Her real name was Stella Huffer and her father owned the funeral parlor, but she made everyone call her Bunny. Her father sponsored our baseball team, so we were nicknamed the Huffer Death Squad, which made sense because we were really named the Pirates after the Pittsburgh team and we had a skull and crossbones on our caps.

Bunny had a great sense of humor. She'd take her double position at shortstop and second base and yell out to the rest of us, "Look alive, you bunch of stiffs." She had about a million dead person jokes. She said her father's spongy felt suit was the color of black lungs. It smelled like pickled onions. When you shook his limp hand he was like a scary doll that whispered, "Good-bye, dearly departed. Rest in peace." Once we had some hamburger spoil in our refrigerator and when I opened the refrigerator door it smelled just like Mr. Huffer. I mentioned it to Mom and she replied that if you think about it a refrigerator is just a coffin for food that stands upright. Then she made me take the rotten meat up to the dump. I threw it to a nest of rats and ran for my life.

Bunny was a great girl who was better than any guy I knew because she was tough, smart, and daring. Because she grew up in a house full of dead people she wasn't afraid of anything. When I was first getting to know her we were in a viewing room at the funeral parlor looking at a new line of cigar-shaped caskets that were called "Time Capsules of the Future." They were made out of polished aluminum and seemed very sleek with a little glass window where the cadaver's face could be viewed. The idea was you were buried with all your favorite things and in a thousand years a relative would dig you up and sift through your rotted remains and stuff. It was kind of a disgusting thought.

But it wasn't disgusting to her. "I'm going to take one to school for show-and-tell," she said. "How much will you give me if I ask old Principal Knox to try it on for size?"

She turned to me for an offer. But I couldn't say anything because the subject of death made me pale and feel cold except for the very tip of my nose, which was heating up like a match head about to combust. I started to back away from her.

She sensed my fear and edged even closer to me. "I think coffins are old-fashioned," she remarked, and made a disapproving face. "I'd rather be cremated and have my ashes blasted into orbit like Sputnik and go beeping around the planet for all of eternity. Now that would be cool. But Dad doesn't like cremation because he doesn't make any money at it except for what it costs him to burn people to a crisp and put them in a Mason jar."

By then I had backpedaled so far I was pressed against a heavy purple velvet curtain that divided the back of the viewing room from the front.

"You're afraid of dead people," she suddenly said. "Aren't you?"

Before I could deny that accusation she reached out with her short muscular arm and grabbed my shirt. "Come on," she ordered, and with her other hand she pulled the center of the curtain to one side. "You need to see your first dead person and then you won't be afraid anymore."

I wasn't sure about that theory. I quickly lizard-licked my upper lip but didn't taste any blood. So far I hadn't humiliated myself, but I knew the worst was still to come.

On the other side of the curtain was a closed coffin displayed on a polished wood platform. Without pausing she went up and with both hands lifted the lid. She propped the lid on a metal rod as if she were propping open a car hood. There was a dead old man in there. He was dressed in a white suit and his face was tinted with flesh-colored makeup. I stared at him. His eyes were a tiny bit open, like an alligator peeking back at me.

Bunny suddenly grabbed my arm. "Touch his hand," she said, and she turned and slapped him hard on his hand. "Touch it—not scary at all!" she proclaimed.

My hand was paralyzed. I probably looked more dead than he did. I couldn't touch him.

"Come on, you wimp," she said, and jerked my hand forward and pressed it against the dead man's neck as if I were going to take his pulse. But there was no pulse. His neck was hard as a fence post, and my legs wobbled and I had to grip the edge of the coffin with my other hand to keep from tilting over to one side. By then the blood was dripping off my chin and onto the white satin lining inside the coffin. I turned and with my last bit of strength I ran out of the room and down the airless hallway and out their front door. I could hear her laughing behind me as the blood swept back across my cheeks and all the way to my ears, like rain streaking over a windshield.

When I arrived at the baseball diamond Bunny and the other four players on our small team were already practicing. They were hitting ground balls to each other and trying to field them.

When Bunny saw me she broke away from the others and threw a fastball directly at my head. "What took you so long?" she asked, with a bit of anger in her voice.

I caught it. "Trouble," I replied, and threw it back at her chunky feet.

"What kind of trouble?" she asked, fielding the ball and bouncing a hard grounder back at me.

I picked it cleanly. "I cut down Mom's corn crop." Even saying that made me wince. I threw her a grounder with some spin on it.

She scooped it up, turned, and threw me a fly ball. "Why'd you do that?" she asked.

I made a basket catch over my shoulder and threw

her a high pop-up. "Dad is making a landing strip for his new plane and he wants me to help him build a bomb shelter."

She caught the ball, then looked at me like I had lost my mind. "A bomb shelter?"

"Yeah," I said.

"A landing strip?" she asked.

"You heard me," I said.

"So what is he going to do—dive-bomb your own bomb shelter?" she asked. "That sounds nuts."

It did. I walked over to the dugout to get a drink.

"Get me some water," she called, and threw the ball to another player.

I poured two cups and carried them back over to the diamond. I gave her one.

"Thanks, pal," she said. "And by the way, I read the Slater obituary in the paper the other day. Dad and I thought you and Miss Volker did an outstanding job."

"How'd you know I helped Miss Volker?" I asked.

"Small town," she said as if "small town" was the answer to every question in Norvelt.

"And because I know you like Mrs. Slater so much I got you a present from her," she said with a sick grin on her face. She dug into her pocket and tugged at something awkwardly shaped. I reached forward and she placed Mrs. Slater's dentures in my hand.

"Here is something you didn't know," she said quickly before I could get a word out of my mouth. I kept staring at those coffee-stained teeth. "When the volunteer firemen found her collapsed by the beehive she was still alive, and she had her dentures in her hand and was tapping out an SOS message in Morse code—*'Help me! Help me!'* she spelled over and over, and then she died."

Bunny had to be lying. But if she wasn't I wished we had used that detail for the obituary. "But didn't your dad bury Mrs. Slater with her dentures in her mouth?" I asked.

"You don't know anything about preparing dead people for a viewing," she bragged. "If you'll notice, the stiffs are always displayed with their mouths closed because my dad has to *sew* their mouths shut. If they don't have real teeth you just sew their gums together which is actually easier, so we keep the dentures. Dad saves them because when he gets a boxful he donates them to the retirement home and some of those old people reuse them."

"You really have to *sew* the mouth shut?" I asked. That stunned me. It seemed so brutal.

"With an upholstery needle and twine," she added, knowing she was making me nervous. "It's like sewing up a turkey after you stuff it, is how my dad puts it."

I felt my blood surge like a tidal wave toward my face.

"Are you always like this?" she asked, and pointed her stubby hand at my nose.

"Yes," I croaked, and wiped away a few drops of blood.

"You should see a doctor," she advised.

"It's nothing," I said. "I have a very sensitive nose. *Anything* makes it bleed."

At that moment I spotted my mother on her bicycle heading in my direction. She must have kicked in the garage door and seen I had escaped out the back, and now it looked like she was coming to scalp me because she had a long wooden cooking spoon clutched in one hand. Suddenly the water in my cup was pink with blood.

I knew I had done something terribly wrong and that I should wait for her to arrive and punish me. She got closer and closer, and as I lifted my shirttail to wipe my nose I knew I was grounded for life before she wheeled into the parking lot.

When Bunny saw the stream of blood running down over my lips and dripping off my chin she nervously pounded her fist in her glove. "What's up?" she asked. "Why are you standing around like vampire bait?"

"I'm dead meat," I replied.

"Then I better call my dad," she said.

"Have him bring a coffin," I suggested. "A small one because when my mom finishes with me I'll be chopped into little pieces."

I might have been joking around but Mom wasn't. She rode the bike up to the backstop fence behind home plate and jumped off. She was close enough for me and everyone else around the diamond to hear her shout, "*You!* Get over here. *Now!*" She pointed the spoon at the ground by her feet.

I turned and ran toward second base. She gave chase. I looked like a bloody turkey with its head cut off as I circled the bases. "Run, Jack, run!" Bunny yelled out. "She's gaining on you." I could hear kids laughing.

Mom was a lot faster than I thought and when she collared me from behind at home plate all she said was, "Mister, you are in deep trouble." Then she clamped one hand around the back of my neck and marched me across the outfield grass and up the Norvelt road. It was about a quarter mile to my house and all I could think of along the way was that from now on I would forever be known by everyone as "the kid who got dragged off the field by his mom." That was going to be embarrassing. And it did make me think that moving out of this town as Dad wanted to do was a good idea, not because I thought the town was a Commie town but because once you got a reputation for one stupid thing it stuck with you *forever*. When my cousin Bruce was a baby boy—long, long before I was even born—he went "wee-wee" in his pants in the grocery store then walked around the store in wet pants shouting, "I wee-wee! I wee-wee!" It was as if he had given himself a new name, and to this day the whole town still calls him "Wee-Wee." I was in the grocery store with him once and in the cereal aisle he pointed to the tile floor and said, "Don't step there. That's where I earned my name." I figured kids on the baseball field would be calling me "Headless Turkey Boy" and when I ran the bases they'd tease me by making clucking noises. And if I was caught in a rundown between bases kids would point and say, "Once again, caught in a rundown by his own mother!"

When we arrived home I tried to distract her as she marched me to my room.

"Hey, Mom," I asked, "how come the doctor said my blood is iron poor but it tastes like copper?"

"You are not funny," she growled. "You are now grounded for the summer! You can only leave your room to do your chores, or go to the bathroom, and if you are lucky, mister, you might have the privilege of having dinner with me and your father. But that is it. And I'm going to call Mr. Huffer and tell him you will no longer be on the team."

"But, Mom," I pleaded, "we only have six kids to begin with."

"Make that five," she replied heartlessly.

"What about seeing Bunny?" I asked.

"It is possible," Mom replied, "that you will have a beard the next time you see her."

"Do you think she'll get any taller by then?" I asked.

"No, but you have every chance of getting shorter," she replied.

"Can I still help Miss Volker?" I asked forlornly. "She needs me." Helping Miss Volker cook her hands and type obituaries suddenly sounded like a wonderful way to spend the summer.

Mom paced the floor and thought about it. "I'm only letting you go down there and help her," she concluded, "because she needs you. Otherwise you can sit in here all summer and think about your shameful behavior. Firing that gun was a dangerous accident but mowing the corn against my direct orders was willful. You deliberately disobeyed me." Then she pointed her finger at my chest and her voice became very throaty. "You took food away from hungry people. From poor people. Nothing can be lower and more cruel than that. Now what do you have to say for yourself?"

I had nothing to say for myself. What I did was wrong, and then what I said next was cowardly. "Dad made me cut down the corn," I whimpered, and dabbed at my nose for sympathy.

"Well, mister," she informed me with no trace of sympathy in her voice, "I'm going to march your father into this room and make him cut you down to size. And when he finishes with you I'll make him wish he had already built that bomb shelter because he might be living in it." Then she turned and stormed out of the room, did a quick pivot, and stormed right back. "Oh!" she said icily. "And another thing! I saw that toy airplane he won in a card game, and mark my words—you will never get in it. *Never!*" Then she stormed out again.

6

It took two days for Dad to march into my room and cut me down to size. He knew he had gotten me in trouble with Mom and so he quickly wrangled a construction job in West Virginia for a couple days of paid work. He thought Mom might cool down, but he could have been away for two years and she would still have been just as angry. It was as if she could preserve her anger and store it in a glass jar next to the hot horseradish and yellow beans and corn chowchow she kept in the dank basement pantry. And when she needed some anger she could just go into the basement and open a jar and get worked up all over again.

When he returned from West Virginia she ambushed him in the kitchen, and after she gave him a tongue lashing a second time around I knew he'd be seeing me next. And then he walked down the hall, one loud footfall after the other in a very deliberate way, as if he was letting me know in advance that he had no choice but to do the awful thing he had been told to do.

My room was as small as a monk's cell. I had a single bed, a dresser with an attached mirror, and a small closet, but I didn't have a Bible. If I did have a Bible I would have been down on my knees and reading it with an angelic look on my face. The only religious book I had in my collection was the Landmark biography *Jesus of Nazareth*. I had it on my lap when Dad pushed open my bedroom door. He quickly stepped into my room and roughly closed the door behind him. But he didn't look angry. It seemed to me that he had willingly retreated to my room after the scolding Mom gave him about the corn and airplane. He took a deep breath and slowly ran his hand back and forth across his mouth as if he were trying to erase it and the lecture he was supposed to deliver.

Before he could get the first word out I sat up and asked, "Hey, Dad, how come we don't have any good information on the boyhood of Jesus?" I held up the book I was reading so he could see what I was talking about. "I mean, it seems that outside of the fact that he was entirely Jewish, we know that he didn't have to go to school and study because God funneled all his preaching knowledge directly into his brain."

Dad shrugged. "I don't know," he said, and pulled up a short stool. "I wasn't around back then. But I wish I could cram some knowledge directly into your brain."

"I guess that would take a religious miracle," I ventured.

"I didn't come in here to talk about Jesus," he said, trying to sound stern. "I came in here to talk about gun safety."

"What about the corn?" I asked.

"Your mom will handle that beef," he said. "I'm here because she told me about you firing off the Jap rifle, and that's *my* beef with you."

"It was an accident," I explained. "Honest. I didn't know it was loaded."

"Don't you remember last winter when we went deer hunting and I taught you about gun safety?" he said, raising an eyebrow. "Don't you remember anything I teach you?"

How could I forget?

It was the first Monday after Thanksgiving. Deer hunting was popular in our area because shooting and dressing a deer provided a lot of winter food for a family, so we had school off for the first day of hunting season.

Through one of his friends Dad had bought me a secondhand camouflage hunting coat, pants, face scarf, and gloves so that if I stood next to a tree you would never see me—which was not good because people sometimes shoot on impulse when they hear something move, and that *something* could be a person.

"Itchy trigger fingers," Dad had said, aiming his trigger finger toward me and giving it a pull, "and stupidity is what gets people killed." So in order for people to see me and not shoot me he had also bought me a large blaze orange cap which kept slipping down over my face. I just hoped there wasn't some hunter who mistook me for Rudolph the Red-Nosed Reindeer and let me have it.

We got into Dad's truck when it was pitch black out. He was eager to get to our tree house in the mountains because sunrise was when the hunting officially started and he wanted to get the jump on the other hunters.

On the moonlit drive through the shadowed mountains he said to me, "I think you are old enough to do this. But I'll teach you all about gun safety, because no matter what, gun safety is the number one concern when out hunting. Of course, good hunting skills are important too. But safety is tops."

"Sure," I said, full of enthusiasm. "Safety first." He smiled, and it made me happy to say things I knew he liked to hear.

"Once you load a rifle," he explained, "and have a shell in the chamber, you always keep the barrel pointed toward the ground."

"Yes," I said.

"And when you are just learning about guns always keep the safety on too," he added.

"Okay," I said. "But what do you do when you see a deer?"

"You won't see one unless you are totally quiet," he said firmly.

I held my pointer finger up to my lips. "Shhhh," I whispered.

"No sneezing," he said.

"Okay."

"No coughing."

"Yep."

"And here is a little-known fact, but good hunters believe it is absolutely essential," he stressed.

"No fake deer talk?" I guessed.

"Yes, that too," he said impatiently. Then he leaned toward me and quietly said, "No *farting*."

"What?" I asked. I hadn't expected him to say that.

"Do you know what that word means?" he asked.

"Yeah. I got it right on my spelling test," I remarked, trying to make a joke.

"Well, don't fart or you'll scare the deer," he continued seriously. "They have very sensitive noses and ears."

"Okay," I said.

"When I was a boy," he continued, "my dad coated me with deer gland scent so they couldn't smell me because I couldn't hold my gas."

"Where do you get deer glands?" I asked.

"From between the toes of dead deer," he explained. "I smelled awful. So for now," he cautioned, "just be quiet and think about what I said. When we get to our deer-spotting tree house I'll go over everything again."

"Sure," I replied, trying to sound respectful, but not as intense as he was.

After that we drove in silence as the sky blued and the few big clouds showed their low gray bellies. We turned off a main road and onto a smaller road and then onto a narrow trail where the long leafless branches of the trees scraped jaggedly against the sides of the truck as we plowed roughly through the heaving snow. Finally we entered a small clearing. We were the first truck there and instantly Dad was in a good mood. He checked his watch. "Ten minutes till sunrise," he said. "I think this is going to be my lucky day."

I threw on an orange backpack, which was stuffed with dry socks, dry gloves, and two Thermoses full of hot coffee. Dad put on his orange hat and vest and we started to trudge up a tree-covered hill. Right away he turned toward me with his finger over his lips, and then he pointed toward the snow where the wind had blown it skin-thin. There were fresh deer tracks. I smiled and he smiled back and gave me a big thumbs-up. We kept climbing, one silent step after the next, and before too long we reached a colossal tree. Dad stopped and pointed skyward. About ten feet above the ground was a tree house platform with low sides. There was no roof. There were ladder slats nailed to the trunk of the tree. Dad brushed the snow off the slats with his gloves and then noiselessly climbed up, and I climbed up after him.

Without talking we cleared snow from a corner of the platform and got our gear settled. Dad opened a Thermos and poured us a cup of coffee. He took a sip then passed it to me. As I took a sip he carefully slipped a brass and copper shell into the chamber of his deer rifle and pushed the bolt forward and over. The keen *click-click* of metal against metal was like a vault locking. We were loaded and there was no way out until he got his deer. "Remember everything I said about gun safety," he whispered.

"Yes," I whispered back, and gave him the last bit of coffee.

"No accidents," he reminded me, and tightly puckered his lips to remind me about the unwanted bodily noise.

"Total silence," I vowed, and extra quietly screwed the top back onto the Thermos.

He raised the rifle and rested the stock on the half-high wall of the tree house. I squatted just behind him, and as his head turned to scan for deer within range, my head turned so I could see exactly what he was seeing—cold black tree trunks, the yellow-lichen-covered tops of frost-gray rocks, and wind-carved waves of white snow. Our heads swiveled back and forth for what seemed like an hour. And then suddenly Dad stiffened. I did too. About fifty yards ahead a white-tailed deer was slowly picking his way across the snow-covered rocks and roots.

As soon as I saw him I knew instantly that I didn't want him to die. He was so beautiful and at ease in the woods. This was his home, not mine, and I suddenly felt like a killer who had broken into his house and was about to shoot him. I watched and held my breath. He would stop and turn his antlered head to listen and then raise his dark nose to sniff the air, and then he would nibble on the tender bark of a thin tree, and then lick some snow, and then take a few more careful steps. The fur under his neck looked so soft, like the neck fur of a cat I had before it went out one night and never came back. I felt as if Dad and I were going to murder nature's tame pet. What I really wanted to do was to go down and stroke his golden brown fur, and name him and give him something to eat and make him see I was not there to harm him.

But we *were* there to harm him. We were going to kill him and gut him and skin him and cut him up and eat him. I turned to maybe say something of what I was thinking when Dad mechanically rotated the rifle in the deer's direction and pressed his eye against the rubber end of the telescopic sight as if he were getting ready to shoot his old WWII enemy. Hitting the deer would be about as easy for Dad as standing at our kitchen window with a target pistol and picking off the finches and cardinals at our window bird feeder.

I knew I couldn't grab Dad's rifle because it would be bad gun safety so I came up with another idea. I thought that if I could silently pass gas I would scare off the deer. But it would have to be silent so Dad wouldn't hear it, and it was hard to tell if it would be silent because I was squatting down. I could think it was going to be silent but then it might suddenly be really loud. You could never be sure. But I couldn't take a chance with Dad because he wouldn't think it was funny. He didn't even want me to breathe. He sure didn't want me to pass deer-spooking gas.

I saw his finger slowly curling around the trigger and it was trembling like a snake about to strike. He kept his eye pressed against the sight as he tracked the deer between the crisscrossing tree trunks, and all I could think about was my twitching sphincter. I was trying to open it just a tiny bit so a whisper-thin stream of gas would noiselessly escape into the air and stealthily warn the deer without Dad knowing it was me. I looked at Dad's tightening trigger finger and the side of his face where his cheek muscles were knotted up as he intently followed the deer and waited for a good chest shot that would cleanly pierce the heart. I knew I only had a moment to act if I wanted to save the deer's life. I took a deep breath, squatted down a bit, and relaxed my bottom. But nothing happened. I took another deep breath and pushed out.

"Come on," I said to myself, "get inspired. You have to save the deer! Think of something."

And just at that tense moment when I was afraid Dad was going to pull the trigger and shoot the deer, a thought shot even more quickly into my mind—a very inspiring thought. I had been reading a great book about ancient explorers before Columbus, and there was a Chinese explorer, a Buddhist monk, who sailed a Chinese junk to the Aleutian Islands by Alaska and landed on an island that was populated by a primitive tribe of people who just happened to be called the Hairy Ainus People. That name alone almost made me howl with laughter, but I kept telling myself not to laugh through my mouth, but out the other direction. I really hadn't planned to think about the Hairy Ainus People, but there I was up in a tree house in the freezing cold and squatting down when my thoughts of the Hairy Ainus combined with a gut desire to save the deer gave me just enough oomph, and I let out a thin stream of gas which sounded roughly like the slow opening of a creaky coffin lid that had been closed for a thousand rusty years. Instantly the deer swiveled his pink ears toward us and cocked one of his strong rear legs as if he was about to bolt.

"What was that?" Dad hissed under his breath and pulled his eye away from the sight.

I didn't answer him because I knew the answer would arrive without me speaking a word. Once that creaky coffin door had opened, the smell of a thousand years of rotting death drifted out through the thick woven fabric of my clothing.

When I saw Dad's nose twitch I knew his question had been answered. Quickly, he pressed his eye back against the sight but I could tell by the way he jerked the barrel to the left and right that the deer had vanished. I had saved his life.

"Good timing," he said sarcastically without even looking at me.

I didn't say a word. I could have said it was an accident but I didn't feel like lying. I wasn't sorry the deer escaped and Dad could see I wasn't sorry.

"You know," he said irritably, "the deer really hasn't escaped. This just means some other guy will bag him."

I hoped not. And even if my hope was false hope, it was better than shooting him ourselves.

"Well, back to gun safety," Dad said, and pulled back and down on the bolt and removed the unused shell from the chamber of the rifle. "You understand never to play with guns, right?"

"Right," I replied, and I meant it. I really did. "Can we go home now?" I asked.

"Are you cold?"

I wasn't. I just didn't want to fake being happy if he shot a deer. I didn't want to see the blood and guts hanging out and everything else. "Yes," I said. "I'm freezing."

"Good enough," he said. "I'll come back tomorrow."

I knew he didn't mind taking me back home early since now he knew he could hunt more easily by himself for the rest of the season. Then we climbed down from the tree and I walked behind him toward the car. It was cold and the snap of each twig breaking sounded like tiny hunters firing tiny rifles at tiny imaginary deer. When we got to the clearing a panel truck full of

Norvelt Gun Club hunters pulled up. The driver stuck his head out the window.

"How'd it go?" he asked too loudly, and even from a distance I could smell whiskey on his breath.

Dad could too. "Nothing to report," he replied, and then the first thing he said to me when we got into our truck was, "No matter what you do in life, *never* drink and use guns—and drive!"

"Sorry about the gas," I finally said. "But the deer was beautiful."

"What you did was nothing," he replied, and reached over and tousled my hair. "Those other guys are the real knuckleheads."

I was thinking about that winter hunting incident and hadn't listened to a word Dad said in my bedroom, but whatever he said, I knew he was right and I nodded my head up and down to show him respect.

Finally he asked, "Do you have anything to say for yourself?"

"I promise," I said as sincerely as possible. "I didn't know there was a bullet in the chamber of that Jap rifle. I had played with it before but there was never a bullet."

"Are you lying?" he asked.

"No. Not even a little," I replied.

"Well, something doesn't add up," he said, standing and pacing the room. "If I didn't put a bullet in the chamber and you didn't—then who did?" He stopped, and just like in the movies he gave me a long, steady look as if I were on trial and now was the moment for me to break down and confess.

I shrugged. "I don't know," I said. "Honest."

"I know I've looked in that chamber before," he said calmly, rethinking his moves. "There is no way it had a bullet in it." He sat back down and his eyes looked vacant. Just as I had drifted off and recalled the old deer hunt, I now guessed he had drifted off thinking about the war and crawling through the sand and finding those dead men and stripping away their weapons and war gear. I looked into his eyes for any sign of emotion. Was he sad? Or proud? Or terrified? I couldn't tell. He looked stuck in time, like an old black-and-white photograph wedged into the side of a mirror frame. Then very quietly he turned and said to me, "You know what the biggest problem was with the marines out in the Pacific Islands?"

I shook my head no.

"When we finally landed on those Jap-infested islands our guys had a hard time shooting the Japs—I don't mean because the Japs were hiding—I mean that they had a real hard time with the idea of having to shoot another person you could look in the eye. Our officers had to threaten to shoot some of our own troops if they didn't fire their rifles."

I had read *Guadalcanal Diary* but didn't remember reading about that problem. All the marines I read about fired their guns like crazy at everything that moved. They even burned the Japs alive with flamethrowers. They killed them every way they could and felt like heroes for wiping them out.

"But the Minutemen shot the British in the eyes at Bunker Hill," I said.

"Stuff like that only sounds good on paper," Dad said dismissively. "But believe me, in real life when you are eye to eye with the enemy you'd rather shake their hand than shoot them."

Dad stood up and looked down over me with his hand on the crown of my head as if he were saying a prayer in church. Then gravely he said, "Don't ever go to war. Even if you win, the battle is never over inside you."

I nodded yes.

Then his mood changed. "I believe you didn't know the gun was loaded," he said, and dropped his hand across my shoulder. "But you shouldn't have played with it or lied to your mom about having my permission. You are still grounded for the summer. Don't worry, though, I might soon be joining you in your room. Your mom isn't exactly jumping up and down with joy about the plane or her corn."

"Move in anytime," I said. "I'd like some company."

"And thank your lucky stars you didn't shoot anyone," he added, and slapped the back of my head.

"I scared Miss Volker," I confessed. "She dropped her hearing aid down the toilet."

"Sorry that old Commie didn't dive in after it," he cracked, and then he slowly left the room to go tell Mom he had really straightened me out once and for all.

7

I was in my room reading *Captain Cortés Conquers Mexico* which was about how Cortés slaughtered the Aztecs and turned them into a Lost World even before Pizarro had done it to the Incas. To me that meant the big lesson Pizarro learned from history was that it was okay to kill innocent people and steal their gold! In fact, Cortés was Pizarro's hero because Cortés and his army of conquistadors used their long swords to hack to pieces so many Aztec soldiers so quickly that fleeing women and children actually drowned in rivers of blood that flooded the streets. Those who escaped from being chopped to bits later died in horrid agony from smallpox the conquistadors spread to Mexico from Europe. The writer of the book called Cortés a great man. As

Miss Volker had once said, "Be suspicious of history that is written by the conquerors." I bet the writer didn't ask any Aztecs what they thought of Cortés.

I was kind of stunned by imagining all the bloody carnage and I slumped back onto my bed pillow when I noticed a bubbling river of blood running out my nose and across my lips. "Dang!" I shouted. "I swear I'm going to drown in *my* own pool of blood." I reached for a box of tissues. I rolled one up and stuck it between my upper lip and gum the way Miss Volker taught me.

I had just stopped the bleeding and hid the wad of bloody tissues behind my bed when Mom came in wearing a crisply ironed summer dress and told me to put on some "respectable" clothes. "I'm taking you out for some fresh air," she said.

"Like walking a dog?" I asked, trying to be clever.

"No funny business," she ordered. "Just get dressed."

I gladly got dressed because I actually needed some fresh air after that awful book. When I met Mom in the kitchen she inspected me up and down, made me change from sneakers to loafers, and then we walked up the street a quarter mile to Dr. Mertz's home office.

Because of Miss Volker's needlepoint map of Norvelt I now looked at the houses differently. Some were well kept and painted nicely with tidy yards and groomed flower beds that Mom admired. But a few were uninhabited and gloomy-looking with dandelions overrunning the yard and limp gutters hanging loose from the weight of soggy old leaves and broken tree branches. Mom seemed to look away from the abandoned houses, but she always brightened up when she spotted a bird's nest full of baby birds who were chirping for lunch. And she laughed as she pointed out the young squirrels dashing crazily across the laundry lines and how the wild brown-and-white rabbits blended in with the dried weeds and Queen Anne's lace that lined the vegetable plots between the houses. Everything good and alive and hopeful made her smile, but what was left to fall into ruin made her tense up and turn her head away. I could read her mind, and I'm sure she was thinking that there was a time when the town was all new and perfect and everyone worked hard and had so much pride in owning their own little Norvelt house. If she had it her way it would all be perfectly fixed up to look as it had been when she was my age. But I could only see what it now was, and it looked like a town whose future was not going to circle back to its past.

Mom hadn't made an appointment with Dr. Mertz but she timed our arrival so we would show up just at the end of his office hours. Dr. Mertz had an elderly receptionist and when we opened the door and stepped in she stopped typing, raised her eyeglasses, and asked if she could be of help.

"I just want to have a quick word with the doctor," Mom explained, using her sweet neighborly voice as if we'd come to borrow a cup of sugar.

"Then please take a seat," the receptionist replied routinely, and pointed toward a row of dark oak chairs before returning to her typing. She was a lot better at typing than I was. She used all of her fingers and I only used two.

"Hey, Mom," I whispered. "Can I ask her to give me some typing tips?"

"Just mind your own business," she said tightly while still keeping a bright smile on her face.

"Well, if we don't have an appointment why are we here?" I asked.

"Because I need to check on something," she said vaguely, then looked away from me and put a lot of attention into smoothing out her skirt. I knew she was up to something but I didn't know what.

I sat in silence and stared at the taxidermed school of fish the doctor had mounted all around the walls. I counted thirty-five of them, and suddenly I wondered if Mr. Huffer could figure out a way to mount a school of old dead people on the wall in order to save space since Bunny had told me the world was running out of burial plots. I turned to ask Mom but she was in the middle of refreshing her red lipstick, and when Dr. Mertz appeared from his office door she quickly hopped up.

"Oh, hi," he said, clearly surprised when he saw us. Then he turned to his receptionist. "Mrs. Woodcliff," he asked, "did I have an appointment I failed to notice?"

Before Mrs. Woodcliff could answer Mom cut in. "No," she said. "I just took a little chance and popped over."

Dr. Mertz knew us from other appointments. He had peered up my nose with a telescopic flashlight which looked like a thin pen that clipped into the top pocket of his white lab jacket. He had also taken blood samples with a syringe, and he was the one who had given me the iron drops to take each night and told me to eat iron-fortified cereal—he had even crushed up a mortarful of the cereal and held a magnet to it and pulled out tiny specks of real iron to show me the stuff that he said was good for me. He also concluded I would need to schedule an appointment to have the inside of my nasal passages cauterized in order to burn away the number of leaky capillaries and stop the bleeding.

"How can I help you?" Dr. Mertz asked after we silently entered his examination room.

"I just thought you might have a few extra minutes to cauterize the inside of Jack's nasal passages," Mom said smoothly. "He's bleeding a lot."

"I see," he replied, then pursed his lips and looked

down at his feet to ponder what Mom was getting at. When he looked up he said, "But you know there will be a charge for that service."

"How much will that cost, Doctor?" she asked. As soon as she mentioned money I pretended to be distracted and fortunately, in the doctor's office, there were plenty of plastic medical models of internal organs to study. I fixed my eyes on a purple human liver that looked just like the cow liver Mom always served me because it was "filled with iron." Even though I tried not to listen to Mom and the doctor any talk of money always got my attention because everything in our house depended entirely on money. Decisions for us were not made on whether we wanted something, or even needed something, but on whether we could afford it or not. Dad once said, "Someday I want to live a life where I won't be bullied by my wallet." I wished that someday would arrive soon because his wallet was a really big bully that said "No" and "Put that back" all the time.

The doctor gave Mom a price and I could tell by the disappointed way she said "I see" that she couldn't afford the operation. But then she quickly switched moods, smiled brightly at him, and asked, "Would you do it for some homemade jarred fruit as payment?"

He smiled widely in return, but his mind was made up. "Well," he said slowly with a touch of regret in his voice, "that is very sweet of you to offer, but I have two cases of peaches left over from last year."

"How about pickles?" Mom was quick to ask.

"Got a basement full of them," he replied just as quickly, and before Mom could offer another barter he said, "I wish I didn't have to ask you for cash, but I do."

"I understand," Mom said in an even voice that showed no sign of regret, and I knew we were finished. A moment later we were out on the sidewalk and strolling home as if nothing embarrassing had ever taken place.

"Why'd you offer him fruit and pickles?" I asked, and looked up at her face which didn't look so bright and cheery. "Doctors cost money."

"You shouldn't be embarrassed," Mom said, knowing that I was. "Money can mean a lot of different things. When I was a kid we traded for everything. Nobody had any cash. If you wanted your house built, you helped someone build theirs, and then they would turn around and help you build yours. It was the same with everything. I'd give you eggs and you'd pay me in milk."

"I don't think it works that way now," I remarked. "If he fixed my nose I don't think he'd want me to do brain surgery on him."

"Not unless he wanted to become Dr. Frankenstein's

monster," she replied with a laugh. "But seriously, it's a shame the way this town has changed. Norvelt was set up so people who didn't have a lot of cash could trade each other for things they needed to make a living. Instead of having to reach for your wallet you'd reach for a hammer and saw, or a plow, or baking pan—something to labor with. Money is just a way of measuring work, but you don't need money if everyone agrees that trading one kind of work for another will do just as well."

"I see," I said, but I didn't. None of the history books I ever read had people happily trading one thing for another. When I read *The California Gold Rush* no one lifted a finger unless they were paid in gold nuggets or gold dust. And Captain Kidd would have had his throat slit from ear to ear if he tried to pay his pirates in fish. When Alexander Graham Bell invented the telephone he did not give it away for free. They all wanted gold just like Pizarro and Cortés and just about everyone else.

"But everyone says cash is king. Not fruit and pickles."

"Cash just means you can be a big shot and cut to the front of the line," she said disapprovingly. "Or get what you want right away. It's true that I wish I had enough cash to have your nose fixed. But for now I'll just save up and we'll pay as we go—that's what regular people do."

She bent down and gave me a kiss on my head which always made me feel better. "It doesn't cost a penny to be sweet," she said, smiling down on me. "Give me your hand." She held hers openly toward me. "It makes me happy to pretend that I'm your older girlfriend."

I grinned, and took a chance. "Then it would be better if your younger boyfriend wasn't grounded so he could take you on a date to the drive-in and buy you presents."

"But you *are* grounded, and not even cash can buy away your trouble," she replied with resolve. "You'll have to work off your punishment the old-fashioned way."

"Can I trade being grounded for a different punishment?" I asked.

"Sure," she said. "You can replant that whole field of corn, tend to it, harvest it, and turn it into food for poor old folks."

I wished I could replant the field, but I knew Dad wouldn't allow that trade. He'd make me mow it down a second time and then I'd be grounded for another year—if I was still alive.

8

I was eating from a jar of pickles in the kitchen and reading my favorite column in the newspaper:

> ***June 23, 1611:*** **Henry Hudson was set adrift in Hudson Bay by mutineers and never seen again.**
>
> ***June 23, 1683:*** **William Penn signed a peace treaty with the Lenni Lanape Indian tribe, covering land that would become part of our Great State of Pennsylvania.**

I was wishing I could sign a peace treaty with my parents when the telephone rang. Mom picked it up and listened, then turned toward me as she said, "Yes, Miss Volker. I'll send him right down."

"I guess being a good neighbor is better than cash," I said brightly, trying to be charming.

"You got me there," she replied, "but after you help her you turn right around and march back home. No baseball or any monkey business. Understand?" Her last word was punctuated with an arching eyebrow.

"Yep," I said, and dashed for the door. "I promise."

It took me less than a minute to run down to Miss Volker's yellow house which was glowing under the morning sun as if it had been carved out of melting butter. It made me squint to look at it, but as I arrived I saw she was waiting impatiently on her porch. She must have had her hair recently colored because it was so blue it looked like a massive hydrangea blossom. "Hurry," she called out, and waved one of her red claws at me. "I just got a call about another possible dead person—a Norvelt original!"

"Who called?" I asked.

"A *spotter*," she said in a hushed tone.

That sounded mysterious. "What's a spotter?"

"One of my network of spies who keeps an eye open on the last of the Norvelt folks. You know—someone who notices if they make it to church, or miss. Or if they go to the grocery store or pick up their mail, things like that. So I got a call today about Mrs. Dubicki over at house number C-27. My spotter has not seen her for a week and I know she hasn't been feeling well, poor thing."

"So?" I asked.

"So, we must go over there *immediately*," she insisted, and leaned her blue bush of hair toward the garage. "I keep dialing her number but no one answers. We must go find out if that phone will never be answered."

"How do we get there?" I asked.

"We'll take the car, and if we can't spot her from the road we'll have to stop and look in her windows, and if we still can't see her then we'll have no other choice—you'll have to sneak into the house," she reasoned.

"What if she's alive and recognizes me?" I said fearfully. "She'll call the cops and I'll be grounded *forever* only in a jail cell. It would be best if you went in because nobody will arrest an old lady."

"I can't go in," she replied. "I'm the medical examiner in this town. When I show up people know I'm going to pronounce someone dead, sign their death certificate, hand them over to Mr. Huffer, and then write their obit. No one *alive* wants a visit from me. These old folks scatter like pigeons when I follow them up and down a grocery store aisle."

"Well, what should we do?" I asked.

"Hmmm," she said, thinking out loud. "It would be best if you wore a disguise."

"I have my Halloween costume from last year," I suggested.

"Of what?" she asked.

"The Grim Reaper," I said.

She threw her head back and her cackling laugh showed off her old-lady teeth which looked like a couple rows of tiny marble tombstones. "You are my perfect partner," she said grandly. "Mrs. Dubicki's going to have to see the Grim Reaper sooner or later, so it might as well be sooner. Now go fetch it—and hurry! I'll wait for you by the car."

I ran back across the yards and sneaked around the pony pen to the back of our garage and opened that half door Dad had showed me. My costume was hanging up in an overflow closet full of out-of-season coats and my grandparents' clothes that Mom couldn't bear to give away. I grabbed the costume, the mask, and the long-handled plastic scythe. I was just sorry I didn't have Mrs. Slater's false teeth with me because that would make it even more spooky. Then as quickly as I had run up to the garage I turned and ran down to Miss Volker's car.

I just figured she would drive because she was the adult, but she was standing on the passenger side. "The keys are in the ignition," she said. "Now open the door for me."

"I've only driven a tractor," I said nervously. "I don't know if I can really drive a car."

"It's the same," she said. "Just go slow and it won't matter if you hit anything."

"But what if I slowly drive off a cliff?" I asked.

"You'll have more time to pray before you hit the bottom," she said impatiently. "Now try to be a man and let's get going."

I threw the costume in the backseat. I opened the passenger door and helped her in, then ran around the front of the red Plymouth Valiant. It was a small car but I was still worried because I was even smaller. When I sat in my dad's truck and pretended to drive I had a hard time reaching the pedals while still sitting high enough on the seat in order to see out the windshield. I could do one or the other, but not both. Luckily Miss Volker's car was a lot tighter inside, and after I scooted the seat all the way forward and stretched my legs out I could reach the gas pedal and just enough of the brake.

"Turn the key," she ordered. "Hurry."

I turned the key and it started right up.

"Now put it in Drive," she snapped. "Come on. You're moving like a snail. That woman might be in trouble, or dead, and if she is I should be the first to know. That vulture Mr. Huffer is always beating me to the body, but it's my job to first pronounce a dead person dead before he calls their family and tries to sell them a casket and all the pricey trimmings."

I pushed a button on the dashboard, which had a big D for Drive on it, and tentatively pressed down on the gas and we inched forward.

"More gas!" she insisted. "Gun it."

I gave it a lot more gas and we flopped back into our seats. I got scared and hit the brakes and we both jerked forward.

"Do you want me to drive?" she barked, and held up her ruddy claws.

"I'll get the hang of it," I said nervously. "It'll just take a minute." I gave it more gas and slowly we crept forward, and I turned out of the driveway and onto the Norvelt road.

"She just lives a few streets down," Miss Volker informed me, and pointed the way with her bent-up fingers.

As I felt comfortable behind the wheel I gave the Valiant more gas. For a second I dared to take my eyes off the road and glance at the speedometer to make sure I wasn't breaking the law. We were going fifteen whole miles per hour.

"I can run faster than you drive," she said, and was so exasperated she suddenly lurched forward and stomped her foot down over mine. The engine revved and my heart beat faster and I gripped the steering wheel as we flew down the road.

"This is more like it," she said.

"Miss Volker, you are scaring me," I said in a nervous voice.

"Hush up and turn here," she ordered, and lifted her foot off of mine as she pointed to the left.

I turned wildly and our tires squealed as we nearly clipped a mailbox, and when I straightened up we went along a curvy road lined with maple trees. Finally Miss Volker reached over and hooked the steering wheel with her stiff thumb and we careened off the road and hopped the dirt curb onto the overgrown weeds, which was really Mrs. Dubicki's front lawn. I put all my weight onto the brake pedal and we slid sideways to a stop. By then I was panting like a dog.

"This is her house," she said. "She hasn't painted it since 1934. I like Mrs. Dubicki because that busybody Spizz gave her a ticket for having a shabby-looking house and she chased him off the property with her dead husband's double-barreled shotgun."

We both stared at the faded green house with dirty white shutters. I'm not sure what I expected to see—maybe a flag at half mast in respect for the dead. "All the curtains are closed," I whispered, "and they are black."

"Those are her old blackout curtains from the war," Miss Volker explained. "It's not a good sign they are closed," she added. "Most people prefer to die in the dark. My guess is that she's history, but you have to go in there and confirm it. Just enter the house and come back with a detailed report on what you find."

"Do I have to?" I asked. I really didn't want to sneak into a house and stumble around like the Grim Reaper who had come to harvest Mrs. Dubicki. What if she wasn't dead and still had that giant gun she was going to shoot Spizz with? Or what if she was dead and I didn't see her and I stepped on her? That would scare me so much my nose would probably explode like a blood grenade.

"Just think how unfair it would be," Miss Volker mused, "if I wrote her obituary and she was still alive. Now that would be cruel if the shock of reading about her own death killed her. Besides, she's on death's doorstep already. I happen to know that she has a heart that's about to quit."

"Okay," I said reluctantly. "I'll do it. But don't you dare tell my mom."

"Cross my heart," she promised, and raked her stiff fingers across her chest.

I got out of the car and opened the rear door. In a moment I had my costume on and was stumbling up the sidewalk. The hooded mask kept slipping down over my eyes and I held my scythe straight out like a lance so I didn't run face-first into something solid. After I made it up the front steps I reached forward and touched the doorknob and gave it a turn. It wasn't locked so I pushed it open. "Mrs. Dubicki," I called out. "Are you alive?"

I heard something scratchy that I couldn't make out.

"Mrs. Dubicki," I called again. "Did you say something?"

Again I heard sounds but they were muffled. Oh cheeze, I thought. I bet a burglar broke in and left her tied up with a gag around her mouth.

With the blackout curtains closed and the mask half covering my eyes it was dark inside the hallway as I shuffled forward with my scythe waving in front of me. I came to a wall and turned left. I was going in the right direction because the scratchy sound grew louder.

"Mrs. Dubicki?" I shakily called. "Hello? Are you alive?"

Once I got a little ways along the hall I could see light peeking out from under an interior door. That was promising. I shuffled down there and *tap, tap, tapped* on the door with my scythe. "Mrs. Dubicki," I asked in a scared-little-boy voice, "are you bound and gagged? Or if you have a gun please take the bullets out. And if you are dead could you please come back to life because I'm really afraid of dead people."

I slowly opened the door and peeked into the dimly lit room. Oh, it was sad. There she was, slumped all the way back in a recliner about two feet in front of the TV. The Pittsburgh news was on and an announcer was talking about where people could receive their second round of polio vaccine. Miss Volker had stressed that if I found Mrs. Dubicki dead to pinch her arm and make certain she wasn't just napping because, as she said, "When old people nap they look like cadavers."

"Mrs. Dubicki," I whispered. "Are you taking an old-lady catnap?"

I wished she'd pop awake and let out a demonic laugh and just go ahead and scare me witless. I mean, what if she was alive? What would I say to her? What?

I stepped forward, took a deep breath, and poked her on the shoulder with my plastic scythe. "Mrs. Dubicki?" I said politely. "If you are still among the living could you please inform me so I don't have to pinch you?"

She didn't move a muscle. I took a deeper breath, reached out, and pinched the spotted old skin on her lifeless forearm.

Suddenly she sat straight up and I jumped back and froze. She was silent at first as she batted her eyes and shook the sleep off. Was she like Lazarus and had just now come back from being dead? Or had she never died to begin with? I didn't know. And then she slowly turned toward me and crossly asked, "Who the blazes are you and what are you doing in my house?"

I guess I should have planned in advance to say something smart to her, but since I hadn't given it any thought I just replied with "Hi, I'm the Norvelt Grim Reaper for the Public Good."

"I can see that," she said, not at all astonished. "I'm not blind. Have you come for me?"

"Someone reported you dead," I replied.

"As far as I know I'm alive," she responded, and took a raspy breath to prove it to herself. "My heart has been giving me fits lately and so I've just been lying low for a few days, but I don't think I'm ready to kick the bucket."

"That's fine," I said nervously because my heart was very much alive and pounding in my chest. I began to back away. "I can come back some other time."

"I'm not afraid of death," she said calmly. "I'd just like to time my earthly exit so I don't miss my grandson's birthday on July third. Would that be okay with you?"

"Oh, no problem," I said quickly. "Take all the time you need. I'm in no rush. There are plenty of other dying people I can visit."

"Well, what about you come back in two weeks," she said, rubbing her chin and thinking about what she just said. "Yeah, two weeks will give me time to wrap up my business, say all the goodbyes I care to say, and then I'll be ready to meet my husband in heaven. Will that fit your calendar, Mr. Reaper?"

"Umm, I'll check my schedule," I quickly replied, "but I think I can fit you in."

"Would you like a cup of tea?" she asked.

"No thanks," I replied, and politely stood there while she chattered on. Finally I looked at my wrist even though I didn't have a watch on. "Time to go," I announced, and took a step back.

"You don't have to go," she implored with a touch of loneliness in her voice. Still, I kept inching back toward the door.

Just then I could hear Miss Volker hitting the car horn. "I'm sorry," I explained to Mrs. Dubicki, "but my chariot is calling for me."

"What?" she asked.

"You know, my chariot with the four deathly black horses," I blurted out, then turned to run.

"Wait!" she shouted. "I just remembered that Karen Linga down the street fell and broke her hip and she's in so much pain she is begging for you to come take her away."

"Thanks for the tip," I said, and once I started running I could not slow down. I bounced off the walls and my scythe whacked some pictures sideways. I had left the front door open, and when I saw daylight I leaped across the threshold and down the few steps.

When Miss Volker saw me she stopped leaning on the horn. "What took you so long?" she shouted. "I could have died from boredom for all the time it took you to take her pulse."

"We have to go," I begged as I ripped off my mask and gasped for air. "She's alive!"

"Dang," she griped as I opened the door and hopped in. "I sure wish these old ones would hurry it up. They need to meet their maker because I'm not getting any younger and there are a few things I'd like to do in this world before my own Grim Reaper pays me a visit."

I really wasn't paying attention to her. My nerves were shot. I started the engine and must have driven a mile in the wrong direction before I gave any thought to where I was going.

"You know," Miss Volker said, "I hope when my turn comes the Grim Reaper is a lot like you. You don't seem too scary."

"I'm not scary," I admitted. "I was scared. Even when she invited me for tea I was shaking. And after she invited me back in two weeks I ran. I don't think I'm a very good Grim Reaper."

"Well, when her time comes remind me," she said, "so that when I write her obituary I make sure to mention she invited the Grim Reaper to tea. That reveals her good upbringing, don't you think so?"

"Very polite of her," I agreed. "And you can add that she loved her grandson whose birthday is on July third."

"Thanks for the good detail," Miss Volker noted, and smiled to herself. "Now, would you like to turn the car around and go home?" she asked. "Otherwise we're heading for West Virginia."

I slowed and made a U-turn in the parking lot of a boarded-up church. On the way back we again passed Mrs. Dubicki's house and saw that the black window curtains were now thrust open.

"I'll have to speak with my spotter," muttered Miss Volker. "He won't be getting a finder's fee for this one!" Then she looked at me and said, "Your nose is bleeding. The next time you come down I'll fix it for you. It's easy—I have all the right tools."

"Did Mrs. Roosevelt give them to you?" I asked.

"No," she replied. "I bought some items at a retired veterinarian's yard sale and the others I made myself."

Cheeze-us-crust!

9

I was reading about King Arthur and liked how he had a round table which made everyone feel equal when they sat in a circle. Usually the king was the boss at the head of a long table and everyone else had to listen and take orders and not talk back unless they wanted to get locked in a dungeon and lose their heads. But King Arthur was different. He respected everyone and believed that if he treated people fairly they would treat him fairly. That was his secret to greatness.

Just then Dad stuck his head through my bedroom doorway. "How would you like to escape your room for a while?" he asked.

"I'd love it!" I shouted, and put down my book. I had really been plowing through the Landmark series.

I figured I might have them all read by the time summer was over. "Is Mom okay with letting me out?" I asked him.

"Well, I'm giving you permission to leave your room so you haven't broken any rules. Now follow me."

"Is she still mad about the plane?" I asked as we walked down the hall.

"Yep," he replied. "And she is showing no sign of getting over it."

"Are you now living in the garage?" I asked as we stepped outside.

"I bought my way out of that trouble," he said. "I took her down to the grocery store yesterday and paid for a cartful of charity food to make up for the corn she was going to trade for groceries."

"Cash is king," I remarked with a little swagger.

"Money makes the world go round," he sang. "Cash is the universal get-out-of-Norvelt-forever card."

"How much will you have to pay her not to get mad that you aren't really building a bomb shelter?" I asked.

"That is still an unresolved subject," he replied. "I can only afford to pay off one debt at a time. So for now we are going to *say* we are building a bomb shelter."

"Mom said you won the plane in a card game. Is that true?" I asked.

"Not entirely. But I got it for a song," he said confidentially. "They were practically giving them away at a military surplus auction. I mean, for twenty-five bucks how could I not buy it?"

I was shocked. "That's less than Mr. Fenton wants for his old car!" I blurted out.

"Next time I'll look around and see how much they are selling Sherman tanks for," he said.

That would be so cool, I thought. I wouldn't have to learn to steer—I could just drive in a straight line and run things over.

By then we were standing at the edge of the ex-cornfield. To one side, where I had cut down the last three rows of corn, Dad had marked off a long rectangle with twine wrapped around stakes in the ground.

"See that space?" he said, pointing.

I nodded.

"And the shovel stuck in the dirt?"

I nodded again.

"Then start digging," he instructed. "I'm going to roll the field flat for the runway." He jerked his head toward a road roller which was hooked up to the back of the tractor.

"Can we trade places?" I asked. "Miss Volker needs me to practice my driving so I can cart her around town."

"Maybe later," he said. "But for now you can practice your digging."

I didn't think that being grounded also included working in the ground.

I grabbed the shovel handle with both hands, then closed my eyes and imagined merry-olde-England in medieval times. "Whoso pulleth out this sword is the rightwise born king of England!" I shouted from *King Arthur and the Knights of the Round Table*. Then I tugged on the handle with all my might. The shovel easily pulled out and for just a moment I imagined that I really would be king, but when I opened my eyes I was still a kid holding a rusty shovel in western Pennsylvania. I had not become the future king of England, but I wished I had. King Arthur only had to deal with plague, famine, and evil knights. Instead, I was just the lone digger of a fake atomic bomb shelter.

"Hey, Dad," I called behind him as he walked toward the tractor. "Which do you think is more deadly? Past history or future history?"

He didn't even slow down to think about it. "Future history," he yelled back without hesitation. "Each war gets worse because we get better at killing each other."

That sounded so true. At first cavemen bashed each other's heads in with rocks and sticks. By the time of the Crusaders it was long swords and arrows, and at

Gettysburg they were blasting each other to bits from cannons filled with lead balls, iron chains, railroad spikes, and door knobs. And atomic bombs made future wars look even more hopeless. *No humans will survive. All the animals will die. Fish will rot in acidic water. All vegetation will wilt in the polluted air. There will be nothing left but enormous insects the size of dinosaurs.* I took a deep breath and pushed the blade of the shovel into the earth and got busy filling a wheelbarrow with dirt. Our only hope for survival might be in building cities deep underground like the one Dad said the army built to protect the president and all the self-important government people.

After a while Mom sauntered out with a pitcher and cups to give us some cold water because it was hot and because she wanted to check up on our progress. We must not have been doing too well because after a quick glance at our work she said to Dad, "Jack, you know I can get some men from the Community Center to help out. This is a big job."

"It's okay," Dad replied, and poured a cup of water over his head then shook it off like a dog. "We don't need any help from the *Communist* Center. We can do this ourselves." He glanced at me. "Right, partner?" he asked, and jabbed me in the shoulder.

"Right," I replied, but I didn't mean it. I'd love to

have a dozen friendly guys run over and finish this job.

"Mr. Spizz and that maintenance crew of his could make this easier," Mom suggested, trying to reason with him. "And faster too. And they might make the runway a little smoother."

The three of us held our hands over our eyes and squinted at the runway. It was as wavy as the ocean.

"It makes me seasick to look at it," Mom remarked as she turned away.

"That's nothing," Dad said dismissively. "This plane was built to take off and land on a ship, so it can certainly land on this."

"Are you sure you don't need just a tiny bit of help?" she asked again.

"Honestly," he said in a firm voice, "I'd rather just keep it in the family."

"Okay," she conceded, giving in to his stubbornness. "Do it your way." And she went over to the pony pen to check on War Chief's hay and water.

Dad turned to me. "If Spizz and those Community Center guys help us, the next thing you know they'll want to help fly my plane and share our bomb shelter. Good God," he said, "think of it. The Russian Commies will be bombing us from above and we'll be protecting a bunch of local Commies in our shelter. Nuts to that!" He hopped back onto the tractor, started it up, and roared off with the roller in tow.

"Yeah," I aped, and picked up the shovel. "Nuts to that." I certainly didn't want Mr. Spizz to come by and ask about paying the ticket.

Just then Bunny came running from around the corner of our house. She looked like the square face on a box of Wheaties—only with arms and legs. I was really happy to see her.

"Hey," she said breathlessly, "what are you doing?"

"Digging our fancy new bomb shelter," I replied without enthusiasm. "The future is going to take place underground."

"Bomb shelters are just family-size coffins," she said like a know-it-all. "When the atomic war comes we'll all die and when UFO people arrive they'll dig us up and study our culture."

"What do you think they'll learn?"

"Who knows and who cares," she replied, and threw her short arms up into the air. "Probably no more than what we know from digging up King Tut."

"Well, we have history books," I reminded her.

"They'll rot like everything else," she countered with a groan, and dropped her hands down to her side. "Nothing will be left."

I was going to say that the presidents on Mount Rushmore would survive when she stopped me.

"Let's change the subject," she insisted.

"To what?" I asked, and leaned on my shovel.

"To what I came here to tell you! The ambulance just arrived and now we have a stranger in the funeral parlor," she said excitedly. "A Hells Angel motorcycle guy who was dancing in the middle of the road early this morning and got flattened by a cement truck down by the pants factory. Guess you could say he got *pressed* flat as pants."

"Ugh," I said. "What's he look like?"

"Like tattooed roadkill only with a long black beard on one end and crushed black boots on the other," she said. "It's not pretty."

I could already feel my nose twitch from imagining what he might look like. "Is he from around here?"

"No one can tell," she said. "He didn't have a wallet and the police don't recognize him. But he has amazing tattoos."

"What kind of *amazing*?" I asked, and looked around to make sure Mom wasn't sneaking up on us.

"Depends on what part of his body you look at," she whispered, and made her eyes get real big like she had seen something off limits. "Dad's just now photographing them for the police, so he told me to get lost."

"Do you think I can handle seeing him?" I asked.

"No way," she replied. "You'd bleed out of your eye sockets if you saw this guy."

That was probably true. But then I had a thought. "Has Miss Volker been there yet?" I asked. "She needs to make it official."

"Nope," she replied.

"Well, do me a favor," I said, and put my hands on her shoulders. "Run down to her house and tell her about the Hells Angel. Then tell her to call me immediately, and that way I can get out of digging and take her down to see the body."

"Sounds like a good plan," she said, getting all wound up and pawing at the dirt with her sneakers. "Meet you in the back of the funeral parlor. But if you plan on looking at this guy, bring a box of tissues because of your nose problem."

"Thanks for the tip," I said as she bounded off like a springer spaniel.

It didn't take long before the telephone rang and Mom called me inside. "Miss Volker needs your help right away," she said at the door. "There was a road accident this morning and she has to examine the poor victim."

"Oh, that's awful," I gasped, and imitated Mr. Huffer's sad face, but inside I was thinking, Great, this will get me out of digging. But before I could make my escape she reached out and grabbed my shirt. She reeled me in and smelled my armpit. "You stink like an old billy goat," she said, and wrinkled her nose. "Hop in the shower, quickly. I'll get your clothes ready. I want you to look respectful at Mr. Huffer's place."

"What do the dead care if I smell?" I asked. "They are *dead* and they're bound to smell worse than me."

"Well, I'm not dead!" she snapped back. "And it is what I care that counts." Then she nudged me toward the bathroom with her hip. "Now don't forget to use soap."

I took the fastest shower I could. I didn't use soap but when I got out of the shower I splashed myself with Dad's bottle of Old Spice. I figured it made me smell like I was Admiral Farragut at the Battle of Mobile Bay. "Damn the torpedoes," I quoted boldly, "and full speed ahead!" I wrapped a skimpy towel around my waist and danced and pranced out of the bathroom and up the hall like I was a Union ship dodging Confederate mines.

Mom was in her room ironing a white shirt for me. "What are you doing?" I asked when I waltzed up to her. "I'm not going to church. I'm going to see a dead Hells Angel whose face looks like roadkill with a beard."

"Don't say that," she said. "No matter who that poor man is he deserves our respect. He was once someone's little angel baby."

"You mean *Hells* Angel baby," I pointed out. "I should be dressed like the devil in honor of that guy."

"Even the devil wears clean underpants," she said, pointing the threatening tip of the hot iron at my skimpy towel. "And put on clean socks, pants, a belt, an undershirt, comb your hair, brush your teeth, and put on your shoes, and when you do all of that I'll be waiting at the door with your perfectly ironed white shirt and then you can leave the house."

"How do you remember all that stuff?" I asked over my shoulder as I ran back down the hall.

"I have it *memorized*," she shouted behind me, "because I'm forced to say it every day of your animal boy life!"

By the time I did everything Mom told me to do she was standing at the porch door holding my shirt out like a bullfighting cape. I wiggled my arms into the sleeves. She buttoned me up the front as I buttoned my cuffs, then I tucked my shirttails in. "Thanks, Mom," I said, and gave her a kiss and fled.

"Hey!" Dad called behind me as I ran past him. "Where are you going? I still need your help."

"Miss Volker called!" I yelled over my shoulder, and kept running toward her house. "There is a dead guy she has to see!"

"If only she were next," Dad hollered back. "Then we'd get some of this work done around here."

* * *

Miss Volker was already sitting in her car. "Hurry," she called from the passenger window. "I just cooked my hands so I can use my fingers to examine the body." She was wearing quilted oven mitts in order to keep her hands warm.

I started the car and put it in Drive. "Hang on," I warned her. "I think I'm getting better at this." I punched the gas pedal to the floor. The back tires shot gravel through the open garage door and we blasted down the driveway. The tires squealed as we turned onto the Norvelt road and about thirty seconds later I hit the brakes and we swerved crazily into the parking lot at the Huffer Funeral Parlor.

"You're a fast learner," she remarked. "You've gone from slowpoke to safety hazard in one day."

I grinned with pride. But that was my last grin for a while.

Mr. Huffer was waiting for us in the back room where he prepared all the cadavers. It smelled of formaldehyde. I knew it looked like a mad scientist's laboratory because Bunny had shown it to me when it was unoccupied. There was a work table topped with a big yellowed marble slab that had a drainage groove carved around it. I remembered seeing that because it looked like one of the Aztec sacrificial altar stones where the victims had their hearts cut out and the blood snaked along the groove and down into a beautiful golden cup that would then be offered up with the still-beating heart to satisfy the bloody appetite of the Aztec gods. But with the Hells Angel on the slab I kept my eyes lowered and stared down at my shoes. I may have been a big talker to Bunny and Mom, but I didn't want to see that dead man. Just the thought of his roadkill body made me queasy and I knew my nose would spew like a busted dike if I even peeked at him.

Bunny stood next to me and tapped me on the leg. "You okay?" she whispered.

"Sure," I said with false bravery, and stupidly took a step forward which was a mistake, because next to my foot was a bucket filled with thick human fluids. Don't look into the bucket again, I warned myself and jerked my head away. I took a deep breath and lifted my head for just long enough to see the victim's mangled boots on display at the far end of the table.

"They had to cut the boots off of him," Bunny informed me. "He was really clobbered."

I looked back down at my shoes and took another deep breath. I closed my eyes but the room began to spin so I opened them a bit.

"Did you see the tattoos?" she asked.

She knew I hadn't and she knew I never would. I hadn't looked at a dead person since she made me touch that man's unnaturally stiff neck.

"Then I'll tell you about them," she said, and without waiting for me to answer she continued. "On one leg is a spiraling black snake with a 666 in its open mouth, and a devil's tail is twisting around his other leg."

I could see everything she said as if it were a wall painting inside the cave of my own skull. Somehow the tattoos were even more gruesome when they were tattooed on the *inside* of my mind. I could run out of the room, but the image of his legs would still be dead inside of me and chasing after me for a lifetime.

I took a step back and quickly touched my nose. I glanced at my finger—no blood yet—but to be on the safe side I kept my hand pressed over my mouth like a window awning. I didn't want to drip blood on my clean white shirt.

"Clearly," I heard Miss Volker say from where the victim's head would be, "there can be no doubt that the main cause of death is a massive skull fracture."

"No doubt about it," Mr. Huffer agreed sadly, and I imagined he struck his classic one-hand-on-hip mournful pose while his other hand reached out to pat someone on the shoulder. That's what made him look like a human teapot. "This is the most massive head fracture I've ever seen," he said. "Even worse than that of Dan Eakins."

"Of course it's worse!" Miss Volker said impatiently. "Dan was only split through the head with the pig shaped weather vane that flew off a barn. Now let me see that police report."

I heard her rustle through some papers for a minute before she began to speak. "It's hard to believe a man could dance this much," she remarked. "Because it says here that he started dancing a jig in a Mount Pleasant bar then danced out the door. Some drivers claimed to have just missed hitting him as he danced all the way here, and that is three miles from where he started. Mr. Spizz was the last to see him—said he was putting air in his tricycle tires up at Bob Fenton's gas station early this morning after poisoning rats at the dump when the stranger strutted by, and a couple minutes later he was flattened."

Mr. Huffer cleared his throat. "And," he began, "the truck driver said the last thing he saw was the man gyrating wildly with his arms and legs pumping up and down as if he was on the dance floor."

Bunny sidled up to me and whispered, "Did you see the big meat cleaver tattoo on his chest?"

"You know I didn't," I replied impatiently, and felt a shiver of fear run up my spine.

"What is great about it," she said, ignoring me as I swayed back and forth in my white shirt like a bowling pin about to fall over, "is that it looks like the cleaver has chopped open his flesh so you can see his open heart, which is black. And in the middle of the black heart is the laughing red face of the devil. Isn't that spooky?"

I couldn't listen to her anymore. My head felt like a balloon that was swelling up and about to blow into another massive head fracture.

"Okay," Miss Volker said dramatically. "I'll sign the death certificate and release the body to you and you can do with him what you will." Her voice had become really loud and I thought it was because I was about to faint. I felt my forehead. It was hot. Hang in there, I said to myself.

I knew that Miss Volker's hands must be cold by now and she'd be ready to leave. I was right, and in a moment I heard the slow scrawling of the pen on the death certificate. "There," she said, "he's all yours."

"I can keep the body in the freezer for a few days," Mr. Huffer said evenly, "but if no one claims him then the Norvelt paupers' fund will only pay for cremation. I'd like to give him a proper burial but no one will pay for it."

"Good enough," Miss Volker said. "We've done all we can."

Bunny tapped me on the shoulder. "Come on," she said. "The show is over and it looks like you just saw a ghost."

I staggered out the back door and into the parking lot and took a deep breath. "I've seen a million dead people in the movies," I said. "But real ones nearly kill me."

"The movies are all fake," she remarked. "They use animal blood. And they never give you the *smell* of death. I do admit this was the deadest guy I've ever seen. I mean, he was really flat."

I was so relieved when Miss Volker came out. Quickly I helped her into the car and started it up. "Do you want me to assist with the obit?" I asked, and gunned the engine as we burned rubber onto the road.

"I'll have to ponder this one overnight," she said, lost in thought. "The dancing part reminds me of something, of some convulsive condition I read about once. I'll do some research. Come down in the morning and we'll tackle the obit." Then she pointed at my shirt. "Your nose is leaking."

I looked down. The big red splotch on my shirt looked like a real bleeding heart.

"Mom's gonna kill me," I moaned. "This shirt is still mostly new."

"Bring the shirt tomorrow," she said. "I have some chemicals in the garage that will send that stain to the Promised Land."

"Great," I said. "Because if Mom sees this she'll send me to the Promised Land."

"We can't allow that to happen," she remarked. "You are my right-hand man."

I glanced at her hands. They were crossed in her lap like two old gloves.

10

The next day, as usual, Miss Volker called early but Mom was up even earlier. It was her day to cook for the Norvelt Meals for the Elderly program, and she was singing along with the radio as she chopped mushrooms she had gathered up in the woods by the town dump. After a quick breakfast I cleaned myself up a bit then hid my bloody white shirt in a bag and walked swiftly toward the back door. "See you later," I called out.

"Not so fast," Mom ordered. "When you come back I want you to deliver these casseroles to the Community Center. Mr. Spizz will deliver them to the ladies who called in for a home-cooked meal."

"Mr. Spizz," I said with disgust. "Doesn't he bug you?"

"Yes," she said. "But in a small town you have to forgive people for their faults no matter if you want to or not."

"I guess," I said, wishing he'd forgive me for forgetting about the weeds and rip up the ticket.

"So don't be too late," she cautioned. "Old people like to eat dinner at four in the afternoon, and they get ornery if they get too hungry."

"I'll be on time," I promised. Then I was out the door. Dad was on the tractor, still working with the heavy road roller in order to flatten the waves out of the runway. In the summer he liked to get started early on chores before the sun blazed down on him.

"Hey!" he yelled when he saw me, and cut the engine back. "You still have some diggin' to finish." He pointed toward the bomb shelter and the sharpness in his voice and the stiffness of his jabbing pointer finger told me he meant business.

"Hey!" I yelled back, and shrugged forlornly. "I still have to help Miss Volker." I kicked a rock toward her house.

"You should be helping me out around here," he said, "instead of working for that nut who's got one foot in the grave."

I pointed toward the kitchen and lowered my voice. "I'm just following orders."

He gave me an I-know-what-you-mean look and put the tractor back to work, and I happily ran down to Miss Volker's house thinking I had really dodged a bullet. Nothing could be worse than digging that fake bomb shelter. It was a project as imaginary as digging a hole to China. At least Dad's work would lead to something. Once he finished the runway he could fly away. Once I finished digging the bomb shelter I would probably be buried in it.

When I entered Miss Volker's living room she was standing in front of the needlepoint map of Norvelt and looking over the small number of surviving original homesteaders. There were medical textbooks opened to various pages and spread out across my little writing desk, the couch, the floor, and anywhere she could find free space. She must have been up all night.

"We have a huge day today," she announced enthusiastically, "and I have it organized just right in my mind. First, we go down to the drugstore to get some supplies for your nose operation and some wax for my hands. Then we'll come back—I'll heat up my hands, do the operation, and then dictate the obit to you. Got it?"

"Yep," I said uneasily, "except I have to make sure to get Mom's casseroles to the Community Center on time."

"Do I get one?" she asked, and held up her hands. "About all I can grab is a cookie."

"Only if you sign up for it in advance," I explained. "Call the Community Center and get on the home meals delivery list."

"Can you request anything you want?" she asked. "I'm a vegetarian."

"Yeah," I replied. "Mom would cook anything for you."

"Well, let's get our day started," she suggested. "It's a big one."

I grabbed her purse and followed her out to the car, happy to drive again.

In less than three minutes we entered the Rumbaugh drugstore. Miss Volker marched toward the back and showed me where the blocks of special wax were kept.

"Can't you just take a pill for your hands?" I asked as we strolled down the aisle of instant fix-it supplies for bad stomachs, headaches, excess mucus, and other ailments.

"Maybe," she replied. "But like the Indians I'd rather discover my own medicines. They were smart enough to make natural remedies, and they knew what would cure you or what would kill you."

"Are you saying the Indians cooked their hands in hot wax?" I asked. "Because I don't think they had wax."

"Use your head," she snapped back. "They had beeswax. And tree sap. They could heat that up. How do you think they waterproofed their canoes?"

"I thought they used animal fat," I guessed.

Suddenly, Miss Volker stopped fast and her face knotted up into a bony fist. "You see that man," she said loudly to me, and pointed her quivering chin at Mr. Spizz. "That man," continued Miss Volker with contempt in her voice, "is the town irritant."

He couldn't help but hear her. "What are you doing here?" he asked with a smirk on his face. "I thought you were sitting around your house all lonely and waiting to die."

"Not yet," she replied. "I'm waiting for you to go first."

"Mrs. Roosevelt gave me the job of keeping this town in good repair and I'm going to do my best till my last breath," he said.

"That can be arranged," Miss Volker whispered to me. Then she turned to Mr. Spizz. "Listen," she said sternly. "Mrs. Roosevelt appointed me to be the chief medical examiner and that is a far more important job than going around scraping gum off of sidewalks or stepping on ants, so you have my permission to do your civic duty and drop dead."

"Look at you," he said, pointing to her cupped

hands, "you can't even feed yourself with those crab claws. How can you keep anyone else in good health?"

"By using my head," she replied swiftly. "And for the health of this town I think you should take a long walk off a short pier."

"You're the one waiting for everyone to die around here, so why don't you set a good example and lead the way," he said.

"Well, I plan to live to be a hundred," she stated.

"I'll be a hundred and one," he said with bravado.

"I'll be a hundred and two," she said, topping him.

"A hundred and three for me," he continued.

"A hundred and four," she said strongly.

I didn't want to get involved, but Mr. Spizz turned to me and said, "If you are her new boyfriend you should know that she is very immature. She always has been."

I looked toward Miss Volker for help.

"That old pain in the neck is just jealous of you," she said, and cackled. "He thinks you are my beau."

"I am your *boy* friend," I said to Miss Volker. "Now come along. Just walk away from this. Don't sink to his level."

She pulled her shoulders back and took a deep breath. "I'll sign your death certificate, mister," she said with confidence. "Mark my words, you should be euthanized like a garden pest."

He pointed at her hands and let out a mean-old-man *har-har-har* laugh. "You can't even swat flies with those hands, much less sign a death certificate. You've had this job too long. You're in a rut, and you should be worried about that because the only difference between a rut and a grave is the depth!"

She smiled. "Good one," she called back. "I'll use it when I write your obituary." Then she turned and marched up to the pharmacy window. On the way she whispered to me, "He's so stupid. Honestly, when he makes alphabet soup it spells out D-U-M-B."

Once we bought the wax and some topical medicine to numb the inside of my nose, we marched back out of the store.

Mr. Spizz was standing outside. "Hey, Gantos boy," he said, pointing at me. "I know you did a lousy job cutting down those gutter weeds and earned your family a ticket."

"So?" I said hesitantly.

"So I heard your dad is building a runway on your property. That's against the zoning laws around here."

"What's zoning?" I asked, looking more toward Miss Volker than him.

"It's what you can build and where you are allowed to build it," she said. "But pay no attention to that bully. In Norvelt you can be as free as a bird—or a plane."

"Just tell your dad," he said, "that I've already submitted his zoning violation to the Community Council meeting."

I nodded, and reached for Miss Volker's elbow and escorted her to the car as gently as I could. Mr. Spizz watched us all the way. He shouldn't have given me that ticket, because now I wanted him to see that I really was her *boyfriend* and that he should be jealous of me.

The moment we pulled out of the parking lot she said, "He and I used to date before Norvelt was built. He wanted to get married but I had my nursing career and held him off. Still, he kept asking over and over to marry me. I guess he wore me down, and in a weak moment I made the mistake of saying I'd marry him once all the original Norvelters were dead and my duty to Mrs. Roosevelt was over. I figured that was safe to say because he'd be dead by now—but he keeps living!"

"You sound pretty upset," I remarked, but I was still confused about their argument in the store because I had read the card he had left on her box of candy and I knew he did like her.

"I'm not upset," she said, and smiled broadly. "I love mixing it up with him. I guess it's a game we play since we both missed out on the joys of marital arguing—keeps my blood flowing."

Now I was even more confused because she said she liked arguing with him. Maybe Dad was right. He said both of them were nuts.

"We can skip my nose if you want," I suggested, thinking of my own good health.

"Oh, no," she replied with enthusiasm. "I've been looking forward to knocking the rust off of these hands and performing an operation to keep *your* blood from flowing," she continued. "So don't you worry. I'll be gentle, and it just takes a moment."

After we entered her house she had me drape a bedsheet over the kitchen table.

"So here is how this is going to work," she explained. "We'll deaden your nose and then I'll cook my hands, and when they are working I'll quickly heat up the cauterizing wire and do the work on you. More than likely my hands will tire and seize up, so I'll have to recook them and heat up the wire and work on you in shifts, but we'll get it. Okay?"

"Are you sure I shouldn't go to a doctor?" I ventured.

"Don't insult me," she said firmly. "I'm a nurse, and I'm telling you that I can handle this. Nothing is wrong with the iron in your blood. It's just your nose capillaries, which are too bundled up and delicate on the inside surface of your nasal passages. I'll burn them off and you'll be fine. You got that? It's easy-peasy."

"I understand," I said. "But are you sure it will work?"

"These hands have delivered babies," she stated. "I've stitched up miles of gaping wounds and set a hundred broken bones and pulled a gallon jar full of rotten teeth—I even had to pop an eyeball back into its socket, so don't question me. Now get onto the table."

I climbed up and took my place on the table as if I were one of Mr. Huffer's cadavers. Next to me she laid out the Q-tips, a magnifying glass, the bottle of anesthetic, and the cauterizing instrument, which was a wooden handle with a six-inch-long thickish wire coming out of one end. On the tip of the wire was a tiny scorched blade. As she turned away to heat up her hands all I could imagine was that she would aim the instrument into a nose hole, have a hand spasm, and drive it up my nasal passage until she jammed the hot little blade into the soft, creamy center of my brain, and I would end up being a babbling idiot for the rest of my life.

"Go ahead and swab your nasal passages with a good dose of the anesthetic," she instructed. "And don't be stingy with it. Believe me, you don't want to feel any of this pain."

I sure didn't.

While I swabbed the inside of my nose with the Q-tip, she got busy with cooking her hands. After she removed them from the pot and peeled off the hot wax, she held them up in the air.

"Watch this," she called, and wiggled her rusty fingers back and forth while singing, "The itsy-bitsy spider went up the waterspout."

That really didn't make me relax. I tried to smile, but I had swabbed on so much anesthetic my lips were frozen in place like fish in a frozen pond.

Then quickly she heated up the wire and pulled it out of the flame. It was red-hot, and a puff of smoke rose from what I guessed was a little scrap of human tissue that had been stuck on the blade from her last operation. I whimpered.

"Don't look at it," she ordered. "You'll flinch and I'll scorch you—and then you'll *really* have something to bleed about."

"How do your hands feel?" I asked shakily as she came toward me.

"Rock steady," she declared. "Now close your eyes."

I did, and waited for the pain.

A few moments later she asked, "Did you feel that?"

"Feel what?" I replied.

"If you didn't feel the map pin I just stuck into the

tip of your nose," she said, "then you are ready. Let's get this done."

I crossed my eyes and looked down at my nose. There was a red-topped pin sticking straight out of my nose, but before I could say anything she came at me. I took a deep breath and clutched the tabletop on either side. I lifted my nose up into the air so she could get a clear view. I felt her dark shadow bend over me. I sensed the beam of her flashlight up my nose, and then slowly she inserted the red-hot wire into my nasal cavity. I waited for the searing pain, but I couldn't feel a thing. The anesthesia was working. However, I could smell something nasty. "What is that odor?" I mumbled, not daring to move my face or neck.

"Singed capillaries." She slowly answered, because she was concentrating. "It's going well. The burnt-flesh smell means it's working."

After she finished cauterizing one nostril she took a break and cooked her hands again. Once her fingers loosened up it didn't take long before I tilted back into position and she came at me and finished the second nostril.

"There," she announced proudly, and with unnecessary flair she plucked the pin from my nose. "I'm all done. It will hurt a little tomorrow and may bleed a bit during the scabbing stage, but you should be fine."

I sat up. "Are you sure?" I asked. "I've been this way all my life."

"Don't question me," she said irritably. "People who question me get crossed off my good list—like Spizz."

"Sorry," I said in a small voice. "Didn't mean to offend you."

"Now come with me," she ordered. "We've got some work to do."

I took my seat at the writing desk after moving all the books to the couch where she sat. I removed a pad of paper and a pencil and stretched my fingers out and cracked my knuckles. "Ready to roll," I said.

She stood upright with her feet firmly planted as if she were going to deliver a fiery speech that would change the course of the nation. And then she cut loose like a wild woman and paced the room back and forth. The more worked up she became the faster she spoke and the faster I had to write. But I kept up with her, and in the end we were both exhausted. She flopped down on the couch and I went into the kitchen to soak my hand in a pot of cold water.

By the time Mom called to remind me that I was late delivering the casseroles, I had finished typing up the obituary.

"Before you leave," Miss Volker instructed, "go into the garage and get the box of hospital bleach crystals so I can soak the blood from your shirt. And while you are out there grab that rusty tin of Compound 1080 poison. I'll need that too. I saw some vermin in my basement and I want to get rid of them—they're feasting on the Great Women in History needlepoints my sister left for me to watch over and they already ate a hole in Clara Barton's Red Cross hat."

I dashed out to the garage and grabbed what she wanted, then returned.

"Should I tell Mom about my nose?" I asked, and set the bleach and poison on the kitchen table.

"Give it a week," she suggested. "And if it heals properly we'll surprise her with the good news."

"Great," I said. "Thanks." And to myself I happily thought that now Mom wouldn't have to save up for it.

I sprinted the obituary to Mr. Greene and was going to turn and dash home but he made me wait while he read it through. Once he finished he made a grim face. "Good grief," he remarked, "this obituary might scare some of these old folks to death."

Might be what she wants, I thought, but instead said, "She's just trying to keep everyone on their toes."

"Well, tell her I'll get it in the paper as soon as I can," he said with his voice trailing off. "I have to help my brother skin the minks at his mink farm this afternoon and I may fall behind a bit."

I didn't want to talk about skinning minks. That might ruin my nose before it had time to heal. I quickly said goodbye and ran home.

Mom was waiting impatiently for me with six casseroles wrapped in aluminum foil and packed into a shallow cardboard box. "They are clearly marked," she pointed out. "This one is for Mrs. Vinyl, who had cataract surgery and can't see her own hands. This one is for Mrs. Linga, who has the broken hip. This one is for Mrs. Sulzby, who has been living on turkey jerky for the last month, and the others are for what is left of the ladies' Fancy Hat Club tea—Mrs. Hamsby, Mrs. Dubicki, and Mrs. Bloodgood."

"All women," I remarked.

"Sadly, yes," Mom said with a sigh. "All the working men except for Mr. Spizz died young from black lung disease after digging in the mines. The coal dust clogged them up and they went early. My dad was the same. I guess the only other old men left are those who owned the mines, and they live in Pittsburgh—in mansions, not mines. Now get going," she said, glancing at the clock. "Mr. Spizz is waiting for you. I'm sure there are some hungry old gals peeking out their windows."

I lifted the box and marched down to the Roosevelt

Community Center as quickly as I could. My hands were full so I kicked on the bottom of the door with my foot. Bunny Huffer yanked it open. She was dressed in her Girl Scout uniform, which she had sewn herself, and it made her look like a shiny green leprechaun. Behind Bunny were two other Girl Scouts. One was Betsy Howdi, who was dressed in a Peter Pan costume, and the other was Mertie-Jo Kernecky, who just had her Girl Scout sash over an outfit that made her look like the Jolly Green Giant. Bunny was the smallest of the three, but her temper made up for her size. "Holy underwear in heaven!" she spat out, and pounded her fist into her palm. "It's about time you showed up! Those starving old people kept calling every two minutes and ruined our meeting."

"I was helping Miss Volker," I explained. "We ran late writing the Hells Angel obituary."

"What is there to say about him?" Bunny snapped. "I could write it in one sentence," and she held up a stubby finger about the size of a Tootsie Roll. "He danced into town and was hit by a cement truck and nobody cared."

"There's more to it than that!" I shot right back. "Miss Volker cares, and she said he has brought a death *plague* into this town and that people better beware or they'll drop dead."

"You read too many books," Bunny replied. "You're starting to sound like a murder mystery for idiots."

Betsy Howdi laughed at that and I turned away from her mocking dark-eyed face.

Mertie-Jo stepped around Bunny and rescued me with her beauty. "Do you want to buy some Girl Scout cookies?" she asked softly, and looked me in the eye as she slowly lowered her head to one side so that her right ear was nearly pressed against the top of her emerald shoulder. She smiled a naturally sweet smile, but it still seemed as if her awkwardly tilted head was the result of a rare medical condition. In order to speak eye to eye with her I tilted my own ear toward my shoulder. "What kind of cookies?" I asked as smoothly as my strained neck would allow, and gave her my handsome smile—the one where she couldn't see my missing tooth. She was cute, and I allowed myself to like her too much because I just knew she would never like me back.

"I have dreamy Thin Mints—twenty cents per box," she replied, and smiled even more brightly.

"I don't have any money, but I bet if you go to Miss Volker's house she'll buy a lot of them," I advised. "She lives off of cookies."

"Thanks for the tip," she replied briskly, and her head popped straight up and she tucked her smile away with one lizard lick of her lips.

I straightened up myself and wiped my smile off against my shoulder. We were suddenly back to where we started.

Bunny glanced at her watch. "Well, girls," she announced in her bossy voice, "this meeting is over. Now go sell some cookies so we can make money to go to the drive-in. My dad said he'd drive us up there in the hearse to watch *Dracula* this weekend if we pay for the tickets."

Just as they ran out the door Mr. Spizz came up from his basement living-and-work studio. I stepped forward and gave him the meals.

"Thank your mom for the food, Gantos boy," he said with his foghorn voice. "But also remind her about the weed ticket. It has to be paid or it will double to six bucks."

I still didn't have a cent. "Can I trade you jars of peaches for it?" I asked, imitating Mom. "You know, barter one thing for another like in the good old Norvelt?"

"I'll have to bring that up at the community meeting," he replied, "and the whole town will have to take a vote on it. And then it will be written about in the *News*. Would you like that?"

"No," I said quickly. "No." Because Mom would surely read about it.

"Then come up with the money," he demanded. "Now I have to get going."

I followed him outside and began to walk up the street. In a minute he rang his kiddy bell as he passed me on his giant tricycle with the red wagon full of meals trailing behind.

11

When I woke the next day my nose was sore to touch and felt a little lumpy. It pulsed hotly inside as if the blood was building up to erupt furiously out of my scorched nasal passages like waves of molten lava, but so far not a drop had leaked out.

"Hey, Mom," I called from my bed when she passed my open doorway. "Can I do anything fun today?"

"Sure. You can study your history books and help out with chores," she said matter-of-factly.

"But I'm young and I'm suffering," I whimpered like a puppy. "I need fresh air. It's not fair to lock your child up."

"What you did to that cornfield was not fair," she reminded me. "Occupy your time with thinking about hungry people. And if you need fresh air just open a window." She raised an eyebrow to punctuate her point then walked down the hall, and I heard her descend the cellar stairs to the laundry room. She wasn't having much fun either.

When I heard the washer start its gyrations I hopped up and went to the kitchen and grabbed the jar of peanut butter and a box of Nilla wafers, a knife, and a tall glass of milk. I turned on Mom's kitchen radio, but it was that awful air raid warning test so I turned it off then scampered back to my room. I made a checkerboard of peanut butter wafers and slowly began to eat my breakfast as I searched through the newspaper. Mr. Greene was late getting in the obituary but This Day In History was really good:

> ***June 26, 1541:*** **Conquistador Francisco Pizarro was assassinated in Lima, Peru, and got what he deserved for killing Atahualpa and all those Incas.**
>
> ***June 26, 1945:*** **The United Nations signed a charter and pledged to create peace around the world. The not so hopeful news is that there seems to be a new war about every other week and millions have died since the charter was signed.**

"And in 1962," I said, looking up from the paper and bemoaning my fate, "the longest grounding of a boy named Jack continues to go unnoticed by history."

When I finished eating there wasn't much left for me to do but read history as Mom ordered. I picked up *John F. Kennedy and PT-109* off my pile of Landmark books and decided to spend the day in bed and let my nose heal. It turned out that reading was a great idea because the book was terrific.

During World War II, Kennedy and his torpedo boat crew were on night patrol in the sea around the Solomon Islands when a Japanese destroyer came roaring at full speed out of the mist and sliced their boat clean in two. Eleven men survived the collision but some were burned badly from the fuel fire that took place after the crash. Kennedy had been hurled across the deck and fractured a vertebra in his back but he could still move.

Fortunately, half of the PT boat floated for a while as they hung on to it and made a plan. Their only hope of survival was to swim miles away to a small island that they hoped was not covered with Japanese soldiers. Kennedy tied one end of a belt onto the most wounded man's lifejacket and put the other end of the belt in his own mouth, and then he swam the breaststroke for five hours before he got the man to the island. There was no food or fresh water.

After several days of hunger they ate snails, which were bitter tasting. At night it rained and they licked the water off of leaves, and in the morning they saw that the leaves were covered with bird droppings. Everyone was becoming sicker and their wounds were infected. Night after night Kennedy kept swimming out into the ocean to try to spot any Allied ships, but he had no luck. He was worn down but he had not given up hope.

Finally he and a sailor swam to another island and discovered a hidden camp where some native islanders had kept fresh water and hardtack and crackers. They were also lucky enough to find a canoe so they could deliver the supplies to the other men. Still, without soon being rescued they were sure to die, because their wounds were so infected their flesh had begun to stink and rot.

But just before the men lost all hope, the native islanders tracked them down. They were friendly and wanted to help, so Kennedy scratched a rescue note on a coconut and gave it to the islanders, who paddled their war canoe to an Allied base. More days passed, and just when Kennedy and his men thought they all would die, they were rescued by soldiers from New Zealand.

Kennedy became a hero for his effort to save his

men from the Japanese. And now that he is president, he keeps that very same coconut on his Oval Office desk.

"Hey, Dad," I hollered when he passed by my room that evening. As he turned toward me I saw the top of his head was white from his helping to paint the War Veterans' Club ceiling. I held up the book for him to see.

He smiled. "That is a great story," he said, and waved his speckled hand over his brow in a snappy salute.

"Weren't you in the Solomon Islands?" I asked. "Did you know him?"

"Sorry to report that we never met," he replied. "But like about a zillion other soldiers who never knew each other, we fought on the same side—the winning side—of the greatest country in the world. And I'm proud of it."

I smiled. It felt good to be an American.

By the next morning Mr. Greene had printed the Hells Angel obituary in the paper. I sat down on the front steps and read it.

> **UNKNOWN MOTORCYCLIST**
> **By E. Volker**
> **NORVELT—As many citizens of Norvelt are aware, a Hells Angel died in our town. He was**

struck down by a ten-ton cement truck and died instantly of a massive skull fracture on the Norvelt road early in the morning on June 24. He was taken to the Huffer Funeral Parlor to be identified, but there was no identification on the body except for many colorful tattoos which revealed his devil-worshipping ways. Mr. Huffer has documented the tattoos, and the photographs can be viewed by adults only at the police station. It is hoped that someone will recognize the tattoos and identify him so his family can be informed.

He was a stranger to our town, but what is even more strange is how he died. From the police record it appears that he was eating a ham-on-rye sandwich and drinking a beer at the Mount Pleasant Polish American Club when suddenly he dropped his bottle and began to dance rather spastically, as if in acute pain. He danced out the door and danced down the road and was seen by many witnesses, who have all testified that he was dancing for the entire three-mile stretch from Mount Pleasant to Norvelt. This is all we know about him before his inner music was abruptly stopped.

What we should be concerned with is that this person may have brought into our community a terrible plague. I do not think it is a coincidence that June 24—the day of our stranger's death—is also the same day of the year in 1374 when the plague of "St. John's Dance" erupted in Germany. This dancing plague began with a single maniac who could not stop dancing for days. Soon he was joined in the streets by others until hundreds of people were afflicted. There were many theories about the dancing plague, but the most popular theory, put forth by physicians and priests, was that the Devil himself—the original Hells Angel—had cast an evil spell upon the citizens.

The dancing plague traveled to France in 1518. To hasten a cure the community constructed a stage and musicians were hired to play soothing dance music so that the dancers might slowly waltz themselves back to good spiritual health. But quite the opposite results were achieved, as the dancers danced themselves to utter exhaustion, and one by one they began to expire from heart attacks, strokes, and complete organ failure. Not one person with the dancing plague survived, but with their deaths the plague vanished. However, throughout history, the plague has reappeared.

Remember in 1284 when the Pied Piper of

> **Hamelin who, when the king refused to pay him for ridding the town of rats, turned the irresistible music of his pipe toward the children? He danced them uncontrollably through the town and into a bat-filled cave where they disappeared forever. And do not think we Americans are immune from this mysterious plague of dancing possession. Remember our Puritan ancestors in Salem, Massachusetts, who were stricken with convulsive dancing, twitching, uncontrollable smirking, and spastic pagan gestures, which were judged to be the signs of Devilish Possession and which led to the Witch Trials where twenty citizens were put to death.**
>
> **And perhaps now we have had the plague's modern advance scout—a Hells Angel—come to Norvelt. What infection did he bring? What curse, disease, or epidemic has he unleashed in our town? Beware! Death has reached our doorstep!**

That was an intense obituary. A lot of people are going to read it and be upset, I thought, and just at that moment I heard something that sounded like a swarm of angry bees. I thought Dad had started up the J-3 and I was hearing the high-pitched sound of the engine.

But it wasn't Dad's J-3. It was an engine-roaring

swarm of Hells Angels coming up over the hill past wormy Bob Fenton's gas station. They must have read the obituary too.

I ran down the front steps and across our property so I could watch the long line of them pass. There must have been fifty of the meanest, toughest guys I had ever seen. They were wearing zippered black leather jackets with HELLS ANGELS spelled out in chrome studs across their backs. They had on greasy blue jeans and thick boots with heavy silver buckles running up the sides, and on their hands some had face-smashing brass knuckles, and to let everyone know they were evil, a few even wore black Nazi helmets.

For some crazy reason I started doing jumping jacks and yelled out, "Welcome to Norvelt! We are a friendly town!"

No one could hear me over the sound of the engines but one guy who had a skull painted on the gas tank of his bike turned toward me and ran his finger across his neck, like he was a pirate and was going to slit my throat.

"Sorry," I said in a small voice as I crouched down behind a lavender delphinium.

Toward the bottom of the hill they downshifted and the engine roar was so loud a few petals fell off the blossoms. The noise rippled in waves across my skin, like when you throw a rock in a pond. There was no where else they would be going except to Huffer's Funeral Parlor, and I knew that meant trouble. I wanted to run down there so badly and spy in the back window and see what was up. This was one bit of *whisper history* I really wanted to know about. But if I did Mom would kill me. Instead, I just ran back and forth across our property line like a guard dog on a tight leash.

It didn't take too long before the motorcycles started up again and soon the entire swarm of them revved up the hill and passed me as before, only this time one of the motorcycles had what looked like a torpedo from PT-109 strapped on top of a sidecar. The dead Hells Angel had to be in it. His gang of friends must have come to get his body in order to give him a proper Hells Angel burial, whatever that might be. I didn't wave to them this time. I just flopped down on my belly and watched until they were gone.

I was still on my belly when I turned and saw Bunny running up the Norvelt road. I stood and when she got close enough I could see she was in her pink-striped pajamas. She kept glancing back over her shoulder as she hopped the gutter and zigzagged up through our yard, like someone had been shooting at her from behind. With all the running her face should have been bright red, but it was as white as a bowl of milk.

"Oh my God!" she shouted as the sweat ran down her forehead like a waterfall. "You should have seen what just happened. They all came stomping into the funeral parlor and demanded to see my dad, and then they made him pull the body out of the freezer and then they just *stole* a coffin off the display table and put the frozen Hells Angel in it and took off."

"I saw the coffin," I said. "It looked like a silver torpedo."

"That's the Time Capsule coffin!" she blurted out. "The top of the line!"

"Wow," I said, taking it all in.

"Dad called Mr. Spizz," she added, "because he's a volunteer cop. He'll track them down to their clubhouse, or cave, or devil hole they live in and arrest them all and make them pay for the coffin and send them to jail."

As she said that I looked straight over the top of her head and down the road. There was Mr. Spizz on his giant tricycle. As he labored up the Norvelt road incline and past us I saw that he had a police badge pinned to his khaki shirt. I didn't see a gun on his belt, but I spotted a baseball bat rolling around in the little cart he towed behind him.

"Hurry! They went thataway!" Bunny hollered, and pointed up the road. "Show those devil-worshipping lug nuts that they can't get away with stealing our dead people and coffins."

Mr. Spizz just nodded. He was out of breath and sweaty, and I figured he really didn't want to catch up to the Hells Angels and try to arrest them with a baseball bat. Plus, it must have been a little embarrassing that they were on really fast motorcycles and he was pedaling an adult tricycle.

"I think he's getting too old for this job," Bunny whispered to me as he barely made it up and over the hill.

"I think so too," I replied. "Dad says his next bike is going to be a wheelchair."

"You know what else the Hells Angels did?" she asked, knowing that I didn't. "They said the dead guy had bought an empty Norvelt house and was going to turn it into a Hells Angels clubhouse. Can you believe that? Before they left, the leader stood up on a table and said he thought their 'brother' was intentionally killed to keep him from opening a clubhouse here, and to avenge his death he put a devilish curse on the town. He said we'd all die painful, agonizing deaths and that then they'd come back and take over this town and rename it Hells Angels Town."

"Wow. Miss Volker said to look out for a curse when she wrote the dead guy's obituary," I reminded her. "And that sure is a nasty curse."

"Then for once she might be right," she agreed. "I'm going to call a special Girl Scout meeting tonight so we can spread the word about the curse so people aren't scared to death."

Then she turned and ran toward the funeral parlor in an odd dancing sort of way—skipping and clapping her hands and spinning around.

12

Thursday afternoon Mom was down the hill at the Norvelt Pants Factory filling out the paperwork for a sewing job. She had grown up with the factory manager and was sure she'd get the position and make a little extra money for "odd and ends," as she put it. Before World War II the factory made heavy cotton pants and shirts for farmers and coal miners. During the war they made snappy-looking dress uniforms for the army. Now they were down to what Dad called a "skeleton crew" that made either brown or gray slacks for office workers.

Dad was in the garage painting the identification numbers on his J-3, and so when the phone rang there was no one to pick it up but me.

"Hello?" I said eagerly.

It was exactly what I hoped it was—my ticket out of the house.

"Help! Quick!" Miss Volker shouted over the phone. She was breathing hard but it was difficult to tell if it was because she'd gotten the dancing plague she predicted or if she was just worn out from dialing the phone, because when she dialed she had to knock the phone onto the floor and then use her big toe to turn the rotary dialer to the number she wanted. It took her about five minutes to finish a five-digit number and by then she was tuckered out.

"What is it?" I asked.

"There are dead ones everywhere," she shouted. "Come help me, quick."

"Who is dead?" I asked. "Did Spizz catch the Hells Angels and slaughter them with his baseball bat?"

"No!" she shouted. "The *vermin* are dead. Rats! Mice! Even a possum! Oh my God, it's an old-fashioned massacre, so come quickly."

"I'll be right down," I promised. "Don't go into the basement without me."

I returned to my room and laced on my heavy winter boots. I didn't want a poisoned rat to have one last spasm and bite me through my sneakers. Then I ran out to the garage where Dad was working. He had everything painted on the J-3, but the wings still needed to be bolted on. He'd have to tow the J-3 out of the garage for that final job.

"See you later," I cried out. "Miss Volker needs me real bad."

"She needs a lot more than you," he said in a wise-guy sort of way. "She needs a boyfriend her own age."

My face turned red and I spun around and ran. In about two minutes I was thumping my boots across her porch. There was a big vase of flowers with a red ribbon tied in a bow around the vase. Spizz was still trying to wear Miss Volker down. I bent over to read the card and was just touching the envelope taped to the vase when Miss Volker shoved the door open with her shoulder and the edge of it cracked me flat on the side of my head. I fell over to one side then quickly popped up and dusted myself off.

When she saw the flowers she threw her bad hands up and got them tangled in her hair. "Not again!" she groaned. "He's driving me nuts."

"Who?" I asked. I was sure it was Mr. Spizz but I wanted her to say so.

"Don't make me spit out his fizzy name," she said hastily. "Now hurry, maybe some of the vermin are only stunned."

I followed right behind her.

"Grab the fireplace poker and go down into the

basement, and if any of those vermin are twitching hit them with the poker and knock them into the Promised Land," she ordered.

I just stood there. I didn't want to go down into that damp basement and beat in the cute heads of little furry rodents any more than she did. I turned and said to her, "I'm afraid of dead things."

"Buck up!" she ordered. "I don't want some of them to get away and breed."

"But when I'm afraid my nose blows a gasket," I whined.

She looked me right in the eye and propped her hands on her hips. "Mister, I need you to be a man," she said with iron in her voice. "Don't disappoint me."

I wanted to be a man. I didn't want to be afraid of dead things. And I certainly didn't want to disappoint Miss Volker, so I took the fire-blackened poker and opened the cellar door. I turned on the light and slowly descended the wooden steps.

"Hello," I whispered, as if mice and rats and opossums and chipmunks could start up a conversation. "If you are alive, it would be best for you to run away to your happy homes, because I'm supposed to kill you." I thumped on the first step with the fireplace poker. Then I stood still and listened. I didn't hear any scurrying off into the dark corners.

"Remember," I sang out. "I'm more scared of you than you are of me." Then I walked all the way down the steps, and when I reached the bottom I knew why there had been no scurrying sounds. They were all dead! Every one of them—small mice and big rats and the opossum. They were splayed out crazily across the dirt floor as if they had suddenly dropped dead in the middle of a wild dance party. It made me sad.

"What do you see?" Miss Volker called anxiously from upstairs.

"A bunch of dead ones," I called back. "What did you do to them?"

"Do you see an open red box of Valentine chocolates?" she asked.

"Yes," I yelled.

"Well don't eat any, 'cause I sprinkled some of that 1080 vermin poison on them and the critters must have got a powerful dose of it."

I looked at the chocolates. They were chewed up, and brown bits and pieces were scattered around the box.

"Don't you like sweets?" I asked.

"I don't like sweets from that old simian sourpuss," she replied. "Besides, I like the Girl Scout Thin Mints I bought from Mertie-Jo. I had a whole sleeve of them for dinner."

"What should I do with the critters?"

"Sweep 'em up and put them in the box and we'll bury them out back," she said.

"You're going to bury them after what you did to them?" I asked incredulously.

"Well," she reasoned, "like most murderers I'm full of regret. If we give them a proper burial I'll feel less guilty about poisoning them."

I took a deep breath and swept up the little rodents and the rest of the chocolate bits and scooped them into the box, but the opossum wouldn't fit so I looked around the basement and found a grocery store bag. I used the red ribbon from the chocolate box to grab the opossum's droopy tail and dropped him in. That gave me the creeps.

When I took the box and bag upstairs Miss Volker had me set them out on the porch. "You can put them in the ground later," she said. "I have something else for you to do."

Great, I thought, because sitting around my house was driving me crazy.

When I came back inside she was in the kitchen. She nodded toward the big box of Girl Scout cookies she had bought from Mertie-Jo, and toward a stack of waxed-paper sandwich bags. "We need to bag up some cookies," she said, "and you can take them over to the

Community Center and then add them to your mother's casseroles for the old folks."

"That is nice of you," I remarked as I washed my hands.

"I'm really not that nice," she replied. "Deep inside I'm wishing that they would all drop dead and then my duty to Eleanor Roosevelt would be over."

"But then you'd have to marry Mr. Spizz," I reminded her.

"You have a point," she considered. "But if he were a true gentleman, he'd just vanish and let me off the hook and then I could go visit my sister."

"Mrs. Dubicki said she is ready to depart this world, so maybe you'll get to Florida sooner than you think," I said, trying to cheer her up as I counted out five Thin Mints, put them in a bag, and pinched over the waxy top.

"Perhaps," she replied. "But they aren't dying fast enough."

"My dad said the same thing," I added, "only my mom was going to clobber him."

"Well, he's right," she agreed. "Honestly, this poor town is in trouble. We old ones just hang on and on. We don't do anything for the community. Our houses are like inhabited tombs. If we don't get any new young people to move in here this town is just going to disappear. Norvelt was built so that families would have a fresh start in life, but now those people are old as the hills and the longer they hang on the less likely it is this town will survive. I'd rather have the people drop dead than have the town drop dead and vanish from history."

"Like one of the Lost Worlds," I remarked.

"Exactly," she agreed.

"Maybe Norvelt can build a coal mining theme park with underground roller coasters zipping through the old mine shafts," I suggested.

"No one cares about digging coal anymore," she said. "Besides, it will kill you."

"Then what about building a Roman colosseum or an Egyptian pyramid—like a Lost Worlds theme park?" I said.

"We don't need a theme park!" she shot back. "The best thing to do is what I did. I sold my sister's empty house to a nice young man a few months ago and I'm hoping he attracts more young people. He said he had a lot of friends."

"That sounds like a good start." I didn't want to get her worked up.

"I hope so," she replied. "There are a lot of empty houses that could be homes to young couples."

After I bagged about a dozen servings of cookies she stopped me from doing any more. "We don't want them to get stale," she said, "and I'm tired. Time for my nap."

"Then I'll take these over to Mr. Spizz and circle back around and pick up the rodents. I'll bury them up at my house since I'm already digging up the ground."

"Tell Spizz not to eat any of the cookies," she said harshly. "He can buy his own. These are for those old ladies. As much as I hate to say it, a good cookie is like medicine that makes you live longer."

"I'll tell him," I promised.

"And one word of advice," she added. "Don't plant any vegetables above where you bury those rodents. They got enough poison in 'em to bring down an elephant."

"Thanks," I said, while thinking that I better bury them up by the dump if they were so toxic.

13

It was the first Sunday in July and I had a smile on my face because it was my birthday and the one gift I had asked for I received. Mom bought me some industrial-strength petroleum-based grease remover that they used at the pants factory. It came in a round tin and looked like black Vaseline, and she said it worked miracles at removing everything—even bloodstains on my T-shirts and airplane oil off of Dad's work clothes—and would certainly get rid of the itchy painted circles on War Chief. She gave me the gift the night before in case I wanted to wake up before church and get started on him.

I did get up early and was in the pony pen rubbing the paint remover onto War Chief and scrub-brushing it in big glistening circles over the paint and then rinsing him down with soap and water. The paint was dissolving and War Chief seemed pretty happy and I was too. After about a half hour Mom joined me with a bacon and cheese sandwich wrapped in newspaper to keep it warm. "I thought you could use a little something," she said, and gave me a goofy love look, like she was remembering the morning I was born.

"I am hungry," I replied, and put the brush down and washed my hands in the soap and water. I unwrapped the sandwich and took a bite, but because my hand still smelled of petroleum the sandwich tasted like my hand.

"You better wash them again," she said.

"Could you hold the sandwich and feed me?" I asked.

She smiled. "Just like a baby bird," she cooed, and as she held the sandwich for me she stroked my hair. Normally I wouldn't like all this kind of Mom attention, but it was my birthday and we always acted like it was her birthday too, because it was the day I was born and the day she gave birth to me. So I was as sweet to her as she was to me.

"I also came out here to tell you something else," she said as she took a napkin and wiped my mouth. "I called a farrier to see if he would trim War Chief's hooves."

"Did you offer to pay him in pants now that you work at a pants factory?" I asked, and looked her directly in the eye.

"Hey, I wear the pants in this family, so don't you be a smarty-pants," she said, and poked me on the shoulder. "I offered him *you.* I told him I'd trade an hour of his time for three hours of yours. I thought that was fair."

I stopped chewing. "What'd he say?"

"He laughed. And when he finished laughing he said that he lived in a 'cash only' world." She didn't sound surprised.

"But didn't you know he would say that?" I asked. "I did."

"Yes and no," she replied. "I told him he could teach you the business and he said that nobody wanted to learn his business anymore. He called himself an antique. I told him that when I was a kid, antique men were the best because they knew how to take care of a horse, farm the land, build a house, and fix a car."

"And I bet he said those days were dead and over with," I cut in.

"Exactly," she replied.

"Are you ever going to realize this barter stuff doesn't work anymore? That people want cash? They've always wanted cash—or gold. I haven't read one book where people didn't want *something* valuable for their work."

"What about a caveman?" Mom suggested. "Did they want gold?"

"No, they wanted food and fire and safety—these things were as good as gold to them."

"Well, they are as good as gold to me too," she reasoned. "So are you calling me a caveman?"

"Cave*woman*," I said, correcting her.

"Who is a cavewoman?" Dad said loudly as he came around the corner of the barn and into the pony pen. He was carrying a plain brown package under his arm.

Mom pointed at Dad and gave me a knowing look. "He's definitely a caveman," she whispered.

"Happy birthday, son," he said, and tousled my hair.

I smiled, until Mom gave me that serious look that meant she needed to educate me about something before I was allowed to have fun. "Now that you have turned twelve," she started, "I know you'll appreciate what I have to say about birthday gifts and gift giving. My mother taught me this and it is the old Norvelt way."

I dared to glance at Dad for a moment and could tell he was not about to interrupt her.

"We always got three gifts," Mom explained. "They were *good*, *better*, and *best*. A good gift was always something *useful*, so your dad and I each got you something useful."

At that moment Dad scooted outside the pony pen and grabbed something out of sight, and when he returned he handed me a new round-nosed shovel with a nice blue bow tied around the handle. And before I could squawk he also gave me the package that was wrapped up in brown butcher paper.

"Open it," Mom allowed, with a beaming look across her face. Right away I knew it could not be fun.

I was right. I ripped off the wrapping paper and inside a box were a set of three cotton dish towels hand-stitched with my name on them.

"Don't worry," Mom said quickly before I could blurt out some complaint. "These are the good, useful gifts. The more you use them and pitch in around the house the more you can understand how the whole family works as a team."

"That is a gift?" I asked, incredulous.

"Don't be an ingrate," she said playfully. "There is still the *better* gift to come."

That was hopeful news and so I waited for the *better* gift to be revealed, but it was a gift I couldn't even see!

"The *better* gift is basically a good deed you do for free," Dad said.

"Or," Mom said in her upbeat voice despite the melted smile on my face, "it's a deed you do because helping others makes you a *better* person. Your dad and I thought you should volunteer this fall at the Frick

Hospital in Mount Pleasant. You've been doing a lot of reading and we signed you up to go to the hospital to read to patients who can't read for themselves. You were born in that hospital and everyone took such good care of us, so this is a way of saying 'thank you' to them and the community."

"Okay," I said. I knew it was a good deed to read to sick people, but there was still nothing wrong with wanting a real gift just for me.

"And now," Dad announced, "here comes the best gift—the gift that we think *fits* you best."

I was sure it was going to be a pair of underpants or socks or T-shirts that just happened to *fit* me *best*.

But then Dad reached into his back pocket and pulled out the smallest white envelope I had ever seen. It was about the size of a matchbox and it fit in the palm of his hand.

"It's all yours," he said with much fanfare, and bowed deeply as if I were the emperor of China.

"So what do you think is in there?" Mom gushed as I held it by the corner and waved it back and forth like a tiny white flag. "Take a guess."

I wanted to say, "I surrender." But mostly I wanted to guess the right gift because it would make Mom very happy to know that she made me happy.

"Well?" she asked. "Cat got your tongue?"

"Come on, son," Dad chimed in. "Take a wild shot at it."

But I didn't know what to say because my mind was screaming, *I hope it's a car, car, car!* And then it came to me in a flash. "A ticket to the Viking Drive-in!" I shouted.

Her smile flattened. "Good guess," she said without much promise. "Now open it."

I ripped the envelope down the side and gave it a shake. Three thin handmade tickets slid into my palm. I looked down at them. The first one read: GET OUT OF JAIL FREE. Before I could say anything she explained, "It's a pass to get out of your room for a day," she said. "An un-grounded ticket."

"Like, for twenty-four hours?" I asked.

"Yes," she confirmed.

"That's great!" I shouted, and my cheeks swelled up so much they blocked my vision, but in my mind I could see myself running free all over Norvelt.

I paused for a moment, then looked down at the other two tickets. One read: ONE FLIGHT IN THE J-3.

Mom suddenly shot Dad a dirty-bird look. "I thought we agreed you were going to give him a ticket to the carnival so he could go on the rides," Mom said.

"I figured the J-3 would be a better ride than some

old Ferris wheel," Dad replied, and looked away from Mom and toward me. "Right, son?"

"Right, Dad," I snapped back.

"But I fly it," Dad confirmed. "And I'll give you a few *tips*."

The way he said *tips* made me think he had some fun on his mind that he couldn't tell me about in front of Mom, who was not looking real happy.

The last ticket read: DOUBLE FEATURE AT VIKING DRIVE-IN.

"I guessed it!" I said, grinning. "I really did!"

"Of course you did," Mom said, and leaned forward for a kiss. "You stare at that tiny screen so much I fear you'll ruin your eyes. But keep in mind that I had to barter for the drive-in ticket. You can see the movies for free, but when they are over you have to stay behind and pick up all the trash that people throw out their windows."

I couldn't tell if she was joking or not. "Really?" I asked in a small voice. "Do I have to pick up trash for my birthday gift?"

"Just kidding," she said. "I tried to barter your work for the ticket but then they reminded me about the child labor laws. Darn! So your dad and I thought we'd better start you off with an allowance before Mr. Spizz caught you working around the house and put *us* in jail."

Dad pulled out a two-dollar bill and set it right in the middle of my hand. "You do a lot of work around here, so you deserve some reward," he said.

"Wow," I said, and I stared wide-eyed. I had never seen a two-dollar bill before and now I knew that President Jefferson was on the front side.

"Hey," Dad said, "I hate to break this party up, but Miss Volker called a little while ago and said she needs a ride to her church. Jackie, can you drive her?"

"Sure," I said. Normally I walked down the hill to the Norvelt Church of Christ with Mom and Dad. But getting to drive Miss Volker was as good as a birthday gift, because her small Catholic church was out in the country and must have been about a half-hour trip.

Mom stepped out of the pony pen and looked up into the air. She could judge time from the range of blue shades across the sky. "You better wash up," she advised. "You have to be there in a half hour and you smell like kerosene. If they light candles you'll go up in flames."

"Then we'll have holy smoke," I said, and was in such a good mood I laughed at my own joke. "And thanks for the great gifts," I added, and then ran off to get ready.

It didn't take me long to wash up and Mom had already laid out all my clothes, so I was dressed and running down to Miss Volker's house in no time. I opened her porch door and she was waiting for me with her back turned.

"Can you button up my dress?" she asked. "I'm gettin' to the point where I'm just going to wear a bathrobe everywhere. Buttons, zippers, hooks and eyes—I just can't do them anymore."

"That's why you have me for your boyfriend," I said, and I buttoned her up in a jiffy.

"I think you are more pet than boyfriend," she cracked, "which is good. At my age a pet is all I need."

I got her into the car and then ran around to the other side and started it up. We were no sooner out of Norvelt than she said, "You know I can't write."

"I know," I replied.

"But if I could write here is what I'd put down onto paper. I want you to have this fine little car," she said.

I almost drove off the road and into a mailbox. "Really?" I said, and gently patted the steering wheel like it was my tender new baby.

"Don't get too excited," she continued. "You can't have it until I'm dead."

"But I'd rather have you alive than the car," I said.

"That's sweet of you," she said without much sweetness. "But you'll find the car will be more useful. And I have a bit of birthday advice to give you."

“What’s that?” I asked.

She pointed at my nose. “I hope you aren’t still taking all those iron drops,” she said gravely.

“I am,” I said. “Mom makes me take spoonfuls of the stuff.”

“Well, pour it down the drain,” she ordered. “Immediately! I did some research on your nose. There is a disease called hemochromatosis, which you get from having too much iron in your blood! It destroys your liver and pancreas and causes severe depression—guess who had it?”

“No idea,” I said.

“Ernest Hemingway!” she hollered out. “The great American writer who shot himself last summer with a loaded rifle!”

“Was it an accident?” I asked, thinking of my own little accident.

“No,” she said matter-of-factly. “Suicide.”

That was a totally depressing birthday warning. I was wondering how I could keep Mom from making me take the iron drops and I started driving so slowly that Mr. Spizz passed us on his tricycle and was already inside the church by the time we arrived.

After I very carefully parked the car-which-someday-would-be-mine I escorted Miss Volker to the front door. She had a special “old folks” seat close to the altar and strolled up the center aisle to take her place. I stayed behind like her chauffeur, and sat in the back pew. From there I could keep an eye on all the grown-ups who were fidgeting or falling asleep or adjusting their fancy hats or singing off key. But the best part of sitting in the back was that my mind could wander aimlessly, because church was so dreamy. Real life was lived like doing a math problem: one and one always equaled two. But church had a different kind of math. You could never be sure what anything added up to, which meant that what was in your imagination while sitting in a pew was just as important as what the preacher was saying—maybe even more important. It's like when you read a book and you know that the words are important, but the images blossoming in your imagination are *even more* important because it's your mind that allows the words to come to life.

Because I had gotten a bunch of nosebleeds in church, I spent a lot of time sitting in the pew with my head thrown all the way back and my eyes looking straight up at the brilliant white ceiling, which was sort of like God's movie screen where I could imagine what heaven might look like.

For me, heaven mostly looked like the pictures in the Landmark book I read about Julius Caesar in ancient

Rome. Everyone wore colorful robes and drove around in chariots and lived in massive stone buildings with tall columns and statues of famous leaders and generals and thinkers. The noon sun was always parting the clouds to show off a robin's-egg-blue sky and people didn't so much walk as they drifted just an inch above the all-white stone paths and roads, and they never went the wrong way because in heaven everything you did was always the right way and everything ended the way it should. For some reason the only food in heaven was bread, but the bread came in every shape you can imagine. There were tiny loaves for dolls, and warm dinner rolls, and long French bread, and braided rings of bread, and thick loaves as big and round as wagon wheels, and even entire wheat-colored cottages of crusty bread which when you lived in them were more like yeasty caves in a gigantic mountain of bread, and all you had to do in order to feed yourself in heaven was pull a hank of soft, moist bread right out of the wall. And there was never such a thing as a "last supper" because every night while you slept your bread house was made fresh all over again, and as my mother always said, if you had fresh bread each day then you'd never have a worry. And not having a worry in the world was the definition of heaven. Dad said that he wanted to move to Florida where he could buy a little piece of heaven, and Mom had said Norvelt was heaven on earth. I guess for me heaven was everything good I could imagine. It was always so beautiful to stare up at that white ceiling and imagine only clean beautiful places, where the reward for living a pure life was a great loaf of warm bread.

But then, when church was over, everything in my imagination seemed to collapse into the dust of a lost world that on the following Sunday I would have to mix up with some live yeast and bake into another vision of heaven.

14

That night my birthday celebration continued. Mom, Dad, and I had cake and ice cream and played Monopoly, which Dad declared was the greatest game ever invented. "It is the American dream in a box," he said, pleased with his tidy summation.

Mom disagreed. "It teaches you how to ruin other people's lives without caring," she countered. She owned the low-rent properties—Baltic and Mediterranean. I owned the railroads, the utilities, and the orange properties. Dad owned the red, yellow, and green properties and had them loaded up with hotels just waiting to bankrupt us out of the game. The rest of the properties were split unevenly among us.

Mom and I teamed up on a handshake and gave

each other free rent. Still, it didn't take long for Dad to own us both. He didn't gloat, but he grinned and sang one of his favorite songs about hard work. "You load sixteen tons, what do you get? Another day older and deeper in debt." Then he carefully packed up the game, as if he were packing up the town and getting ready to hit the road before he got older and deeper in debt.

Sometime after I went to bed I heard the motorcycles swarm up over the hill and down toward the center of Norvelt. I could tell they were not returning to the Huffer Funeral Parlor but to some other place a little farther out. They had to have awakened everyone as they downshifted loudly, and even at a distance their roaring engines rattled our windows. I didn't know why they came back but I knew it couldn't be good. They didn't stay long, however, and it seemed like only a few minutes passed before I heard them rev their engines and come growling back up the hill and branch off toward the road to Mount Pleasant, where the first Hells Angel had danced in from.

Maybe they were lost, I guessed. But that was just wishful thinking. I should have remembered the plague they brought, because I had almost fallen back to sleep when the stabbing whistle of the volunteer fire department went off. I jumped out of bed and ran to the hallway just as Mom and Dad dashed out of their doorway. It was if we were on the *Titanic*. We all went into the living room. Mom pulled the curtains to either side of the windows. I half expected to see waves and fish and icebergs. But immediately we could see the fire beyond the Community Center.

"It has to be a house in section D," Dad announced, and he doubled back to his room. In a few moments he came out in his work clothes.

He gave Mom a quick kiss.

"Be careful," she said as he went out the front door. I heard his boot steps quicken as he tramped down the front porch. In a moment we saw the headlights swing by the windows as he turned his truck around, shifted into first gear, and headed off to join the other volunteers to help put out the fire.

Mom and I were both nervous and kept staring blankly out the window. From our distance we couldn't make out any telling details, other than that the fire seemed to grow.

Suddenly, Mom turned to me as she remembered. "Go get me those Japanese binoculars," she ordered, and gave me a little shove toward the back door. "Hurry! But don't you dare touch the rifle."

"Of course I won't," I cried out. "I'm not a suicidal maniac."

I grabbed the flashlight from under the kitchen sink and turned it on just as I started down the back porch steps. The air was thick with humid summer heat which seemed to rise off the grass like steam. The paving stones under my bare feet were warm and smooth as I leaped from one to the other, silently counting them like Monopoly spaces all the way to the garage. Dad had left the door unlocked and half open. I slipped inside and in one motion pulled the hanging string switch for the overhead light as I trotted around the sleeping J-3 and over to the chest where the souvenirs were kept. I lifted the lid and leaned it back against the garage wall. The rifle was wrapped up in the Japanese flag, right on top where Dad always kept it. I could just see the dark barrel poking out from the white silk of the flag. I swung the flashlight and could make out the shining lenses of the binoculars in the far corner of the chest. I quickly grabbed them then reversed my steps back to the kitchen.

"Let me have them first," Mom said urgently, and took the binoculars from my hand. She stood at the kitchen window and held them up to her eyes as if she were the captain on the bridge of a battleship.

"What do you see?" I asked anxiously.

"The whole house . . . is on fire," she replied slowly as she concentrated on what she saw through the lens. "And the garage too."

"Whose house?" I asked. Mertie-Jo lived in that direction, along with a couple other kids I knew from school.

"Miss Volker's sister's old house," she said.

"But Miss Volker sold it," I replied. "To some young guy."

Mom lowered the binoculars and gave me a very serious look. "She sold it," Mom said grimly, "not to some 'nice young guy' but to the Hells Angel who was hit by the cement truck. It turns out he was dancing his drunken jig to his new home when he was run over."

"That's interesting," I said, wide-eyed. "Real interesting. Because Bunny told me that when the Hells Angels showed up to take his body away they were really angry."

"I saw Mrs. Huffer on the way to the pants factory and she was worried," Mom added. "She said they swore they would return for revenge."

"Did you hear the motorcycles tonight?" I asked.

"That had to be them," she agreed. "I bet they returned to set the house on fire."

"But why would they set their own house on fire?"

"To scare us," Mom said. "Burning down a house is about the most terrifying thing you can do to someone because it says you have no respect for human life, or anything."

I don't know why but at that moment I thought of the *Lost Worlds* book. Invading armies would always burn a city down. Why wouldn't they just want to conquer the city and keep it as their own? Why would the ancient Greeks burn Troy? Or why would the invading Goths burn Rome? It seemed like the smartest thing to do would be to capture the city and keep it for yourself. If the Hells Angels moved into that house and lived in our town that would be more frightening to me than burning the house down. But maybe what Mom said is right—burning something down is the most terrifying thing you can do because burning a house down to the ground is the same as putting a person six feet under.

"This is just too sad," Mom said with a shudder as she turned away and handed the binoculars to me. "Watching it burn is like watching someone being tortured. I can't look."

"Could you see Dad?" I asked.

"No," she replied, and poured a glass of water from the sink. "The fire truck is there, but nothing can be done. The house is a complete loss."

"Should I go tell Miss Volker?" I asked.

"Let her sleep," Mom said with mercy in her voice. "It will be bad enough for her in the morning. Just return the binoculars before your dad gets home. I'm going to bed."

I took the binoculars and went out the back door but I didn't go to the garage. I trotted over to the picnic table and used the bench to step up and stand on the tabletop as I had done the night I fired off the sniper rifle.

I held the binoculars up and focused on the small house. I could see the flames leaping into the air, and the confetti of glowing ash that floated above the flames as if a magical fairy celebration were taking place in some ancient world under a dark night. But it wasn't a celebration. The blistering flames rising above the house were just waving goodbye to everyone who was watching. And even for those not watching it was a piece of history dropping to its knees before disappearing forever.

It was too sad, so I swung the binoculars toward the Viking Drive-in. As usual, a war movie was playing. American and Korean soldiers were machine-gunning each other to bits across a shell-pocked field. Fiery explosions tossed bodies through the air to bleed out and nourish the exhausted dirt. It was an American-made movie and I knew we would win, but still I could feel myself getting all worked up. My heart pounded and my breathing was rapid and my eyes were glued onto each American soldier and I could feel myself wanting to shout "Come on, kill them, kill them all," and when one of the American stars got shot I jerked away from the screen and lowered the binoculars.

I was panting like a dog and passed my hand under my nose to feel for blood. Nothing. Maybe Miss Volker had fixed my nose, but it didn't stop me from wanting to watch war movies. That was the weird thing about death. In real life I was afraid of it. In the movies I couldn't get enough of it.

I swung the binoculars back toward the burning house at the moment when the roof caved in and the final golden crown of flames rose up through the air. I felt as if I were trapped inside that house, as if I couldn't escape the broiling walls—as if my life and the life of that house were burning down together. I stood there for a minute because that cruel moment had captured me in its tight fist, but after a while the harsh feeling weakened and I lowered my head as I stepped down from the table and across the wilted grass and returned the binoculars to the chest and went to my room. Watching that house burn was the torture Mom claimed it was. It felt like we were cursed. And after I crawled into my bed and got settled under the sheet it wasn't easy to fall asleep.

As soon as the phone rang I shouted out, "Tell her I'll be down in a minute. I have to brush my teeth."

I got out of bed and dressed and dashed to the kitchen where Mom gave me half of her egg and butter sandwich.

"Did Dad say anything when he got home?" I asked with my mouth full.

"You better get a move on," she replied. "Believe me, if there is anything to be said about last night Miss Volker will say it."

When I arrived on her porch there were about a half-dozen big ceramic pots by her door. They were covered in black soot and all the plants were leafless and charred. One pot was in the shape of a large owl's head, and growing out the top were just the spindly burned stems of something that had been alive the day before. There was a card between the stems and I knew I had to read it. I put my ear to Miss Volker's door. I didn't hear any movement. I reached down and quickly opened the card. *Sorry, these were all I could rescue. —E. Spizz, Volunteer Fire Deputy.* I closed it up and put it back between the stems. He was always leaving her presents and he must have saved these from her sister's house.

I opened her door. "Miss Volker," I hollered, "are you dressed?"

"What would it matter?" she replied glumly. "Today I'm not a person—I feel like a box full of cold ashes."

When I entered the living room she was sitting on the couch wrapped up in a large knitted afghan. The tears ran in uneven channels down the wrinkled maze of skin on her face. Watching an old person cry is not the same as watching a young person cry. Old people don't really seem hurt so much as they seem hopeless, which is worse.

"I heard about your sister's house," I said quietly. "You can have it rebuilt. My dad could do it."

She wiped her face against her bony shoulders. "No," she replied softly. "It's gone for good. But not forgotten. Sit down and get your pencil and paper. Today we are going to write a different kind of obituary."

I took my seat and got my pad and sharpened my pencil. "I'm ready," I said, and licked the tip of the lead.

"This is not your normal obituary," she started, and I could hear the strength return to her voice. Then she pulled herself up like a drum major about to march at the head of her words. "This is the obituary of a house—a home that was born of love and died by the hands of hatred. The little house on parcel number 11 in section D on Larkspur Circle was born in 1935. Mrs. Roosevelt was the godmother and a great one she was. When the government offered to help poor people build houses in Norvelt the architects drew up plans to have entire families live like farm animals in one barnlike room with a bathroom outhouse and a kitchen that was nothing but a wood-burning cook shed on the back of the property. The government's idea of helping poor people was to give them some shelter to survive, but not to allow them to live a life of pride.

"But Godmother Roosevelt came to the rescue. She made sure people had real houses—little New England–style houses—and they had bedrooms and a living room and a useful kitchen and a bathroom with a bathtub, and even a laundry room with a washing machine. The government called this luxury living. But Mrs. Roosevelt called it living with dignity.

"My sister and I lived together here in my number 3 house in section A until she met and married Mr. Chester Hap in 1941. He was an original Norvelt member who was accepted into the new town because he was an electrician and was needed. He helped folks wire their houses and in return they helped him build his house. In true Norvelt fashion he bartered his skills for their skills until the two hundred and fifty houses were fully built.

"Many good times were had in the Hap home. All the holidays were celebrated with artistic decorations, as my sister was head of the Federal Art Project in Norvelt and she taught ceramics and painting and the decorative arts in her garage art studio, and up at the school and Community Center. Their home was a Babylonian garden of beauty. They had a grape arbor, beds of asparagus, lettuce, tomatoes, and potatoes, as well as fruit trees and a field with corn and soybeans. The grounds were graced with raised beds of mixed bouquets, and the full perimeter of the property was edged with azaleas, which fit the house like a gilded frame fits a beautiful painting.

"In such a fertile home devoted to beauty, love, and understanding, only one thing was missing—a child. My sister was a little too old for motherhood, but in 1942, after the bombing at Pearl Harbor when Japanese Americans were being rounded up and sent to internment camps, a Japanese couple with a new baby arranged for their infant son to be adopted by my sister and her husband. This way the child would have a loving home and not have to be sent to a prison camp and suffer the hardship and shame of that life. I remember that beautiful baby and the love my sister and her husband graced upon him. They had an angelic six months together until the federal government tracked that baby down and took him away, all because he was of Japanese origin—an enemy of America in diapers!

"We never knew what became of the baby nor did we forget the heartlessness of our own government," Miss Volker said with her arms folded in a tight X across her chest. "It cut us so deeply, as we loved that little innocent boy who lived in a house devoted solely to his innocence. And now the house has been burned to the ground by a gang of Hells Angels who have turned their obscene hatred toward our town. They poured gasoline throughout the house and garage and lit them on fire and like cowards they fled in the night. It is a sad death for a house to become nothing but ashes and dust and earth, but we in Norvelt will never forget every splinter of the life it lived."

I had tears in my eyes but Miss Volker looked revived, as if a few hot embers of the house were glowing within her. "Boy," she said as she tried to close her hands into two bony fists and punch out at the air, "I love it when I get mad! I feel like I'm ready to take on the world—I'd like to show a few of those Hells Angels a thing or two."

I hurried up and typed the obituary and ran it down to the *Norvelt News*. Mr. Greene took it from my hands and read it. "An obit for a house?" he questioned as he relit his pipe. "Has she lost her mind?"

"No," I said. "She just speaks her mind."

"Amen to that," he remarked.

15

Mom was reading the house obituary in the newspaper and taking the last sips of her coffee before she went to work. "This is really a sad obit," she remarked when I entered the kitchen and opened the refrigerator door. "Honestly, Miss Volker should just leave and go live with her sister in Florida."

"But she won't until she's the last original Norvelt person left standing," I explained, and pulled out the milk. "She promised Mrs. Roosevelt she'd nurse this town to the end."

Dad overheard us on his way out the door. "Well, when she finds out about my new top secret job," he said in a muffled voice full of intrigue, "she might change her mind. 'Cause there'll be no town to nurse."

"What do you mean by that?" Mom and I called out.

"You'll see what I mean—later," he said, teasing us as his voice trailed off. Then he was gone.

I turned back to Mom, who shrugged. "Well," she said as she rinsed her coffee cup. "I'd hate to see these old folks move on to the next world, but for some of them it might be for the best."

"How can dying be good for you?" I asked.

"When living is worse," she replied matter-of-factly. Then she turned toward the door. "Clean up your room before you do your outdoor chores—and don't forget to feed the turkeys," she said. "They get mad when they're hungry and they take it out on War Chief."

I nodded. Once I finished eating I slunk back to my room to put on my work clothes, which were stiff with dirt. Then I went outside and with my new birthday shovel I got back to digging the bomb shelter. I had asked Dad what size it needed to be and he said the hole should be as large as a swimming pool. So far it was about the same size as a bathtub.

I had just thrown a shovelful of dirt out of the hole when I noticed a human shadow hovering over me. I looked up and it was Mr. Spizz. He had a camera pressed against his squinty face.

"What are you taking a picture of?" I asked.

I heard a click and he lowered the camera. "Gantos

boy, take a look at that runway," he said loudly, and pointed accusingly at it. "That airplane and runway are going to be trouble for your dad."

I looked over at the runway. Dad had it flattened out and he had the J-3 almost ready to fly. All he had to do was connect the wings, start the engine, and take off right out the back door. I knew he would be really upset if Mr. Spizz turned the town against his plans.

"I can see by the look on your face that you don't want to disappoint your dad, do you?" Spizz asked. "I also heard that he's been taking flying lessons over in Kecksburg, so I'd hate to make him plow up this new runway."

Dad had told only me about his private flying lessons. He didn't dare tell Mom, but somehow that nosy Mr. Spizz seemed to know everything.

"You're right," I said. "I don't like to disappoint my dad."

"Then I have a way you can help him avoid trouble and keep his runway," he barked.

The louder he spoke the more I lowered my voice. "What's that?" I asked.

He turned his ear toward me. "Trot down to the hardware store and buy me a tin of 1080 poison—I got some vermin to kill up at the dump." He pointed toward Fenton's Gas Station. The dump was just beyond it and sometimes the rats came out of the murky old mine shafts and swarmed over the dump and then spread out into everyone's house and garden. It was disgusting to find knots of them gathered hungrily on the back porch.

"Why can't you go down there yourself?" I asked. "On your tricycle."

"I hurt my leg," he groused, and pulled up his pants leg. The side of his calf from his ankle to his knee was darkly bruised and swollen. "When I went after those Hells Angels one of them was lagging behind, and he drove by and kicked me in the leg and I crashed my trike—which reminds me. While you're at the store, get me a tube repair kit for my tire. Boy, if I'd've had that baseball bat in my hand I would have knocked that Nazi helmet off his head."

I thought it was probably pretty good that he didn't have the bat. The Hells Angel would have taken it and knocked his head into the next county.

"And then at the fire the other night," he continued, "when I was trying to rescue some ceramic pots, I tripped and hurt it again."

"Well, I'm grounded," I explained in a whisper, and shrugged my shoulders. "Can't leave the property."

"What'd you say?" he shouted, and screwed his finger into his ear then popped it out and stared at the waxy amber tip. "Now, are you going to help me? Or do you want me to make sure your dad is *grounded* too, if you know what I mean?" His awful voice made what he was saying even more of a threat.

"What about the gutter ticket?" I asked with my voice raised so he could easily hear me.

"I'll make that fly away too," he said reluctantly, grimacing a bit because of the pain in his leg.

I had planned to offer him my two-dollar bill as a partial payment on the ticket, but now I could spend it on myself. "It's a deal," I said, and pulled myself out of the hole. When I stood up I stuck out my hand and he slapped five dollars into it. I gave him the shovel. "Lean on this," I suggested. "I'll be right back."

"And not a word to your *girlfriend*," he said in a gruff way. "Or else."

I took off running through the backyard paths and behind hedges. When I passed Miss Volker's house I ducked way down as I ran because I didn't want her to ask what I was up to and then get it out of me that I was doing a favor for Mr. Spizz, which would trigger a tirade I didn't have time to endure. I was quick and when I got close to the hardware store I made a mad dash for the front door and scooted inside, because if Mom saw me from the open pants-factory windows across the street she'd ground me for another year. I caught my breath then quickly got the tube patch kit from the shelf and went up to the cash register. I didn't know the man behind the counter, because the hardware store had been bought and the new owner hired people outside of Norvelt.

"Can I help you?" he asked as he cleaned his fingernails with a small red pocketknife.

"Yes," I replied, and looked at the tiny spirals of dirt rolling along the stained blade of the knife. I gulped for breath. "May I have a can of 1080?" I put the tube kit and crumpled five-dollar bill on the counter.

"You'll need a note from your parents before I can sell poison to you," he said plainly. "That stuff is deadly."

"It's for Mr. Spizz," I explained. "He works for the Public Good. He hurt his leg and I'm helping him out 'cause he has to kill all the rats." I pointed like a scarecrow toward the dump.

"I guess that's okay," he allowed. "I know old Spizz. But you still have to sign this sheet saying you bought some—it's a new law."

I would have signed anything. I just wanted to slink out of there as quickly as I could before anyone entered the store who knew Mom or Dad and might mention they saw me there.

As I read down the list of names on the sheet I saw that Mr. Huffer was the last man to sign it. The thought of rats living in his coffins knotted my stomach as I signed my name. When I looked up from the paper the man was staring directly into my face as if he recognized me from a post office Wanted poster.

"Your nose is bleeding," he said slowly, and pointed at it with the blade of his skinny little knife. "On the left side."

Just then a drop of blood slid down my lip and plopped onto the soft paper where a moment before I had written my name. I stared down at the red spot of blood as it spread through the paper fibers. I didn't like how that looked.

I wiped my nose on my forearm and saw a ruddy streak from my wrist to my elbow. "Thanks," I said, sniffing loudly. And then nervously added, "I have Hemingway's liver disease."

He looked at me like I was already insane.

I grabbed the bag off the counter and quickly turned toward the door. Once I was outside there was more blood. I thought maybe my nose was bleeding because of all the running I did. But I had a feeling it was more than that. The blood drop on my name was a bad omen. Maybe it was because I had broken the rules and left the yard and I was worried about it. Or maybe it was because I didn't really trust making deals with Mr. Spizz. Then again, maybe it was the way the hardware store man made me sign my name on the paper like I was up to no good. Or that seeing Mr. Huffer's name gave me creepy thoughts. I wasn't sure. All I knew was that I was bleeding on one side and I didn't want Miss Volker to try and fix me again. Her hands were getting worse and worse.

I trotted back up the path and found Spizz sitting awkwardly on the picnic table bench. He was rubbing his sore leg and grimacing. When I stopped in front of him I was pinching my nostril shut with one finger and whistle-breathing through my other nostril. I gave him the bag.

"You should get yourself a tricycle like I have," he suggested. "It's a great way to get around without wearing yourself out."

I didn't want to say anything that might offend him, like "Tricycles are for kindergartners—grow up!" So I just said, "I'll ask Santa for one."

He reached out and patted me on the head. "I hope you're on the good list," he roared, then let out a booming *ho-ho-ho* Santa laugh.

I didn't think I was on the good list.

Then he painfully stood up and winced when he put weight on the bad leg. "I should move to Florida," he said, grunting with every word. "And if that Miss Volker knew what was good for her she'd move there too."

"But she's determined to be the last original Norvelter standing," I said.

"Don't remind me," he said impatiently. "I know all about her stubborn promise to Mrs. Roosevelt."

"Yep," I confirmed. "She's dedicated."

"Well, some of those old ladies might live past a hundred," he said.

"I thought you said you'd live to be a hundred and three," I reminded him.

"That's just bluster," he replied, and squeezed his eyes together when he moved his leg. "For now I better limp up to the dump before those rats multiply and take over the town. What would Mrs. Roosevelt think of that?"

I pointed toward the runway. "Thanks," I said, "for not causing trouble."

"One good turn deserves another," he replied, and began to hobble away. Then he turned and stopped. "Really," he said. "Don't mention to anyone I was ever up here or they'd know I saw the runway and it would cause me some trouble. And if I'm in trouble," he said, pausing and pointing toward the runway for effect, "then you're in trouble."

I turned my back and the moment I unpinched my nose the blood gushed out like a busted pipe and spattered all down my jeans and over my sneakers. It made me nervous. I just knew something bad was headed my way.

As soon as Mom came home from work she dropped her purse like dropping anchor and marched down the hallway.

"You disappoint me!" she hollered before she even reached my doorway. It was one of the worst things she could have said, and then she stomped into my room. I could tell by the stern look on her face that she did not come to kiss me. "Hand over your get-out-of-jail-free card," she ordered, and held out her hand. "I saw you running out of the hardware store from the factory window."

I didn't dare argue with her because then I might have to tell her everything about Spizz and the ticket and the 1080, so I just looked her in the eye and said, "I'm sorry. I had to get out of the house and run around a bit. It was stupid of me."

"That was stupid, but at least you aren't a liar," she said. "But you did violate my trust. And if I can't trust you then it makes me realize that you can't trust yourself to make good decisions. Remember, a person first lies to himself before he lies to others. Think about that." Then she turned and stomped out the door.

I knew she was more disappointed with me than angry, and that really hurt most of all. But I just couldn't tell her the whole truth about the ticket and Mr. Spizz and his threat to have Dad's runway closed down. One lie always leads to another. At the moment that historic truth seemed like a *historic* curse.

16

"We're in business!" Miss Volker hollered over the phone before I heard the receiver drop and bounce across her floor like a fish flopping around. "Dang useless hands," she growled in the background. "Get down here!"

I made it down there pretty quickly. "What's up?" I asked, and put the beeping receiver back onto the cradle.

"We lost another one today," she said excitedly. "Confirmed. An original Norvelt homesteader."

"Who?" I asked. She seemed so delighted I was sure she was going to say it was Mr. Spizz. But I was wrong.

"Your Grim Reaper friend, Mrs. Dubicki," she revealed, still sounding all bubbly. "You predicted it and my spotter confirmed it this time. Said he 'touched' her and she was stone cold. They already have her down at the Huffer Funeral Parlor, so if she isn't dead they'll finish her off."

"I guess we have to do her obit," I suggested, and headed into the living room to take my place at the desk.

"And I have good history for today too," she said with enthusiasm. "But first we'll start with her personal stuff."

I picked up my pencil and wrote as she paced back and forth and spoke wildly off the top of her head while her arms sliced through the air like karate chops.

"Mrs. Rena Dubicki, who died today at age eighty-six, was born in Slovenia in 1876. During a deadly wheat famine her farming parents decided to immigrate to America. They took their savings and purchased the cheapest tickets they could on an ocean liner and gathered up what little food they could for the long journey. Their tiny room was in the dank bottom of the boat and it took weeks to travel down the Adriatic Sea and around the boot of Italy and across the Mediterranean Sea and through the Strait of Gibraltar and across the Atlantic Ocean.

"Partway through the trip they ran out of food and were living on handouts and kitchen scraps and were barely half-alive by the time the boat pulled into New

York City. They were thrilled with having made their way to a new country and cried tears of joy as they passed the Statue of Liberty. But they were also crying from a terrible tragedy. Somehow, along the way, they lost their daughter. Mrs. Dubicki was six years old and tiny and her parents had not seen her in days. They were afraid to tell anyone that she vanished for fear they would be arrested and sent back to Slovenia to starve. Mrs. Dubicki was a sleepwalker and her parents worried she had wretchedly stepped overboard one night and been eaten by sharks or swallowed by a whale. After a final futile search for her they had to disembark along with the rest of the passengers. The boat took on cargo and turned right around and went back to Slovenia. Her parents were heartbroken. Where could their daughter be, they asked, without an answer. But they did not give up hope.

"Well, about the time the ship pulled back into the Slovenian port, the fattened-up Mrs. Dubicki slipped out of her hiding place within the captain's private kitchen pantry. Weeks before she sneaked in and hid while the door was open, but got trapped when the door was locked. She had been feasting on the captain's good food, and when she made her way onto the deck to locate her parents she declared to a sailor that Slovenia and New York looked exactly the same. It was soon discovered that she was a lost girl who had failed to get off in New York, so she was assigned to a host family, and when the boat turned around and headed back to New York she remained on board. At immigration her parents were tracked down and she was reunited and this is how Mrs. Dubicki came twice to America—and as she liked to say, 'Twice was enough so I never left again.'

"She married Taduz Dubicki and together they had seven children and five grandchildren. Mr. Dubicki was a coal miner in Calumet and passed away from black lung disease. The children who lived with them after they moved to Norvelt have all moved away, but Mrs. Dubicki stayed in her Norvelt home. In recent times she had been ill with a muscular disease which gave her the shakes, cramping convulsions, and uncontrollable spasms that led to her death from cardiac arrest the day following her grandson's birthday on July 3.

"She was a member of the Roosevelt Food Bank for the needy, a devout Methodist, a Girl Scout den mother, and a cook for the volunteer fire department. She will be missed by all who knew her. She will be cremated at the Huffer Funeral Parlor on July 5, and soon a burial ceremony will take place at St. George's Cemetery."

I wrote all that down. "Is there more?" I asked, because I was a little tired of Mrs. Dubicki.

"Yes," Miss Volker replied, "but that is enough about her. We've got other things to think about because dying on July 4 really brings up some interesting history which we have to get into the newspaper. So write this down, but I'll keep it short."

I quickly sharpened my pencil, cracked my knuckles, yawned, stretched my arms, and was ready.

"Amazingly," Miss Volker began with her usual physical enthusiasm, "John Adams (our second president) and Thomas Jefferson (our third) died on exactly the same Fourth of July day in 1826, which was the fiftieth anniversary of the signing of the Declaration of Independence. When Adams died his last words were, 'Jefferson survives.' But Jefferson had already died two hours before and his last words were, 'Adams survives.' Their fight for freedom turned them into blood brothers. Both presidents were great patriots and signers of the Declaration of Independence, and it is a majestic coincidence that they would both die on the day all Americans celebrate as the birth of this country. At times the two men were bitter political enemies—especially over the issue of slave ownership—but as they aged they grew into great friends, for it is the American way not to focus on differences, but on what we have in common: life, liberty, and the pursuit of happiness."

The moment she paused to catch her breath, I raised my hand like I did in school. "Excuse me, Miss Volker," I called out.

"What?" she snapped. "I'm speaking."

"Is it really true what you said about Adams and Jefferson having almost the same last words at almost the same time?"

She exhaled and looked at me as if I were an idiot. "Most all of what I say is true," she replied. "But if you don't know your history you won't know the difference between the truth and wishful thinking."

"Well, which is this? Truth or wishful thinking?" I dared to ask.

"Look it up for yourself," she said impatiently, and turned her back on me. "Now, let's continue the obit, shall we?"

"Okay," I said quickly, and lifted my pencil.

"Mrs. Roosevelt," she said loudly, "was especially fond of a Jeffersonian principle that shaped the planning of Norvelt. Jefferson believed that every American should have a house on a large enough piece of fertile property so that during hard times, when money was difficult to come by, a man and woman could always grow crops and have enough food to feed their family. Jefferson believed that the farmer was the key to America and that a well-run family farm was a model for a well-run government. Mrs. Roosevelt felt the same. And we in Norvelt keep that belief alive."

After speaking her last word Miss Volker bowed her head in prayer. When she finished she plopped down onto her couch like a string puppet that had been cut loose. All her jumbled pieces slumped into herself, and with her forehead pressed against her tucked-up knees she fell into a deep sleep.

But I still had work to do. I typed up the obituary and history lesson then went over to the map and put a final red pin on Mrs. Dubicki's house at C-27. "Sorry, Mrs. Dubicki," I whispered. "You were very nice and I hope the real Grim Reaper was kind to you."

Just then Miss Volker lifted her head from her knees and peeked up at me as she yawned loudly.

"Anything I can get you before I take off?" I asked.

"Yes," she replied. "I want you to take a sleeve of Thin Mints and line them up on the edge of the kitchen counter and then when I'm hungry I can just bend over and sweep a cookie into my mouth like I'm scoring a goal in hockey."

"What about milk?" I asked.

"Just put a straw in a bottle and leave it on the counter. That will make a nice dinner."

"Sure," I said, and after I got her set up I ran down to the newspaper office where Mr. Greene was smoking his pipe. A cloud of smoke hung over his head like a cartoon thought bubble full of swirling, unformed thoughts. I gave him the obituary, and after he read it he lowered the pages and smiled at me.

"Nice job," he declared.

"Miss Volker does all the work," I replied. "She's really good at thinking up the obits."

"I don't mean the obit," he said. "I mean the typing. You are getting better."

I beamed. "Thanks," I said, and tapped my fingers on the counter.

"If you have any spare time I could always use an extra hand around here," he offered. "I could teach you how to work the press."

"I'm grounded for the summer," I explained. "But let me see what I can do."

"Let me know," he said. "I'll be here."

17

“Your whole summer is wasting away,” Bunny complained the following week in that wilting tone of disgust she was so good at. “Think about it. This is the summer of your life when you did *nothing*! Oh, I take that back,” she said suddenly, and pointed her accusing finger at the bomb shelter. “This is the summer you dug your own grave!”

Her attack almost succeeded in turning me against myself, but after I thought about my last month I said, “You’re wrong. I’m having a very interesting summer.”

She did not like to be disagreed with and she never gave up easily. She seemed to compress down into an even smaller version of herself so that she looked like an angry tree stump with short stubby branches for arms.

"No, you are wrong," she said, shooting forward and poking me hard in the chest. "You are supposed to be my friend, and we've done nothing together."

"You held my hand when I was around the dead Hells Angel," I reminded her.

"Only because you were sick as a sissy," she replied. "Why can't we do something that's fun?"

"Like what?" I asked.

"Like playing baseball," she suggested. "We have a game against Hecla this afternoon and we only have five players. We're going to get our butts kicked. Mr. Spizz said he'd be our pitcher but that is too weird to have an ancient old guy on a kids' team."

"He's not that old," I said slyly. "He rides a tricycle."

"You know what I mean!" she said, and gave me a shove. "Now prove you're my friend and do something."

"Hold on then," I said to her. "I'll be right back."

I ran into the house and down the hall to my room. I pulled my T-shirt off and put my Huffer Funeral Parlor baseball shirt on, then grabbed my glove and hat and my ONE FLIGHT IN THE J-3 ticket. Mom was in the kitchen chopping mushrooms and dill for a chicken soup she was cooking for the old ladies.

I walked up behind her and tapped her on the shoulder. When she turned around I asked, "Can I trade in this ticket and go play one game of baseball?" I asked. "Bunny needs me on the team."

At first she didn't look hopeful, but once she recognized the ticket I was holding she brightened up. "We can do an even swap," she said. "Besides, I think it is for your own good not to get into that plane. It scares me." Then she glanced at the stove clock. It was just before noon. "But don't make it too late, as you have to help Miss Volker sack up bags of cookies for tonight's dinners."

"You're the best," I said, then dashed out the door and nearly knocked the gum out of Bunny's mouth as I slapped her on the back with my glove. "Follow me," I shouted. "I'm free as a bird." We took off for the ballpark.

It felt so good to just run and not have to think of a thing but playing ball. Being grounded had beaten me down and it was as if being a kid had become a Lost World for me. But the more I ran and smiled and thought of baseball my old kid self was found again, until we passed by Miss Volker's front porch and I heard her faintly call my name. I kept running. And then I heard it again.

"Jackie!" This time she split the air with her demanding voice.

Bunny shot me a look. "Play like you didn't hear it," she chuffed.

"I can't," I replied, and slowed down. "She needs me."

"Don't you dare mess this day up," Bunny warned, and spit at my sneaker. "Ignore her!"

I couldn't and peeled off toward Miss Volker's house. She was standing on the porch. "Jackie!" she called out again, and waved one of her misshapen hands. "I'm afraid we've got another original down for the count. Mrs. Linga. Section E, house number 17. Let's get going."

"Good grief!" Bunny cried out. "I live with dead people all day long. I don't need to see another one."

"Come on," I begged, "this will be something we can do together."

"Okay," she groaned, "but make it fast. We have a game in an hour."

"No problem," I said, but I was uncertain about that. Miss Volker always liked to take her time. The hands on her kitchen clock were just as useless to her as her own two hands.

As soon as I got both of them in the car we took off for Mrs. Linga's house. It didn't take us long to get there, but Mr. Huffer had beat us to the body. Thankfully he had already covered Mrs. Linga with a white sheet. The sharp peaks of her stiff knees and elbows made the sheet take on the shape of a small iceberg. I looked at it for a moment too long and began to think of the frosty remains of small animals I'd find in the woods just as the spring snow thawed.

I looked away from the sheet and noticed one of Mom's partially eaten casseroles on the kitchen table along with an open bag of Thin Mints I had helped Miss Volker package up.

"Hi, sweetie," Mr. Huffer said as Bunny dragged herself though the doorway.

"Hey, Dad," she replied glumly as she stepped casually over Mrs. Linga on her way to open the refrigerator. It was empty except for the moldy smells that rolled out and were more deadly than the wavy odors rising off of Mr. Huffer's spongy suit.

"What do you think was the cause of death?" Miss Volker asked him as we all stood in the kitchen around the sheet. I glanced from the table to the orange linoleum floor, which looked like the inside of a grilled cheese sandwich.

"Complications from that broken hip," he said matter-of-factly as he held a partially carved wooden duck and a carving tool in his hands. "Looks like she was eating while carving and somehow slipped out of her chair and hit her head." He pointed toward the corner of the table where there was a swipe of fresh blood. The instant I saw the blood I looked up at the cotton-white ceiling and covered my nose.

"I think you are right," Miss Volker agreed as Mr. Huffer reached into his jacket pocket and removed the medical examiner paperwork and certificate of death.

"Can you sign this," he asked, "or do you have to cook your hands?"

Miss Volker frowned at him. "Jackie," she ordered, "get that pen and hold it in my hand."

Mr. Huffer leaned awkwardly over Mrs. Linga's cold body and held the paperwork on the kitchen table corner right where she had hit her head and dropped dead. I pressed the pen between my hand and Miss Volker's twisted palm and together we managed to slowly scrawl her name, letter by letter, as if we were receiving it from a Ouija board.

"Voilà!" she said to Mr. Huffer when she finished. "Now you can take her away."

That was just what he had in mind.

On the way out the door I glanced into the living room, and there must have been about a hundred carved ducks. They were so lifelike it was as if a flock of mallards had flown in the window and settled all over her furniture.

"Pretty cool, don't you think?" I said to Bunny, who was pacing around by the door. "I'd love to be able to carve ducks."

"God, how I wish there were more kids in this town

so I wouldn't be forced to hang out with a kook like you," she replied. "Now let's get to the game!"

But when we got in the car Miss Volker was ready to dictate the obituary. Bunny sighed unhappily as I pulled a pad of paper and a pencil from the glove compartment.

"Mrs. Karen Linga died on July 9 at the age of seventy-two," Miss Volker began. She couldn't pace back and forth in her living room like always, so she just tapped her feet as if stamping out a campfire. "Mrs. Linga had a wonderful, gentle husband with a beautiful wooden leg, and it meant a lifetime of love for her. When he was still a single man he lost his leg in a coal mining cave-in and when the stump healed he had to have a new leg fitted for him. At the time there were people who carved legs, and Mrs. Linga was a carver. As everyone knows, she is a champion duck carver and carved the portraits of all the presidents that hang in the school library. So she carved a new leg for Mr. Linga and that is how they met and from there they were married.

"He continued to work in the mines, but not at digging coal. He took care of all the mules that lived in the mines and pulled the small rail cars filled with coal through the tunnels and to the elevators, where the coal was lifted up to ground level for sorting and shipping.

The mules, once they entered the mines, seldom ever saw daylight again until they died and were hoisted up to the ground and sold to animal processing factories. Mr. Linga took particularly good care of the mules and Mrs. Linga would often go with her husband down into the mine to help groom the mules and feed them treats and clean their stalls. The two of them provided the mules with affection and doctoring and kind company. It was cold in the mine shafts and Mrs. Linga sewed feed bags together and made blankets for them. After Mr. Linga died she continued to volunteer her time to care for the mules until they were gradually replaced by more modern machines."

I was just writing that last sentence when I looked up through the windshield and was stunned to see Dad slowly driving a big flatbed truck with a Norvelt house on the back of the double-wide trailer. He slowed down even more and waved at me. "Hey, Jackie," he hollered gleefully, "say goodbye to a piece of old Norvelt."

"Where are you taking it?" I hollered back as I jumped out of the car and ran toward him.

"Eleanor, West Virginia," he said loudly—loudly enough for Miss Volker to hear. "A crew of us have been hired by some folks down there who are buying up all the empty Norvelt homes and adding 'em to their own Roosevelt town."

I quickly turned to catch Miss Volker's reaction. "You-you-you—!" she stuttered as she tried desperately to open the door handle, but her fingers were so rusted together she gave up trying and leaned out the open window. "You should be ashamed of yourself! These are Norvelt homes," she shouted. "Mrs. Roosevelt said our homes should stay right here in town and never, ever be destroyed."

"I'm not destroying anything," Dad shouted back. "I'm just moving the dead parts of this town to a new location that's still alive! Besides, take a look at the back of the house—it's burned. The Hells Angels must've got to it, only this one was put out by a neighbor before it was gutted."

"Hey!" Bunny shouted to my dad as she slipped out of the backseat. "How about giving me a ride to a new location?"

"Hop on board," he replied. "Just sit on the back of the trailer, and when I pass through town you can jump off."

Bunny turned toward me and I could see the disappointment in her eyes.

"I'll play next time," I replied, but my voice sounded phony. "I really want to."

"You are worse than one of Dad's stiffs," she shot back. "At least they know they are dead. You don't even know you're alive." Then she ran after the trailer.

I was afraid to get back into the car because I knew Miss Volker was fuming and would be so angry with my dad she might take back her car. I wouldn't blame her. For her entire life she had done nothing else but keep her promise to Mrs. Roosevelt to watch over the health of our town. Now to see it being sold and hauled off to some better Eleanor Roosevelt town must have hurt her feelings.

"I've been thinking," she said angrily when I got enough courage to take my seat behind the wheel. "We should have Mr. Greene print up a request to start a Protect Norvelt fund and collect money to buy what empty houses there are and keep this town from being sold or burned down."

I started the engine. "That's a good idea," I said, and put the car in gear, but at the moment I didn't know anybody with money in Norvelt except for Mr. Huffer, and he only had money because everyone was dying off.

"You can't write and drive at the same time," Miss Volker said to me, "so I guess we'll skip the history at the end of the obituary."

"Sure," I said, hoping that maybe if we got back to her house I could still find time to run down to the ballpark and play a few innings and make Bunny happy.

"But if I were going to add a little history to Mrs. Linga's obit it would be about a great love story," she said. "I like a love story."

"Is it a good one?" I asked. "You know I like history."

"One of my favorites," she said. "It is about Alexander Berkman and Emma Goldman—two great American anarchists who wanted to improve the lives of all Americans."

"I never heard of them," I said.

"Because schools don't teach the history of social reformers who were real American heroes and fought for workers' rights and justice," she said angrily, with her hands already chopping at the air as if she were fighting off hornets. That was a sure sign she was warming up to her subject. "Anyway," she continued, "let me tell the story."

"Okay," I agreed, and drove slowly enough so that the squirrels could run relay races back and forth between the wheels of the car without getting flattened.

"Alexander Berkman was a handsome and fiery revolutionary young man who wanted better pay and safety for miners and factory workers. He was full of hotheaded ideas—too hotheaded, really. In order to gain equality for miners and steelworkers he decided in 1892 that all he had to do was assassinate the incredibly wealthy Henry Frick, who owned a lot of coal mines and factories where men and children were poorly treated. He figured once Frick was killed then the mistreated workers would rise up and start a revolution to take over the country and give everyone a good, safe job and education and a house and everything else they deserved."

"That sounds like some of Eleanor Roosevelt's thinking," I interjected.

"They may have thought alike," replied Miss Volker, "but they sure didn't act alike. Mrs. Roosevelt did not approve of violent revolution."

"What happened next?" I asked.

"Well, depending on who you talk to, Berkman got an appointment with Frick at his Pittsburgh office and during the meeting Berkman pulled out a gun, but he was nervous and his hand was shaking and when he fired he only nicked Frick a few times in the neck. So then he pulled out a knife and stabbed Frick a few times in the leg. Or, another story has it that Berkman pulled out a gun and it jammed so he pulled out a knife and tried to stab Frick. Either way, what happened is that Frick and a helper wrestled the gun and knife from Berkman, who was then arrested and sent off to prison."

"Was there a revolution anyway?" I asked.

"No," she said. "No one cared, which really depressed Berkman."

"So where is the love in this love story?" I asked.

"I'm sure Frick didn't give him a hug and kiss for trying to kill him."

"Hold your horses," she replied. "I'm not finished."

"Okay," I said.

"Anyway, Berkman's girlfriend was Emma Goldman, who I admire. She was a really famous social reformer who did all kinds of good things for women, and she decided to help him escape from prison. Berkman sent her letters filled with secret code for a brilliant plan. First, Emma and some friends rented a house across from the prison walls. Second, they hired a piano player to sing and play loudly all day long. Third, they began to dig a tunnel from the basement of the house toward the prison while the piano playing covered the sound of the digging. They dug under the road and under the prison wall and, depending on who you talk to, two things happened."

"What?"

"One story has it that their tunnel came up to a little patch of prison ground where only Berkman was allowed to exercise. Emma was waiting for him to take his daily walk, and then he'd sneakily drop down into the tunnel and off they'd flee to freedom and live a romantic life fighting for workers' justice all over the world."

"But that didn't happen, did it?" I suspected.

"No. Unexpectedly, a guard stepped into the hole

and discovered the tunnel and everyone fled for the hills," she said flatly.

"What is the other story?" I prodded.

"Or else they were digging the tunnel when two kids who were playing around the house went in to listen to the piano player and discovered the tunnel and ran away and told their father who was a prison guard and everyone had to disappear. Either way, Berkman did fourteen years in prison."

"So what happened to his girlfriend?" I asked.

"She was a great gal," Miss Volker said with admiration in her voice. "She continued to travel the world fighting to improve the lives of poor people, but in the end she was at the train station when Berkman was released."

"That's a pretty good love story," I said as we pulled into her driveway. "Why can't we add it to the obituary?"

"Well," she said, "depending on who you talk to there are different dates on the bungled escape. One says it was on July 5 and the other on July 16, so it's hard to link the story to Mrs. Linga's death date."

"Too bad," I said. "But it would be really cool to have a tunnel out of my basement so I could escape from being grounded."

"And I wish someone would dig an escape route out

of here for me too," she said, staring vacantly out the window. "I'd love to step into a hole and vanish with a handsome revolutionary and live a life of exotic adventure."

"Like with Mr. Spizz?" I asked. "He seems to want to take you away."

"He's not a romantic man," she said scornfully. "He's a dud. His idea of a revolution is coloring outside the lines. Ugh! What a bore."

"Well, you won't need a tunnel out of here once all these Norvelters pass away," I said. "Then you can do anything you want with whomever you want."

"Believe me," she replied with a heavy heart, "I know that all too well. And by the way, your nose is bleeding, but only on one side."

"I hate this!" I cried out, and ran my hand under my nose. My fingers were covered with blood.

"Get the flashlight out of the glove box," she ordered.

I pulled the car over and got the flashlight out and tilted my head back and shined it up my own nose. "Oh, yes," she said peering up my dripping nostril. "I can see where a bundle of capillaries has ruptured. We'll take care of that easily."

Take care of that easily echoed back and forth across my mind, and when the echo stopped I knew it was not going to be easy.

18

Without my GET OUT OF JAIL FREE card I was stuck waiting for Miss Volker to call me down for some obituary work, but all the old ladies were doing just fine. They were breathing and eating and talking and singing and not at all making plans to die. I couldn't blame them because I didn't want to die either, even though boredom was killing me. Then, after a few more sun-scorching days of hard digging in the backyard, I suddenly remembered Mr. Greene had said I could work for him at the *Norvelt News*.

But when I asked Mom to let me go work for him she said, "No. You have chores to do right here."

"But he'll pay me," I said.

"And we are now giving you an allowance for your

work around here. Besides you are still grounded." She was tough.

"I'm now going to go cry," I said with my voice rising as I headed out the back door to continue digging the bomb shelter. "If you come outside you won't see any tears because the sun is so blazingly hot my sad tears evaporate before they even have time to leave my swollen red eyes."

"That was nicely spoken," she said, and cracked a smile. "Too bad you didn't put that much thought into not mowing down my corn."

"Please," I begged. "Let me help Mr. Greene."

She softened. "Maybe later," she said. But later never arrived. I was stuck in a world where time had come to a standstill except for my digging. My nose bled on and off, so I worked with a corner of a white handkerchief shoved up my one bad side. I had used a yellow pencil to pack it in there good and tight. From a distance it looked like I had been playing badminton and had a shuttlecock jammed up my nostril.

Every morning I hoped it would rain, but the sky remained clear blue and the temperatures hovered around ninety degrees. At breakfast one morning something seemed wrong when I read This Day In History. Then I realized Mr. Greene had repeated a column from the previous month. He could definitely use my help at the newspaper.

> ***June 16, 1829:*** **Geronimo was born. He became a great Apache warrior who fought for Indian freedom.**
>
> ***June 16, 1858:*** **Abraham Lincoln delivered his "a house divided cannot stand" speech in Springfield, Illinois, which meant the country could not be partly for and partly against slavery.**
>
> ***June 16, 1903:*** **The Ford Motor Company was started. Henry Ford declared that the perfect assembly line factory worker would be a blind man because he could learn one exact task and repeat it endlessly for the rest of his life.**

That was me. I could close my eyes and dig a hole for the rest of my life.

After breakfast I washed out my handkerchief, packed it back into my nose, and went out to the bomb shelter. I loosened up the hard dirt with a pick and then with my shovel I flung the dirt into the wheelbarrow, and when it was full I wheeled it over to where Mom had marked out where she wanted new raised flower beds.

I dug and dug until the whole perimeter of the shelter was about as deep as my knee. By about two o'clock each afternoon I wished the Russians would bomb me out of my misery. As I shoveled I worked on my obituary. "Jack Gantos," I said a little breathlessly, "was born at the Frick Hospital in Mount Pleasant, Pennsylvania, and raised in Norvelt, Pennsylvania, which is a town that is slowly vanishing, and like some Houdini trick it will soon be found in West Virginia. Jack was a good student but learned more from reading books than from staring out the window at school. His parents were total strangers who took him away at birth."

As I spoke out loud I didn't hear Bunny sneaking up on me.

"Are you adopted?" she suddenly asked, which startled me, and I jumped into the air like a crazed cat.

"No," I said after I landed on all fours then sprang back up. "No. I'm *not* adopted."

"Then why'd you say your parents were strangers?"

"Because they were," I said right back. "I had never met them before the moment I was born."

"You are the strange one," she said, and pointed at my face. "And that bloody thing hanging out of your nose is beyond strange."

"Sorry," I said, and turned away as I tugged the blood-crusted handkerchief from my nose then jammed it into the back pocket of my jeans.

"I came here," she said, "to see if your mom will let you come to my house. My dad needs help cleaning the embalming room after he worked on some of those bus group people who died in that head-on collision at the Unity Bridge. He'll pay you."

I swallowed hard. "Will the mess look worse than what was in the Hells Angel's bucket?" I asked.

She counted up the dead people on her stubby fingers. "Five times worse," she said. "Not including the pet dog who we didn't embalm."

I suddenly felt faint. The air was hissing in my ears and it was snowing just behind my eyes. I took a deep breath as I reached for her shoulder to steady myself.

She stepped away. "Don't touch me with your bloody hand," she cried.

I dropped down to my knees and pulled the handkerchief from my pocket. "See this blood," I said faintly, and waved the handkerchief back and forth. "It's my own blood and it makes me dizzy. As much as I want to get away from my house and make money, I can't work for your dad. I'll bleed to death and your father will toss me onto that Aztec altar and embalm me."

She shrugged. "Look, I'm here to give you another chance at doing some fun stuff together," she said. "You are already punished and have to dig this bomb shelter, so how much worse can they make it for you?"

"They could make me dig two bomb shelters," I said.

"Don't be so depressing," she said. "I've got a plan. Now that you can drive, let's borrow Miss Volker's car and cruise into Pittsburgh and go to a Pirates game. I have money for tickets."

"Money is not the point," I said. "If I drive to Pittsburgh I'll be arrested and put into jail. The cops aren't stupid. They'll know I'm a kid. And my parents will kill me."

"As my dad says, 'You have to die sometime,' so why not while you are having fun?"

Suddenly I remembered something we could do at my house without getting into trouble and it would be fun too. "Come in my room," I said with enthusiasm. "And I'll show you something cool."

"Cooler than your bloody nose rag?" she asked, and wrinkled up her face.

"Much cooler," I said as I slowly got back onto my two feet. "Come on."

She reluctantly followed me into the house and down the hall and into my bedroom. "Look," I said proudly, and pointed to the back corner of my room where I had been busy. "I built a little igloo out of my books."

"That looks more like a doghouse," she remarked.

"It's an igloo," I said. "Made out of blocks of books."

"When you were born it's a wonder your parents didn't reject you," she said. "I would have."

"Do you want to read for a while?" I asked. I was eager to keep her in the house after I had spent days digging by myself. Dad had helped haul another empty Norvelt house to West Virginia so he wasn't around, and I always felt guilty in front of Mom so I avoided conversations with her.

"You know I hate reading," Bunny said.

"You want to know a secret?" I asked.

"Sure," she said halfheartedly.

"I love to sniff the insides of books," I said in a whisper. "Because each book has its own special perfume."

"Now you are getting even more weird," she whispered right back, and stepped away from me.

"Let me show you," I said. I grabbed *Thirty Seconds Over Tokyo*, flipped it open, shoved my face into the gutter of the book, and inhaled deeply through my stuffed-up nose. When I lifted my face from the book I swooned and said dreamily, "Ahhh, that was a good one. Now you do it."

She reluctantly grabbed *Custer's Last Stand*, flipped it open, and stuck her little curled-up cashew-size nose into the gutter. She gave it a good sniff, then dropped the book and staggered against my dresser. "History," she said, gagging a bit, "has to be the worst smell in the world. Maybe that's why when you die and people say you are history they mean you smell as bad as a rotten old dead person."

"History isn't dead," I said. "It's everywhere you look. It's alive."

"Well, I'm looking at history," she said, pointing at me. "You used to be a friend, but now you stink as a friend! I came here to give you a second chance and you make me smell the crotch of an old book."

"I'm sorry," I said. "But I'm just trapped here. As soon as I can prove I didn't know there was a bullet in that gun I'll be ungrounded, and then we can do anything normal you want."

"Okay," she said. "But how can you prove you didn't put a bullet in the gun?"

"I have no idea," I said. "None."

"Great," she said in a huff. "Well, Mr. Genius, when you figure it out call me, but I can't sit in your little doghouse and sniff books all summer long because then I'd know I had gone insane!"

She started to walk out of my room. "Don't go," I begged. "Please."

She lowered her shoulder and stiff-armed me out of the way and stomped down the hall and out the door.

From the other end of the hall my mother called out, "Jackie, who was that?"

“A stranger,” I muttered.

I jammed my handkerchief back up my nose and went outside. Before I started digging I fed the turkeys, made sure War Chief had water, then picked up my shovel.

That evening when Dad returned from West Virginia he came into my room. “Hey, Jackie,” he called out. “Are you in here?”

“I’m in the igloo,” I said.

He walked to the back corner of my room. From where I was curled up in my igloo I could just see his work boots.

“That looks more like an outhouse,” he remarked. “Or a tomb. An igloo is round but your books are square, not curved. Do you need glasses?”

I knew what I was thinking was wrong, even evil, but for the first time in my life I wished that another old lady in Norvelt would drop dead at that moment and get me out of my room.

“I found out something interesting,” he said. “Guess who actually is buying up all the Norvelt houses and moving them to West Virginia?”

That stumped me. I couldn’t think of anyone who would do that but my own father. “Who?” I asked.

“Mr. Huffer,” he said, and hooted out loud. “He’s

selling all the houses but keeping the land. Why do you think he'd do that?"

I stood up and my igloo fell apart and settled at my feet. "Maybe he's planning to turn Norvelt into one big cemetery," I guessed.

"That's a possibility," he said, and winked at me. "But he won't have to work too hard at it. The place is already half-dead."

"I'll ask Bunny," I suggested.

In a minute I called her on the phone. The moment she heard my voice she hung up.

19

I called her on July 17th and she hung up.

I called her on the 18th and it sounded like she threw the phone across the room.

I called her on the 19th and she was softening. "You know what I'm doing?" she yelled.

"No," I replied.

"Dropping the phone in the *human innards bucket*!"

I heard something like a splash and a gurgle. I hung up and went directly to the bathroom. My nose was right on time. I looked in the mirror and the first drop was just sliding down over my upper lip.

I called her on the 20th. I was wearing her down. She held up a pair of dentures and made them chatter while she made spooky ghost sounds in the background. Then she hung up.

I called her on the 21st.

"Okay," she said, sounding a little exasperated. "Do you know who put the bullet in your rifle?"

"I'm working on it," I said. "And do you know why your dad is buying and moving all the Norvelt houses to West Virginia?"

There was silence, but I could hear her brain operating. "Okay," she said. "Here's the deal. My dad said to keep it a secret, but I'll tell you. Only you have to sneak out of your house tonight and go on Girl Scout fire patrol with me. It's my night to keep an eye on the empty houses so the Hells Angels don't burn them down."

"Can't you just tell me over the phone?" I asked.

"Nope! Show some backbone and sneak out," she said.

Then I made a decision that almost got me killed forever. "I will sneak out," I quietly replied. "Just tell me where to meet and what time."

"On the other side of the school," she said. "We'll start with section D at ten o'clock."

"Ten?" I repeated.

"Be there or be-ware!" she said, and slammed the phone down.

I went back into my rebuilt igloo and gave the evening a lot of thought. Then I did a little planning and preparation and when it was nine-thirty I jumped into action. I walked into my mom's room and kissed her good night.

"Sleep tight," she said.

"You too," I replied, hoping she would. Then I walked back down the hall, past my bedroom to the basement door, which I had left partway open because of the noisy latch. I slipped sideways through the doorway and picked up the flashlight I had left on the top step. I turned it on and carefully went down the basement steps. I passed the washing machine and furnace and entered the old coal bin which was no longer used. There was a coal chute, like a sliding board, that went up to a metal hatch like a bigger version of a mail slot where the coal had been delivered. I scampered up the chute. I opened the latch and swung the hatch open. It didn't creak because I had earlier oiled the hinges. I turned my flashlight off and wiggled my way out and gently lowered the hatch behind me. I jammed the flashlight into my back pocket and walked quietly behind the garage, where I had a bag with my Grim Reaper costume. I put on the black robe and kept the mask pushed back on top of my head for now.

I stepped out from behind the garage and saw my mother's light was already off. If my dad came home late he would never check on me. I picked up my pace and headed for the school.

Bunny was already there and was smoking a cigarette.

"Well, look who decided to be a man for a change," she remarked when she saw me. She held out the pack of smokes. "Want one?"

"No wonder your growth is stunted," I said, and pushed her hand away.

"I can still kick your tail so watch your mouth," she started up.

"Let's just get going," I said. "And put out the cigarette. We're not here to start fires."

She threw it down and ground it out with her shoe. "Okay," she said. "Since you showed up, here is the deal with my dad. He buys up all the empty Norvelt houses and is selling them to Eleanor, West Virginia, because that is a bigger town and more people die there and business is better there. He figures he is going to have to shut down here and we'll move there."

"Well, that makes sense," I said. "But moving the houses is driving Miss Volker nuts. She loves this town and can't stand to see it die off."

"Believe me," Bunny said wisely, "I've seen a lot of people looking at things that have died off—and they get over it. So she'll get over it too."

"What about the land?" I asked. "Are you going to build a huge cemetery?

"No. My dad wants to build a big development called Hufferville," she said.

"Are you pulling my leg?" I asked.

Just then Bunny grabbed my shoulder and we stopped walking. "Listen," she said.

"It's a car," I said. "Not a motorcycle."

"They've been sneaking up on the town in cars," she said. "There have been a half-dozen small fires that haven't been reported because Dad doesn't want to scare people."

The car was slowly heading our way. We ducked down behind a hedge until it passed and then the brake lights came on. A Hells Angel got out of the passenger side and popped the trunk open.

"What do we do next?" I whispered.

She didn't answer. Instead she showed me the silver whistle she had on a string around her neck. "The secret signal," she whispered back.

The Hells Angel grabbed a can of gasoline and walked over to the porch of the house and began to slosh gas onto the boards and railing.

I looked at Bunny but she didn't move. I elbowed her. She reached into her pocket and pulled out two fist-size rocks. She gave me one. I nodded. Then she stood up and yelled, "Hey!"

The guy stopped and turned toward us and she threw her rock. It hit the house. He dropped his gas can and I heard his metal lighter flip open.

"Hey!" I yelled, and threw my rock. I had no idea

where it went, but in an instant the entire porch burst into flames as if I had thrown a grenade. Bunny was blowing her whistle and the Hells Angel with his wild hair and bushy beard could see me in the firelight.

He pointed at me. "Kid," he growled, "I'm gonna kill you!"

That was the moment I realized my mask was pushed up on my head and he could see my face, and I could see that he was running in my direction.

"Run for your life!" Bunny cried out, and she took off.

I ran in another direction. I don't think the Hells Angel followed because I could hear their car take off and peel rubber as it hit the main road.

I slowed down for a moment and that was when I could hear Bunny's whistle start up again, and then other whistles followed. The Girl Scouts had a system set up, but I didn't have time to admire it because I knew that the fire department would be called and that fire whistle would go off and wake the entire town and I knew Mom would hop up and the first thing she would do is dash into my room and check on me to make sure my room wasn't on fire.

I ran as hard as I could with the costume bunched up under one arm. My mask went flying off my face but I didn't stop. Just when I got past Miss Volker's house I heard the loud fire whistle. I knew Mom wouldn't find me in my room. I couldn't get there fast enough. There was only one thing I could do. I ran to the back of our garage and opened the little door. I ripped the costume over my head and threw it to one side, then I quickly opened the souvenir chest and grabbed the binoculars and ran back out the little door and around the garage and up the steps to our back door and in a flash I was in the kitchen. Mom was just flicking on the light.

"Where were you?" she asked, and I could see the concern on her face because she had been in my room.

"Here," I said, avoiding the question as I held out the binoculars. "Quick. Which house is on fire?"

She held the binoculars to her eyes, and as she stood at the kitchen sink and scanned the town I slipped down the hall to my room and kicked off my shoes and threw the flashlight on the bed and wiped the sweat off my face with my pillow.

When I returned to the kitchen she was on the phone with Mr. Spizz. The fire had been put out by neighbors almost as quickly as it was started. The house was scorched, but not burned.

By the time she got off the phone I was in the bathroom.

"Good night," she said.

"Sleep tight," I said through the closed door.

20

After that night I just stayed around the house like a good angel. Mom did ask me how I got out of my bedroom so fast to get the binoculars. I gave her that innocent look and just said, "Boy, you must have been in a sound sleep. The fire whistle was going on for a long time before you woke." That seemed to satisfy her and, like any lie, the fewer details you give the better it is.

But it wasn't Mom who I thought was going to kill me. I was just hauling a wheelbarrow full of dirt around the side of the house when a huge man roared up the driveway on a motorcycle. He had a long beard combed down the middle and pulled back over his shoulders and tied together in a knot behind his neck. He looked just like the Hells Angel who said he was going to kill me. I'm dead, I thought when he got off his chopper and reached into one of the black leather saddlebags and pulled out a hammer and spike and swaggered in my direction.

I figured he would pick me up, press me against a tree trunk, and drive the spike through my forehead and leave me hanging there while he burned our house down. All I had to fight back with was a pick and shovel, and I was so tired I could hardly lift either of them to defend myself. My only regret was that I hadn't written down my obituary, but I figured Miss Volker would do a good one. I had read her This Day In History column and July 28 was when Henry VIII had Thomas Cromwell executed, and Robespierre was guillotined, and a U.S. Army bomber accidentally flew into the seventy-ninth floor of the Empire State Building and killed fourteen people. It was already a good day for death, and I was about to go down in history.

"Hey, kid," he called out, and waved his hammer at me as if he were Thor and about to crush my little head with one massive blow. "Where is War Chief?"

"What?" I yelled back, and got ready to run away.

"Your pony," he said as he stomped toward me. "I'm the farrier who is here to fix your pony."

"I thought you were a Hells Angel," I said.

"I used to be," he replied. "But fighting all the time

and being really drunk and nasty got boring. So now I just take care of animals."

"Over there," I yelled back with some relief, and pointed to where War Chief was trying to catch flies in his mouth.

He turned around and grabbed more tools from his saddlebags. Mom was down working at the pants factory, so I just hung around with the farrier. He took off War Chief's old worn-down horseshoes. "Boy, this sure is overdue," he said as he began to carefully clip the hooves and peel away the old layers. He filed them down and shaped them. Then he gently went from hoof to hoof and cleaned the frog. After that he nailed new shoes onto War Chief. Finally he went back to his motorcycle and returned with a bunch of carrots. As he rubbed War Chief's nose and fed him he turned to me and asked, "Is your mom here to pay me?"

This was my chance to escape. "She told me that she was trading me for your work, so you can take me with you," I said in my polite voice. "I'm more valuable than money."

He glanced at me and grinned. "I'm sure you are," he replied. "But it's a lot cheaper to keep money in my pocket than to feed a kid. I'll hold out for the cash."

"I'm sure she'll pay you," I said. "She works really

hard and is the most honest person I know—more honest than me."

"She told me on the phone that if she wasn't here to go to the pants factory," he said, "so I'll go down there."

And then I desperately blurted out, "Do you want to see the igloo I made out of books?"

He looked me in the eye then reached forward and placed his big, soft hand on my forehead. "I think you've been out in the sun too long," he said. "You better go in there and get some rest."

21

Finally the telephone rang and in a minute I was back at Miss Volker's house.

"Who died?" I asked with a little too much enthusiasm.

"No one," she said, and gave me a cross look. "Drive over to Mertie-Jo's house and tell her I need more cookies," she instructed, and waved her hand toward a ten-dollar bill on my desk. "These old ladies really love them for dessert, and since I can't bake anymore it is the least I can do to help your mom out with those great meals she cooks."

"Sure," I replied, and crushed the ten-dollar bill into the palm of my hand. I was eager to visit Mertie-Jo. I loved the way she smiled at me like a dazed sunflower.

It was the first time I had driven by myself and that

made me nervous, and then going to Mertie-Jo's house made me more nervous because I liked her but would never tell her because I couldn't even say I liked her to myself. Even though I drove slowly to her house I felt as if I had sprinted all the way there because I was kind of sweaty and breathing hard when I arrived. I wiped my hand across my nose and checked for blood as I walked from the car to her porch. I was clean. I rang the doorbell, and when she opened the door and saw it was me she smiled her special smile as her head slowly descended, like the sun setting against the beautiful beach of her tanned shoulder. "Hi," she said softly. "Nice to see you."

"Hi," I chirped, and smiled brightly as if I were a blinding sun that had just risen.

She squinted at me and I knew I was supposed to start a conversation, but it was as if I had suddenly had a total eclipse of the sun and my mind faded to black and became wordless. After a few quiet minutes she raised her head back up and asked, "So, why did you ring my doorbell?"

Her question snapped me out of myself. "Oh, Miss Volker needs more Thin Mints," I replied.

"Must be my lucky day," she said, finally delighted by something I said. "I sold a box to Mr. Spizz and one to Mr. Huffer, and now Miss Volker can have all I've got left," Mertie-Jo offered. "We're moving, and I can't take them with me."

"Why are you leaving?" I asked, sounding a little too alarmed.

"My dad needs a job," she explained. "I mean, it's been good that I'm making money on the cookies but it's not enough to keep us going. Everyone in Norvelt would have to eat about a thousand cookies each day in order for us to get by."

"I'd eat a thousand cookies," I said. "If you'd stay."

"It wouldn't make me feel real good to be the cause of your grotesque weight gain," she said, and puffed out her cheeks in a chubby way.

"Well, I'm sorry you are leaving," I said.

"I'm not sorry," she replied. "Norvelt is kind of dead. We're moving to Pittsburgh."

I didn't know what else to say so I showed her the ten-dollar bill, which was a little sweaty, and said, "Miss Volker will buy all your Thin Mints."

"Great! Wait right here," she replied, and closed the door.

In a minute she opened it up and her dad stepped onto the porch with three big brown boxes. "Where do you want these, son?" he asked.

"The trunk," I replied, and pointed toward the car. "I'll open it for you."

"Did you drive here?" he asked as we walked down the driveway.

"Yeah," I said proudly.

"You must be mature for your age," he remarked.

"I am," I said, and proudly puffed out my chest as we reached the car. Then I opened the trunk and when I lifted the lid I let out the most high-pitched girlie scream of my life. "Oh cheeze-us!" I cried out, and jumped up and down with my arms flopping around. "There is a dead old lady in the trunk!"

Mertie-Jo's dad dropped the boxes and hurried to where I was standing. "Looks like she's been dead a long time," he said softly with a puzzled expression on his face. "Why, she's become a skeleton."

It was a skeleton. A very white skeleton but wearing a lady's flowered dress and red shoes.

"Wait a minute," he said, perking up. "This is a fake skeleton—the kind they have in science class." He reached into the trunk, lifted it out by its neck, and rattled it back and forth. "Oo-oooo-oooh," he moaned, and shook the skeleton in front of my face. The jaw broke away and bounced off the toe of my sneaker.

"Ouch," I said, and picked it up. I turned to look at Mertie-Jo but she was back in the house. Through the kitchen window I spotted her on the telephone, and it didn't take me long to realize she was probably calling

Bunny because faintly I heard her squeal, "Oh cheeze-us!" And then she jumped around with her arms flopping up and down as I had done. She was just like Miss Volker making fun of Mr. Spizz. I felt my cheeks redden and for a moment I felt sorry for him until I touched my nose and there was a little smudge of blood on my upper lip. I wiped Mr. Spizz out of my mind just as quickly as I wiped the blood away on the back of my hand.

Her dad dropped the dressed skeleton back into the trunk. "I'll just put these boxes in the backseat," he offered, and I could tell by his hokey voice that he was laughing at me himself. I walked around him to the front seat and slipped behind the wheel.

"Good luck in Pittsburgh," I said after he closed my door. I wanted him to like me even if Mertie-Jo made fun of me. I started the engine and pressed down on the gas to make the engine roar. The moment Mr. Kernecky stepped back from the car I punched the gas pedal and took off like I was a real man and not some spineless kid who was afraid of a plastic skeleton in a dress. When I got to Miss Volker's house I stacked up all three boxes on top of each other and carried them as if I were Hercules. It almost killed me.

After I put the cookies in the kitchen I didn't want to go home, so I began to polish all of Miss Volker's scuffed-up old-lady shoes. That was when the telephone rang.

"Miss Volker's house," I said politely.

"This is Mr. Huffer," he said, and even though I couldn't see him I could tell he was in his sad pose. "Tell Miss Volker that an ambulance has just dropped off Mrs. Hamsby. She looks in rather bad shape and her children called to tell me to go ahead and cremate her immediately. I am preparing to do just that in a short while, so if she wants to examine Mrs. Hamsby she needs to get here on the double."

"Hold on a minute," I said, and lowered the phone.

Before I could say anything Miss Volker stood up and walked gingerly across the floor in her bare feet. "Which one?" she asked, and stared out the window toward the funeral parlor.

"Mrs. Hamsby," I replied.

"I sure liked her," Miss Volker said in a quiet voice. "Ask him if there are any unusual details. If not, tell him to go ahead and later I'll send you by to pick up the paperwork so I can sign it."

I relayed the message to Mr. Huffer. "Tell her it looks like she died of natural causes," he said. "She called the operator and complained of body spasms. The ambulance was sent but they found her expired in the kitchen. Most likely another old-lady heart attack."

"Go ahead with it," I said, and he hung up.

Then as I continued to polish the shoes and buff them, Miss Volker walked over to her needlepoint map and stuck a red map pin into Mrs. Hamsby's roof at A-41. She continued to stand by the map and tidy up the pins, but I knew there was nothing to tidy up. She was just letting time pass as she collected her thoughts.

"Better sharpen your pencil," she called over to me. "I'm in a mood today. Mrs. Hamsby was one of the good ones. I hate to see her go—though it is for the better."

It was always hard for me to think that death was for the better, but there was nothing I could say to Miss Volker to change her mind because I knew she thought it was for the good of the town that the old ones move on.

"When the sun goes down each day it turns its back on the present and steps into the past," she started with a strong, even voice, "but it is never dead. History is a form of nature, like the mountains and sea and sky. History began when the universe began with a 'Big Bang,' which is one reason why most people think history has to be about a big event like a catastrophe or a moment of divine creation, but every living soul is a book of their own history, which sits on the ever-growing shelf in the library of human memories. Sadly, we don't know the history of every person who ever lived, and unfortunately many books about historic people, like the lost Greek and Latin and Arabic texts, are gone forever and are as lost as the lost world of Atlantis.

"But here in Norvelt we had one of those librarians who collected the tiniest books of human history. Mrs. Hamsby, who died today at age seventy-seven, was the first postmistress of Norvelt and she saved all the lost letters, those scraps of history that ended up as *undeliverable* in a quiet corner of Norvelt. But they were not *unwanted*. Mrs. Hamsby carefully pinned each envelope to the wall, so that the rooms of her house were lined from floor to ceiling with letter upon letter, and when you arrived for tea it appeared as if the walls were papered with the overlapping scales of an ancient fish. You were always welcome to unpin any envelope and read the orphaned letter, as if you were browsing in a library full of abandoned histories.

"Each room has its own motif of stamps, so that the parlor room is papered with human stamps as if people such as Lincoln, or Queen Elizabeth, or Joan of Arc had come to visit. The bedroom has the stamps of lovely landscapes you might discover in your dreams, and the bathroom has stamps with oceans and rivers and rain. Each stamp is a snapshot of a story, of one thin slice of history captured like an ant in amber. There is history in every blink of an eye, and Mrs. Hamsby knew well that within the lost letter was the folded soul of the writer wrapped in the body of the envelope and mailed into the unknown. And for this tiny museum of lost history we citizens of Norvelt thank her."

"That was a good one," I said quietly with admiration, finally looking up from my pad. "I'd love to see the inside of her house."

"You might," she replied. "Or maybe your dad will haul it off to West Virginia, where I bet they'll rip every one of those letters down and toss them in a furnace."

"They wouldn't do that," I said. "Would they?"

"It's been done before," she said. "Which is why we have to save the history we have. You never know what small bit of it might change your life—or change the whole world!"

I turned my pad to a clean page and sharpened up my pencil. She looked me in the eye. I looked her right back. "Hit it!" I said.

"On this day in history, August 1, 1944, a book of letters written by a child was close to being destroyed in the blink of an eye. This was the day that Anne Frank, a fifteen-year-old Jewish girl, last wrote in her diary of the two years she and seven of her family and friends hid in the secret rooms above her father's office building, while the Nazis searched for Jews to deport to concentration camps. Three days later they were betrayed and captured. Anne and her sister, Margot, were sent to the Bergen-Belsen death camp.

"Anne's diary, which the Nazis thought was so meaningless, was thrown onto the floor of her hiding place. The diary was recovered by a friend and carefully preserved so that someday she could return it to Anne, but Anne and her sister died of typhus in the concentration camp just weeks before the camp's liberation.

"Only her father, Otto Frank, survived, and he was given the book when he returned to his building after the war. After reading the diary he decided to have it published, even though many people did not find it worthy. But in the United States, one person who felt the true power of the diary—a diary as loud as the six million Jews who lost their voices—was our own Eleanor Roosevelt. She wrote the introduction to the first American edition and was so deeply moved by this young girl's words that she said the diary was 'one of the wisest and most moving commentaries on war and its impact on human beings that I have ever read.'

"We are proud in Norvelt that our men and women fought in the war to liberate oppressed people and allow their found voices to record the history of that terrible time."

"That was really important," I said to Miss Volker as I raced to get her words down on paper.

"Anne Frank can never be forgotten," she replied with reverence. "And it is yet one more reminder why I stay to take care of this town. Mrs. Roosevelt is the greatest American woman who ever lived and she has always been devoted to those who suffer. And to this day she herself is suffering from a terrible illness, so how can I give up my duties when she has given so much of her life for us?"

I got this one typed up as Miss Volker stretched out on the couch and took a restorative nap. She always needed to recharge her batteries after a passionate obituary. She was still sleeping when I finished. I covered her with the old knitted afghan and walked down to see Mr. Greene.

"It can only mean one thing when you walk into my office," he said as he tapped out his pipe.

"Yep," I said, and handed him the obituary.

He read it on the spot. "Those old ladies seem to be dropping like flies," he said, and pressed more tobacco into the charred bowl of his pipe. "A real shame. Someone should look into all these deaths."

"Isn't that what the newspaper is for?" I asked. "To look into things?"

"I'll take that under advisement," he said. Then he lit a match.

22

"It's time," Dad announced, and rubbed his hands together as he stood up from the breakfast table, "to get an elevated perspective on Norvelt."

"What's that mean?" Mom asked suspiciously, looking up from Mrs. Hamsby's obituary with tears in her eyes.

I knew what Dad meant.

"Time for me to join the birds," Dad said smoothly as he flapped his arms. "Just look out the window."

I leaped from my seat and nearly cracked the window glass with my forehead. The J-3 was sitting at the beginning of the runway and was polished, painted, and poised to fly. "When did you pull it out of the garage?" I asked without taking my eyes off the plane.

I just had to take a ride in it. And secretly I wanted to fly it!

"Early this morning," he said casually, and tilted back in his chair, full of satisfaction from finishing a job Mom thought he couldn't complete. "When I returned from dropping another empty Norvelt house in West Virginia, I had a couple of the workers help me move the J-3, then lift the wing in place so I could bolt it on."

"Can I go with you? Can I? Please?" I begged. I wished I had never traded Mom my ONE FLIGHT IN THE J-3 ticket.

"No, you can't get in that plane," Mom said firmly, and she meant it. "It's not even inspected."

"Oh cheeze-us-crust!" I grumbled.

"I wish you would stop that fake cursing," she scolded. "It's just as rude as the real thing."

"A test flight is all the inspection it needs," Dad replied. "But Jack can help me get her ready."

"Whatever you need," I said excitedly. "I'll be your ground crew."

"Then follow me," he replied.

"If you don't mind, I'll watch from the porch," Mom informed us, and stood up to clear the table. "That is, unless you need me."

"I'll handle it," I said to her. It was finally my chance to be a part of the airplane crew. Dad didn't want me hanging out in the garage with him because it annoyed Mom. She thought that fixing up the J-3 was too much fun for a kid who was being punished. She liked it a lot more when I was digging the bomb shelter in the sun.

In a few minutes we were standing in front of the J-3 as Dad explained my duties with military precision. "Your job will seem scary," he said, summing things up as he put his hand on my shoulder. "But it's not dangerous as long as you do everything the right way—just like gun safety. Follow the rules, okay?"

"Okay!" I shot back, then took my place standing at the rear of the plane. I didn't want to mess anything up like I did when we went hunting.

Dad placed both hands on the varnished wooden propeller. He rocked it back and forth a few times to get the fuel flowing into the engine, and once he smelled it he put his entire weight into a big swing. The engine started, and the sound of the spinning propeller was as loud as a thousand-pound wasp. My hair blew straight back but the plane didn't budge forward because Dad had the wheels chocked with big wedges of firewood. I gripped the tail and watched him make sure to stay out of the path of the propeller as he trotted around the wing and back to the fuselage, where he opened the flimsy cockpit door. He hopped up into his seat, closed the door, and stuck his hand straight out the window and gave me the thumbs-up.

That was my signal. I dropped to my hands and knees and crawled forward alongside the humming body of the plane. The prop wash peppered me with stinging bits of loose dirt and small gravel, but no big rocks. When I reached the left-side wheel under the fuselage I pulled away the wood chock in front of the tire. Then I rolled over twice under the belly of the plane to the other wheel. Once I removed the chock I scampered back to the tail and waited. When Dad waved the back flaps up and down that was my cue. I ran and jumped into the shallow bomb shelter, then flipped myself over and peeked up over the edge. He gunned the engine and the J-3 began to jitter and lean forward, and once it started rolling down the runway it quickly picked up speed. I jumped out of the bomb shelter and ran after it like I was Orville Wright chasing after his brother, Wilbur.

"Wait for me!" I yelled. Maybe he had waited, but I couldn't tell because by the time I reached the very end of the runway I didn't know if he was off the ground or under it because I was covered by a thick brown cloud of loose dirt. I squinted and coughed and covered my face.

"Jackie!" Mom shouted from the back porch. "Where is he?"

I still couldn't see him but I could hear him. "I'm not sure," I shouted back, and scanned the sky for any trace of him. "Maybe he's going to Kitty Hawk." I had been reading about the Wright brothers. "Or to New York to fly circles around the Statue of Liberty." Wilbur had done that and I was sure it was a stunt that Dad would try.

"He'll be back," Mom reasoned. "He has more empty houses to truck to West Virginia. And knowing him, he won't pass up the chance to make this town disappear so he can fly out of here for good."

In the distance we could faintly hear what sounded like a mosquito coming our way. It was quickly growing louder and we knew he was circling back, but before we could spot him he flew in low over the house and Mom and I hit the deck.

"Jerk!" she yelled, and waved her white-knuckled fist at him as she popped up from the porch, but by then he was already beyond Fenton's gas station.

"That looks like fun," I gushed. I just couldn't wait to fly the plane.

"*Dangerous* is what you mean," she remarked as she brushed dirt off her knees. "He keeps saying that plane is our ticket out of here," Mom said derisively. "But all I want to do is slap it out of the sky."

"Are you afraid he'll crash?" I asked.

"That is a really foolish question," she said with her voice rising sky high. "Of course I'm afraid. He's my husband and your father and he's flying around somewhere up there like a kite that broke away from its string. Now go get me those Jap binoculars again. I want to see what he is up to."

I dashed off to the garage and ran inside and flipped open the trunk and grabbed the binoculars and was heading out the garage door when he came in low over the rustling trees and just missed the back porch. Mom screamed and her legs buckled as she plopped down on her rear.

"I'm going to kill him for that alone," Mom swore as she swatted more dirt off the back of her pants.

"He's just playing," I said, trying to make her relax even though my heart was pounding.

But she was serious. "You better tell Miss Volker to start writing *his* obituary, because he is sure to kill himself." She reached for the binoculars.

"But he's not an original Norvelter," I said as she scanned the air. "It won't matter to her."

"Now what is he doing?" she asked in her huffy voice as she concentrated her attention through the binoculars.

I looked where she looked and to me he was about the size of a toy. He was dive-bombing a house like the Japanese did when they bombed Pearl Harbor. He was roaring down toward the roof, then he would pull up and circle around and do it again.

"He's really lost his mind now," Mom uttered. "I

think he just buzzed one of those empty houses and threw his shoe out the window as he flew by."

"Really?" I asked. "He threw his shoe at a house?"

"Yes," Mom said, confirming what she had seen before. "Now he just threw his other shoe!"

"He's like one of those flying aces from World War I who would just throw the bombs at their targets like hand grenades," I said.

"Or," she said without enthusiasm, "he is like a mentally ill criminal who should be locked up!"

"He's just having fun," I cried out.

"What if you lived in that house?" she asked. "Would you think it's fun?"

"You said it was empty," I reminded her.

"I hope I'm right," she said. "If some old lady is in there she just might drop dead."

That was a good point. Then suddenly I saw him in the distance as he nosed the plane down toward the far end of the runway. I could feel my chest tighten as the wheels got closer and closer to the ground. "You can do it," I said to myself. "Come on. Bring it in!" And then the wheels touched down and he bounced up a bit but stayed in control, and in a minute he cut back on the throttle and rolled right up to our end of the runway.

Once the prop stopped spinning I ran up to greet him. "What were you doing?" I asked. "We watched you buzzing that one house over and over."

"Oh, I was off having a little fun," he said with a grin. "I have to move that house to West Virginia so I was just using it to practice my dive-bombing technique."

"Well, I'd say you blew it to West Virginia," I confirmed.

"Next time I'll get some balloons," he suggested. "And fill 'em with water. That'll be fun."

"We can drench them from the air," I said, including myself in the bombing raid.

"No, you won't," Mom said from over my shoulder. "You will not be doing that with your father, so don't even ask."

Just then the telephone rang.

"I'll get it," I yelled, and took off for the kitchen.

It was Miss Volker. "What is your father doing?" she hollered in a voice as shrill as the fire whistle. "I just got a call from Mrs. Vinyl and she said she thought Norvelt was being invaded by the Russians and that she was having a spell."

"Did you call the ambulance?" I asked.

"Of course not," she replied. "I told her to take a Bayer aspirin and have a glass of dandelion wine and relax in a hot bath. And why does your father have a plane anyway?" she asked.

"He wants to fly out of town and never come back," I replied. "He said his slice of the American pie is too thin in this town."

"He doesn't know what thin is," she said with a great helping of scorn in her voice. "In the Depression you had pie made out of grass clippings. Believe me, if he leaves he'll find out it's a dog-eat-dog world out there. The grass clippings are not always greener on the other side."

"That's kind of what Mom says," I replied.

"Well, let's hope he is wise enough to listen to her," she said, and then the phone dropped and clattered across the floor.

"Are you okay?" I yelled into the receiver.

"Dang hands!" she hollered from a distance, and I could just imagine her pitching a fit. "Goodbye," she hollered again, and the phone went dead.

23

Maybe something else went dead too. Over the next few days Miss Volker had me telephone Mrs. Vinyl's house about twenty times to check up on her like we did with Mrs. Dubicki. Finally Miss Volker was worried enough to call me down to her house. All the way there I was filled with fear that Dad had killed Mrs. Vinyl.

"You don't think my father gave her a heart attack?" I asked when I let myself into Miss Volker's living room.

"No," she replied. "Because I spoke with her the next day and she had one of your mom's casseroles for dinner."

"That's right," I said, recalling that I took it to the Community Center and gave it to Mr. Spizz.

"Well, we better drive to her house and pay her a visit," she suggested. "Help me out to the car."

"Do you want me to wear my Grim Reaper costume again?" I asked, and took her hand.

"Don't bother," she said. "I have a suspicion the reaper has already paid number B-19 a visit."

That reminded me of something. "Why do you have a dressed skeleton in your trunk?" I asked as we turned onto the Norvelt road.

"My sister left it in there," she said. "She used it for a drawing model."

"Well, it scared me half to death," I said.

"Thank your lucky stars it was only *half* to death," she replied. "You could have gotten the full dose."

When we entered Mrs. Vinyl's house we saw the result of a *full* death. Mr. Huffer's stretcher on wheels was already in the hallway.

"That man has a nose for death," Miss Volker said, noticing the stretcher.

"No kidding," I replied.

"She's in the bedroom," he called out when he heard our footsteps. His respectful, whispery voice sounded like air leaking out of a crypt. "I've already called her daughter."

"Did she opt for cremation?" Miss Volker asked.

"Yes," he replied with a disagreeable tone in his voice.

"All these kids live too far away to care about giving their mothers a proper service. It's just cheaper and easier to have me mail them the ashes so they can put mom in a mantelpiece vase, or in a shoe box in the back of the closet. But mark my words, people will still want to be buried in the ground. A tombstone is a carved page in a book of human history. It will last forever. A jar of dust just looks like something you emptied out of a vacuum cleaner." After that unusual outburst he struck his sad little teapot pose. I didn't know how sad he really was, because now he could buy her house and move it to West Virginia. But I didn't say that to Miss Volker because she would have put him in a shoe box.

"How did you know she was dead?" I asked Mr. Huffer.

"Spizz told me," he replied. "He stopped by to collect the newspaper money and found her."

"That busybody is into everyone's business," Miss Volker remarked with contempt. "He probably helped her kick the bucket."

"I don't think so," Mr. Huffer said. "Looks like she had a fit of some kind while having a midnight snack."

"Jack, you stay here," Miss Volker said as she and Mr. Huffer stepped toward the bedroom. "She may not be properly dressed and I promise you don't want to see a naked old dead person."

I didn't argue that point. I stayed in the kitchen, and like Bunny I opened the refrigerator. Aside from some wrapped-up pieces of Mom's dinners, there wasn't much. I was just going to take a slice of mushroom and cheese casserole when Miss Volker came out complaining about how some people were selling their houses to Eleanor, West Virginia.

"Well," Mr. Huffer said without giving himself away, "this town can't remain a museum piece. Plus there is a lot of good land here that could be useful again."

"I don't want it to be a museum," Miss Volker said. "I want it to be a shining city on a hill—an example of what a Roosevelt community should strive to be."

"Times change," Mr. Huffer said weakly.

"Time has nothing to do with it," Miss Volker said strongly. "We have a choice! It is the people who live here that can change Norvelt for the better or the worse."

"Nothing lasts forever," said Mr. Huffer as he shrugged.

I just knew what Miss Volker was going to say. I could hear the bile in the pit of her stomach boiling and the words steaming up in her mouth before her lips parted. And then she fired off the red-hot words. "History lasts *forever*," she snapped. "And we'll be judged by our history."

"History may last forever," Mr. Huffer said in his humble sad-man voice. "We just won't."

Miss Volker lifted her hands and put them around Mr. Huffer's neck. "If my hands were good enough I'd strangle you," she said, and then smiled.

So did Mr. Huffer. "Are your hands good enough to sign this death certificate?" he asked.

Miss Volker nodded at me. "He's my hired hands," she said with a chuckle, and as we had done before, we held the pen between my hand and hers and managed to scrawl out a signature.

We left Mr. Huffer behind to collect the body and returned to Miss Volker's house. I took my place at the desk, and she began to breathe deeply and pace the living room and twist herself left and right and all around like a Slinky, and before long I was writing the obituary as quickly as I could.

"Seventeen years ago," Miss Volker joyously cried out as if she were addressing a theater audience, "Mrs. Vinyl had the best birthday party of the year. This was during the war and so having a birthday cake was pretty rare because of the rationing of flour and sugar. We all had eggs and milk because of our chickens and dairy cows. But somehow the friends of Mrs. Vinyl managed to save up enough tablespoons and teaspoons of flour and sugar and they made her a huge cake, and it had to be huge because they also made their own hand-dipped wax candles which were thicker than normal birthday candles and colored with cherry, dandelion, and grape juice—and there were sixty candles! It was a splendid cake and we all gathered around for the lighting of the candles and the singing of the birthday song. But before Mrs. Vinyl could make a wish and blow out the candles, those little flames joined together into one massive flame that was tall enough to scorch and melt the light fixture hanging over the table. I think the wicks in those candles must have been taken from a roll of dynamite fuses. They sure burned hot and fast, and while everyone was trying to save the light fixture the heat from the candles burned a coal black crater into the top of the cake. Well, it looked awful, but that didn't stop us from eating it. Afterward everyone had crusty black lips as if they had eaten a plateful of ashes. We just laughed and laughed and Mrs. Vinyl laughed the loudest. She was a great woman and her sons both served honorably in the war and as a nation we honor her."

Then Miss Volker lowered her head in prayer and after a quiet space of time, when she once more began to speak, her voice had dropped as if a shadow had passed over her heart.

"Given that this is August 6 it would be impossible

not to remember that this is the anniversary of the dropping of the first atomic bomb on the city of Hiroshima. Most people think that the atomic bombing of Hiroshima was necessary for ending the war," she continued. "And there is some truth to that, given that the Japanese were prepared to fight to the last person to protect their country. But what the atomic bombing of Hiroshima should teach everyone is that you don't win a war by being more moral or ethical or nicer or more democratic than your enemy. And God has nothing to do with winning or losing. There are over four thousand religions in the world, so it is impossible to claim that one God is more powerful than another God. Keep in mind that there are plenty of good civilizations full of God-worshipping people that are now lost to history. The American Indians were nicer than the settlers and look where it got them. Dead! No, you win a war by being tougher and meaner and more ruthless than your enemy. You beat, burn, and crush them into the ground. This is the historic rule of winning a war. Look what we did to the Japanese. Hiroshima was not a big military target. Nor was it even a battle. It was an out-and-out sneak-attack slaughtering of innocent people. It was a massacre. We killed seventy thousand civilians in one atomic blink, and seventy thousand more died a little later on. No nation has ever before been this cruel and inhumane and killed more people so quickly in the whole bloody history of the world.

"So as we remember Mrs. Vinyl and honor her heroic sons, let us remember that the only way to turn enemies into friends is with respect," she stated firmly. "Never call them 'Japs' again. That won't do. Remember what the Bible teaches us, 'Thou shalt not avenge, nor bear any grudge against the children of thy people, but thou shalt love thy neighbor as thyself.' "

I typed it up as she settled down on the couch like a cat curling into a comfortable shape. Then she wrapped her afghan around herself and bowed her head as if it were the lowering of a theater curtain. After I typed a page I looked back and her eyes were closed. Her breathing was like a cat purring.

I finished up and ran the obit down to Mr. Greene. He skimmed it over, and with his pipe jammed deep into one tobacco-stained corner of his mouth he spoke out the other. "Mrs. Vinyl was only seventy-seven," he remarked as he rocked back and forth on the soles of his heavy black boots. "A shame how the good die young."

"What about Marilyn Monroe dying yesterday?" I said. "She really died young."

"That was a crime," he insisted, and removed his pipe then sharply pointed the stem at me. "Mark my words, there is something fishy about the way Miss

Monroe died and I think there is something fishy going on in this town." He pulled the pipe out of his mouth and poked the air with it as if typesetting an exclamation point on his accusation.

I stepped away from him as he kept his hard eyes fixed on me. When I reached the door I turned and sped home.

The next morning Mrs. Vinyl's obituary ran in the paper.

As Dad read it I could read his face and I knew he was annoyed. "Ex-soldiers like me who fought in the war," he said with checked anger, "are busy trying to forget what horrors we went through and she's just reminding us of how bad it was." He pressed the paper down on the table with both hands, then stood straight up. His face was like a movie screen of unhappy memories.

"Maybe she thinks that remembering it is a good thing," I suggested. "Because if you do something bad and forget about it, then you might do the same bad thing again. But if you always remember it, then chances are you won't do the bad thing twice."

"I suppose," he said, and cracked his knuckles out of habit. "But believe me. Nobody has forgotten Hiroshima. If fact, what we did to the Japs is what we fear the Russians will do to us. See," he said pointedly to me, "one war leads to another and another and each just gets worse. Speaking of wars," he added, turning on me in the only way he could, "you need to get back to work on that bomb shelter. Now that Miss Volker has got us all worked up about the atomic bomb, we have to put our energy into surviving it."

"Why can't we just put our *energy* into not having any atomic bombs?" I asked. "Wouldn't that be a lot easier?"

"It would be a lot easier if everyone just listened to me," he suggested, and jerked his thumb toward the door. "Now go dig the shelter."

"But you said it's a fake shelter," I replied. "So why bother?"

His voice jumped right back. "Because now that I've been reminded of Hiroshima I don't think the shelter should be fake. See, Miss Volker has changed my mind already. Her talk of history has me fearing the *future*!"

I could tell that it would be a lot better if I just went outside and dug the shelter. "Hey, Dad," I asked, "can I borrow your transistor radio?"

"I just got it," he moaned. "It was expensive."

"Well, I could listen to the Pirates game," I said, "while I dig."

"They don't play ball in the morning," he said. "Nice try."

"Can I listen to the news?" I asked.

"The battery is low," he said.

"I could run to the hardware store and buy a new one," I offered. "With my allowance."

"That reminds me," he said. "I have to move Mrs. Linga's house. The guy at the hardware store also works for Mr. Huffer and he's going to help us."

"So can I use the radio?" I asked one last time.

He gave in. "Sure," he said reluctantly. "But just turn it off when the commercials come on so you save the battery."

"Okay," I said. "Thanks!"

24

The battery slowly faded over two days but I could still hear a tiny voice in the radio when I tuned it to my country music station, and that was just long enough to keep me company as I dug and waited for the telephone to ring. And it did.

"Come on down," Miss Volker squawked. "We have a duty to perform."

"Who?" I asked.

"Mrs. Bloodgood at F-11 has left the confines of her flesh," she said respectfully. "She's a great combination of Norvelt resident and Norvelt history all rolled into one, so we have tremendous obit material."

That sounded promising. "I'll be right there," I replied, and hung up the telephone.

"Hey, Mom," I hollered. "Mrs. Bloodgood's battery ran out before mine did."

"Be mindful of the dead," she scolded me. "Now that she's in heaven she can hear you!"

"Sorry, Mrs. Bloodgood," I yelled into the little speaker on the radio.

Mom reached out and took a swipe at me. "Just be considerate," she said. "We don't know how Mrs. Bloodgood feels about being dead. I suspect she's probably a little confused about her condition."

"When you're dead can you feel disappointed that you died?" I asked, just guessing. "Or are you just dead and that's that?"

"When you are young," Mom said, "you only see how death affects the living. When you get older you worry about how your death will be greeted by those who are already dead."

"Is that like going to a new school?" I yelled back. "You worry about being the new kid."

I didn't wait for an answer and dashed out the door. As I passed the bomb shelter it made me think of what Mom had just said. I was young and I only wanted to think about the living. If that hole was for a swimming pool I'd be smiling. Instead the bomb shelter made me chew on my lip with dread because it was all about death.

* * *

Miss Volker was waiting for me in the living room. She was frantic with excitement and I had no idea what was going to come out her mouth—but I knew it was going to be good.

"Did I ever tell you how this town got its name?" she asked gleefully.

I groaned. "Yes," I replied a little too impatiently. "You told me about a million times. It's named after Eleanor Roosevelt."

"Right," she continued, marching this way and that across the living room and waving her hands about like a traffic cop directing her thoughts and words. "But there is more to it than that. In an indirect way Mrs. Bloodgood had something to do with the name. This town used to be called Westmoreland Homesteads, which is a mouthful and really sounds more like a mental institution or an old-age home. Once Eleanor got the funding to build this town, the government bought the old Hurst farm which was here. Two hundred and fifty houses were planned and families had to apply to get one of the land plots. Now, you have to realize that these were desperately poor people. The coal mines closed during the Depression. There was no money to be made in farming and a lot of farmers lost their land. So the homestead idea really appealed to poor people who needed a helping hand.

"And then a Negro family applied. They were the first Negro family to do so and by chance their last name was White. Now, as I said, these were all poor white people and they should have seen beyond skin color that everyone had their desperation and poverty in common, as well as the same American dream for a better future for their children. But Mrs. Bloodgood did not want any Negro families in the town. She rallied all the white people and they made sure the Negro family application was denied. But Mrs. White was determined to do the best for her family and so she wrote to President and Mrs. Roosevelt directly and told them about the hopes and dreams she had for her family. The letter so moved the Roosevelts that they made sure the White family received a house and there was no more fuss about the issue of race. Well, when the town was finally built nobody really cared for the name of Westmoreland Homesteads and so there was a contest to name the town—and who do you think won the contest? Well, it was Mrs. White, of course. She combined the 'nor' from Eleanor and the 'velt' from Roosevelt to create a new word for a new town, Norvelt, which was a fitting tribute to the great woman."

"That is a great story," I said, gushing a bit. "A real home run."

"And great justice," added Miss Volker, nodding

respectfully as she recalled Mrs. White and her family. "And as you know, I always have to add a little marble pillar of history to hold up a story and properly show it off, so don't put your pencil down."

I quickly sharpened my pencil and got a clean pad of paper on my desk. "Ready for the history part," I said. "Fire away."

Miss Volker shimmied her hips and shoulders back and forth and high-stepped up and down a little bit as if she were trying to shoo a bee out from under her dress. But she was just adjusting her old bones, and once she was good and warmed up she started talking. "So the interesting thing about this land belonging to the Hurst family is that they were slaveholders who came up from Kentucky and purchased the land from the Penn family—and when they arrived here they brought their own slaves with them. Who would have guessed that years later the farm would become a stop for runaway slaves on the Underground Railroad. And then," she said excitedly, "who would have further guessed it would be Mrs. White—perhaps a descendant of those very slaves—who named this new town which was built on equality."

"Wow! That's something to remember," I said.

She winked at me and dusted the top of my head with a swipe of her ruined hand. "Don't ever forget your history," she sang, "or any wicked soul can lie to you and get away with it."

"Even the dead," I added.

"Now you're catching on," she said warmly. "You're a good listener and a great assistant."

"So where is Mrs. Bloodgood's body?" I asked.

"Mr. Huffer already has his grasping hands on it," she said. "He brought her over already stretched out in the hearse, and I looked her over and signed the papers and I would say that right about now she is about to go up in smoke."

"That was fast," I said.

"Death is not a lazy fellow," she replied, then glanced up at the clock. "But the living have fallen behind. Hurry and type that story up into an obituary form. Quickly, and then you can take my car to run it over to Mr. Greene."

The thought of driving her car got me excited and my fingers rattled across the keys. I typed up a pretty good obituary about Mrs. Bloodgood and the Mrs. White story of naming Norvelt, and the history of the Hurst farmland.

"Get a move on," Miss Volker encouraged from the wall map where she was sticking a red pin into Mrs. Bloodgood's front yard. "I want that obit in the next edition."

I yanked the paper out of the typewriter. I got her keys and ran out to the car and started the engine with a roar and fishtailed out of the driveway and onto the Norvelt road. I floored it and burned rubber and was just picking up speed when suddenly I heard *Ring, ring! Ring, ring!* It sounded like a bicycle bell and I thought there might be a kid on a bike, so I hit the brake and slowed to a stop. I looked to my left and right and then into my rearview mirror. Right behind me was Mr. Spizz on his adult tricycle. He was pedaling madly and waving his arm overhead while his other hand repeatedly rang his little chrome bell. Then I heard him shout, "Pull over!"

I just stayed in my lane since there was nowhere to pull over other than into the gutter weeds. He hopped off his tricycle like a mad monkey and ran up to my window.

"Gantos boy, let me see your license," he ordered.

"Mr. Spizz, you know I don't have one," I replied. "I'm too young."

"Is this your car?" he shot back.

"You know it is Miss Volker's car," I replied.

"I could give you a speeding ticket," he declared. "But I'll let you off with a warning."

"What's the warning?" I asked.

"The warning is I heard the news that nosy Mr. Greene

is planning to call the sheriff about these old ladies dying and so a lot of county cops are going to be snooping around town. If they catch you driving, you are going to be in big trouble and they'll impound her car."

"It's my car," I said emphatically. "She gave it to me."

"We'll see about that," he said skeptically. "There is a lot going on you don't know about—even if you are her puny boyfriend."

You are just jealous, I thought, and tightened my grip on the steering wheel. I really wanted to hit the gas and roar away from him. He might think I was "puny" but he'd never catch me on that tricycle.

"Now that Mrs. Bloodgood has passed only Mrs. Droogie is left," he continued. "So you can drop off your mom's casserole at Miss Volker's house, and I'll just collect that and the cookies at her place and make my delivery to Mrs. Droogie."

"Are you sure Miss Volker will even want to see you?" I asked.

"Gantos boy," he said, and smiled coyly. "She and I have some personal business to finish up that is none of your business. So take the car back to her house and do what you need to do on foot. Really, if you were a smart kid you'd get one of these tricycles. *History* will show that the tricycle will last longer than the automobile." Then he gave his old-man *har-har-har* laugh.

Har-har, I thought to myself. I think history is on my side.

I took the car and left it in the garage, then doubled back and got the obit to Mr. Greene. He just shook his head back and forth when he read it.

"A word to the wise," he said to me. "Things are going to change around here."

"That is what everyone keeps saying," I replied.

"Then it must be true," he said curtly. "Mark my words, change is on the way."

25

The next day I fully understood what Mr. Greene meant when he said things were going to change. He printed an editorial in the paper that stirred everyone up. He asked why all the old ladies were dying so quickly. He wanted to know if there was an investigation. He wanted to know if Miss Volker was up to the job of taking care of them.

> **The town is dropping dead at her feet. All the bodies are cremated before being given a proper medical autopsy. We don't know why they die. Is it just old age? Or is it something else we should be concerned with? It was suggested that it was a Hells Angels curse that was put on this town. But**

that is just fairy-tale thinking. We need scientific answers, which is why I have called in the county police. We are a town built on justice, so we are compelled to get to the bottom of this situation.

Miss Volker took it very personally. I was eating breakfast and reading the paper when she began to kick on the back door with her slippered foot. "Jackie," she growled when I opened the door and found her in her pink chenille bathrobe. "Take a letter. I have to put that ignorant man in his place."

I flew down the hall to my room and got a notebook and pencil and returned to the kitchen table. I raised my pencil above the paper and froze into the same position a doctor holds just before he jabs a scalpel into a patient.

"History," she started with her voice as strong and confident as ever, "often sheds more light on the present than on the past. Many of us remember being plagued by the Great Influenza of 1918 which killed over five hundred thousand Americans and fifty million people worldwide. Out in the coal-mining towns and steel factories where people worked closely together the virus spread rapidly, and thousands died in days. Small towns lost half of their populations or more. Schools were closed. Movie theaters closed. Churches were shut and locked for fear that worshipping God would lead to the death of the congregation. Football and baseball and hockey games were canceled. Entire teams dropped dead. People were forced to wear cotton masks over their mouths and noses as they walked the streets. The whole country was terrified. Everyone pointed fingers at everyone else. The terror created fear and mistrust and neighbor blamed neighbor for the death of their loved ones. But no person was at fault. It was the influenza, which is as natural as the yeast that makes your bread rise.

"And here in Norvelt we've lost but a few ladies of advanced age by natural causes. They lived useful, long lives, so let us not panic like a bunch of Chicken Littles and feel the sky falling, but instead put our energy into keeping Norvelt alive. People will pass on, but we must preserve our history. Stop shipping out the houses and instead sell them to young families. Let us fill every empty seat at the school. Let us farm each acre of land. Let us be good neighbors and build communities where the pursuit of happiness *is* the purpose of life, rather than merely staying alive just so we can cower from fear."

After I wrote this out I slowly escorted Miss Volker down the grassy back path to her house. "What do you think Mr. Greene will say when he reads this?" I asked her as I *click-clacked* away on her typewriter.

"He won't say anything," she replied from her position on the couch. "He's a coward."

"What is he afraid of?"

"What most people are afraid of," she replied. "The truth. These ladies just died of old-lady age. Nothing more than that."

But some people thought it was more than that.

At dinner that night Mom looked at Dad and me as if she were being washed out to sea. "I have a terrible confession to share," she said, and lowered her fork. Her lips quivered and then she cried out, "I think I may have killed those old ladies!"

"What!" I shouted, and the food spit out of my mouth.

"You *should* spit it out," Mom agreed, "because that's how I think they died—from eating my food. You know how thrifty I am. Well, in the evening I've been picking mushrooms up by the trash dump and I think I've been making a mistake between the *Amanitopsis* and the *Amanita virosa*, which is called the Destroying Angel mushroom because it is deadly to eat. One tastes heavenly and the other will send you to heaven. So depending on what I picked, I may have been adding those killer mushrooms to all the casseroles I made for the old folks."

"Should we tell someone?" I asked, and patted her hand.

“Maybe Miss Volker,” Mom guessed. “She’s the nurse.”

“Then she’d have to report you to the police!” I announced dramatically.

“And they’d put me in jail for murder,” Mom cried, and the tears ran down her pale cheeks. “And I’d never see you grow up,” she said to me, sobbing. “And I’d even miss your bloody nose, which, by the way, is bleeding all over you again.”

I grabbed my napkin and held it beneath my nose.

Then Mom turned toward Dad. He was eyeballing us as if we were insane. “I’ll never grow old with you, honey,” she whimpered, and reached out for his face.

Dad slowly shook his head back and forth. “Before you two hopeless cases go off the deep end,” he said bluntly, “may I ask a question: Have you been putting these poison mushrooms in *our* food?”

“Yes,” she blurted out. “Oh my! I’ve been killing you too.”

“Well, I have a news flash for you—we aren’t dead,” I said, “so that shoots down your poisoning theory.”

“Point well taken,” Dad pitched in. “If we eat what they eat, it figures that we’d be dead too.”

“You think so?” Mom asked, and a note of relief buoyed her voice.

“I think you need to settle down for now,” Dad advised. “But don’t tell a soul. This is how awful rumors start. If you tell one person about the mushrooms they will tell others and the others will tell even more, and before long an angry mob will surround our house and burn it to the ground."

"Good Norvelt people wouldn't do that," Mom replied. "People trust each other around here."

"Good Norvelt people wouldn't be suggesting that the old ladies are being knocked off like this is some kind of cheap murder mystery," Dad said. "We have to face facts that times are changing around here, and I'm planning on changing with the times."

"Times might be changing," Mom echoed. "But my values won't."

"I'm not asking you to change who you are," Dad said. "Just where you are. We could sell our house to Mr. Huffer and he'd pay me to move it to Eleanor, and we could keep right on going and leave this town to die behind our backs instead of in front of our eyes."

"Let me think about all of this moving business," Mom said reluctantly. "But for now let's just keep this murder talk in the family. We can trust each other, but something is wrong and I'm not sure why."

When I went to bed I began to think that Mom was right about something being wrong in Norvelt. In a lot of the history books I read, I learned about dates and people and events, but I wasn't always sure *why* people did what they did. *Why* wouldn't the English king and church not share all their land with their own starving countrymen? And *why* did the conquistadors think it was okay with God to kill the Incas and steal their gold? And *why* would the rich coal mine owners work the miners so hard they died young with their lungs hardened up with coal dust? How could history be filled with so much horror and so few reasons *why*?

And now all those old ladies had died. But *why*? If they were poisoned, it had to be the 1080. Miss Volker had killed all those rodents with it and I had buried their bodies by the dump. Spizz used it in traps he set at the dump for the rats that bred in the old mine shafts and came out to swarm the town. Plus I had seen Mr. Huffer's name on the list of people who had bought 1080, and he threw funeral parlor gunk and dead rodents into his trash cans, which were emptied at the dump. And even my name was on the 1080 list. If the police asked me what I did with the poison I bought, I would tell them I gave it to Spizz.

But what if Spizz denied it because he didn't like me anyway? Then I would be the suspicious one—the prime suspect. Everyone else had a reason why they used poison, but I didn't have a reason for what I did with it. I didn't even have the tin of 1080 I bought, which would look to the police like I had tried to hide the evidence. All night I kept thinking it through, and still I didn't have an answer to why all the old ladies were dying.

But somewhere inside me I must have known I was onto something ghastly, because when I woke up in the morning my pillow looked like a big loaf of bread pudding soaked through with blood.

26

On Sunday after church I made an appointment with Miss Volker to fix the leaky side of my nose. I told Mom I had to go down to her house and help with her laundry, which was sort of true because she had trouble getting the washing machine started and she definitely couldn't pin her clothes onto the outside lines to dry.

When I arrived at her house I quickly went into the basement to get a load of sheets going. When I turned on the light I saw that Miss Volker had put out more chocolates sprinkled with 1080. There were a few dead mice scattered around, which only reminded me of the dead old ladies. I tried not to look at their tortured little bodies as I filled the washing machine, added the soap, and got it started.

I dashed up the stairs as quickly as I could and went into the kitchen.

"Would you like some cookies before your operation?" she cheerfully asked, and nodded toward where she had a package of them spread out across the kitchen counter. They were the same cookies she packaged up for the old ladies.

"No—no thanks," I said hesitantly. Mushrooms, casseroles, chocolates, and cookies were suddenly off my food list.

"It's always good to have a little something in your stomach before an operation," she suggested. "How about just one little cookie to help settle you down?"

"I'm just eager to get this over with," I replied. I went to her linen closet and got a sheet for the kitchen table. Then I gathered up her special tools.

She got her bucket of paraffin heated and dunked her hands into the hot wax while I numbed my nose with the anesthetic. Once she got her fingers moving she peeled off the wax, then grabbed the cauterizing instrument and held the sharp tip of it under the flame until it turned a painful shade of bright red.

"Now," she said, pivoting quickly from the stove and staring as she pointed the menacing wire toward my nose, "let's get this done once and for all."

"Are you sure?" I asked in a small voice.

"You know I don't like to be questioned," she said sternly.

"Okay. Do it—but don't make it painful," I begged and gritted my teeth. She looked like she had just one purpose on her mind as she aimed for the dark cave of my left nostril. Maybe she knew I thought she could have poisoned those ladies, and now she had me pinned to the table and she was planning to jab that sizzling hot blade and wire right up into the caramel center of my brain. I'd be dead in an instant and all she would have to say is that I sneezed and jerked my head forward and impaled my own self on the wire.

I didn't know what to do, so I did nothing. She peeked up my nose and then, as steadily as she could, she inserted the tiny blade. I felt the fierce heat inside my nostril and knew that one false move, one little hiccup . . .

And then the telephone rang.

"Don't bat an eyelash," she whispered, and carefully lifted my hand to the wood handle of wire and blade. "Just . . . hold . . . it . . . right . . . there. I'll be quick."

"But . . ."

"Hush!" she snapped, and turned toward the telephone. "Or your hand will move and you'll deform yourself."

She had enough flexibility in her hot fingers to pick

up the receiver. "Miss Volker here," she announced. "Make it snappy. I'm in the middle of a nose job."

Someone said something to her.

"Okay," she said hastily. "I'll be right there. No problem. My driver is with me now."

Just then I had to sneeze. "My nose!" I wailed. "Hurry."

"Don't jerk your hand!" she hollered from the phone.

But it was too late. I sneezed and scraped the blade and wire against the inside of my nose as I yanked it out.

"Bless you," she said.

"I think I sliced half my nose off," I cried. "I'll be a freak on one side of my face and have to walk around in profile like an Egyptian drawing for the rest of my life."

"Relax," she said, standing over me. "It's just a small burn blister at the tip of your nose." Then with her other hand she shined a flashlight up the nostril. "Hey, not bad," she concluded. "Not bad at all. Looks like that sneeze helped you cauterize the rest of the capillaries. You might make a good doctor someday."

I sat up. I still couldn't feel my face. "You didn't stick a pin in my nose this time, did you?" I asked.

"No," she said impatiently. "Now let's get going. I just found out Mrs. Droogie will no longer be sharing air with us on this planet."

We left the house so quickly she didn't see the box of chocolates and note sitting outside by the porch door. It wasn't there when I arrived this morning, so Mr. Spizz must have sneaked over when I was on the operating table.

As usual, I drove and she talked. "Well, this is a day I've been waiting for a long time," Miss Volker said, and sighed as if a great weight was off her chest. "Now it will all come down to me and *him*! We are the last two Norvelters standing."

"Are you going to have a shoot-out at high noon?" I asked.

"That's not how I operate," she replied. "He'll never see me coming!"

But Mr. Spizz did see us coming. When we pulled into Mrs. Droogie's driveway he was sitting on his tricycle with a superior smirk on his face, as if he had just won a super tricycle road race. Behind him were two county troopers standing in front of the doorway and they had their thumbs hooked into their pants pockets. With their puffed-out chests and thick necks they looked like owls rotating their carved faces back and forth. Off to one side Mr. Huffer stood next to a twiggy, water-starved azalea and posed like his usual wilted teapot self.

When Miss Volker stepped out of the car they all stared at her, but she was accustomed to being the center of attention.

"Gentlemen," she announced to the troopers, "this is my jurisdiction and I'll take charge of the examination." They nodded and quietly the five of them filed into the house. I lagged behind and stood in the doorway. Mr. Huffer had Mrs. Droogie laid out on the couch in the living room, where she had died while watching TV after dinner. As soon as I caught sight of the body I hopped back and gazed off to one side, but I could still hear.

Mr. Huffer pulled the sheet back from Mrs. Droogie's heavy body. "No unusual marks on her face," Miss Volker announced, "other than the bruise from where she fell from the couch to the floor. Her belly's not swollen. Her legs are contorted but that is just the rigor mortis having set in." I knew Miss Volker's hands must have cooled down and would be seizing up, but she just took a deep breath and proved to the police that she could complete a thorough job.

Miss Volker went over Mrs. Droogie from top to bottom. I heard Mr. Huffer pull the sheet back up over her, so I stuck my head around the corner. Miss Volker stood fully erect and looked at Mr. Huffer and the unblinking troopers and Mr. Spizz. "It is death from natural causes," she said with confidence. "All very routine. Looks to me like it was a stroke, given the burst capillaries in her eyes. Her gums are badly infected too, and often that infection spreads to the heart so it is possible she had a heart attack. She had high blood pressure, minor diabetes issues, and if you look at her foot you will see that one shoe is partially cut open across the side because she had gout in her foot, and the only way she could get her shoe on was to split the side to accommodate the swelling. Gentlemen," she said, summing up her case, "what you see before you is the result of eighty-three years of growing old."

It was a top-notch examination. She showed off all her skills and perceptions and I was very proud of her. It went well until she turned to Mr. Huffer and asked, "Cremation as usual?"

That was when the two troopers stepped forward and one of them said, "We have an order to take charge of the body and send it to the lab for a full autopsy. After that we'll release it back to Mr. Huffer."

"Suit yourself," Miss Volker said, "but you are wasting your time and taxpayers' money." Then she turned on one heel and marched out the front door with me right behind. She was quiet in the car except to point out, "The dear lady died on a day with some great history. August 12 is the day on which we remember the death of Antony and Cleopatra two thousand years ago."

"I know she was the last Egyptian pharaoh and died from a snake bite," I said. "Poisoned by asps. But how'd her boyfriend go?"

"Self-inflicted wound," she recalled without sympathy. "He and another Roman general, Octavian, were fighting over who would rule the Roman Empire. Once Octavian had conquered Antony and Cleopatra's army, someone told Antony that Cleopatra had been killed during the battle. In grief Antony fell on his sword but did a crummy job of killing himself, so he was very slow about dying. However, Cleopatra wasn't dead. She was hiding in a little fortress palace, and when she heard about Antony she had him brought to her. He moaned and groaned and whined and cried, and after he finally died she allowed the asps to bite her on the breast with their deadly poison."

"Romantic," I said, "wow. Now that's the way to go!"

"Not romantic," she disagreed. "To me it would be romantic if Antony properly fell on his sword and kicked the bucket and Cleopatra escaped and lived a lovely life sailing along the Nile without him and his big ideas ruining her kingdom. She was better off without him."

I knew what she was getting at. It was time for Spizz to fall off his tricycle and onto his sword and leave her alone to live the new life she wanted in Florida with her sister. But I didn't think Spizz was going to just fall on his sword.

When we returned to Miss Volker's home I sat down at my desk, as I had all summer. I raised my pencil and Miss Volker fell back into an easy chair.

"Mrs. Droogie," she started up, and already her voice sounded tired, like a cold engine that didn't want to turn over. She paused and took a deep breath and began again, and this time her engine sputtered to life. "Mrs. Droogie was a lovely woman and lived a long and satisfying life. She loved her family, her community, and her country and in return she was loved and respected by all who knew her. As a child she was a violin prodigy who at the age of eleven played with the New York Philharmonic. She went on to perform with the world's greatest symphonies, but by the age of twenty-three she set down the violin and never picked it up again. When asked why she quit she replied that one day she realized she was only playing to please her parents and that she really didn't enjoy it. Instead, she retreated to Norvelt where she married Mr. Droogie, who was best known as a clown at children's birthday parties and was famous for his sense of humor—and

Mrs. Droogie became famous for her laughter. They were a perfect couple."

I waited for Miss Volker to continue but she had run out of gas and slumped back into her chair. "That's all I have to say," she said. "Mrs. Droogie was a lovely woman who proved that you don't have to do what your parents want or what your boyfriend wants for you to be happy. You just have to be yourself, for there is no love greater than self-love."

"I'll type this up," I said dutifully, and then I asked something that had been on my mind for a long time. "Miss Volker, now that all the original Norvelters are dead, doesn't that mean you have to marry Mr. Spizz like you promised him?"

"I've been thinking about that," she replied with a wry smile. "And I realized that I failed to inform that bonehead of one key fact—I'm an original Norvelter too. So I guess he'll just have to wait until I drop dead to marry me. Like I said, his alphabet soup only spells out D-U-M-B."

"Well, I don't think he'll be very happy about that," I said. "Because he already left you a little gift by the back door."

Instantly her face stiffened. "Go get it for me," she snarled. She looked even more tired. "I expect it's more mouse bait."

I went out to the porch and retrieved the box of chocolates and the note and brought them to the living room.

"Read the note," she instructed.

I pulled the tape off the package and opened the envelope. *"As God intended, it is just the two of us left in this Garden of Eden. Marry me. —E. Spizz."*

There was a knock at the door.

"To quote Cleopatra," Miss Volker sang out, "'The enemy is at the gate.' Believe me, if I had a snake I'd use it on him. Now go answer it."

It was Spizz. "Gantos boy," he bellowed. "Figures you'd be here." He stared down at me as if I were a piece of gum he might scrape up.

"I was just leaving," I said to him, and stepped onto the porch. I hadn't gone far when I heard his foghorn voice holler out, "Hello, good-lookin'. Looks like we're the last two old birds at the party."

I knew she was about to let him have a piece of her mind and I didn't want to hear it. I had heard enough already. I took the obituary down to Mr. Greene.

He was wiping ink off his hands with a rag. "I told you there was something suspicious going on," Mr. Greene said, feeling pretty proud of himself and puffing up a noxious cloud of cherry tobacco smoke, which burned my eyes. "We'll know soon enough if someone has been killing those old ladies."

"Or not," I added.

"How much do you want to bet? I say that Miss Volker killed them," he declared as he pulled out his wallet.

I pulled out my two-dollar bill. "I say she didn't," I replied.

He took my money and his and put them in a desk drawer. "Winner takes all," he said, puffing excitedly.

"Takes all," I repeated, then walked straight home. I was exhausted.

I didn't know what to do but try to distract myself by reading while waiting for the autopsy report. I looked over all my books but every one of the histories reminded me of Miss Volker. *The Crusades*, *The Magna Charta*, *The F.B.I.*, *Women of Courage*, *Custer's Last Stand*—I could just hear her voice behind each book, linking the past to the present and the present to the future. But what was her future? That question was why I couldn't read a word, because I was looking out the window and toward her house and trying to read her mind. I wanted to sneak back down there and snoop but I was still grounded.

Police cars had been coming and going. Spizz's tricycle was parked by her back porch. Men had been carrying boxes and bags out of her house and loading them into trucks and driving off. Mom wouldn't let me call her, so my only hope was that Miss Volker would call me. And so I waited.

When the telephone rang I ran for it and picked up the receiver. "I'll be right there," I cried out to Miss Volker.

Only it was Mr. Spizz. "Gantos boy!" he hollered so loudly I could smell his breath through the phone. "I got some bad news for you."

"Is it about Miss Volker?" I asked nervously. "Is she okay?"

"She asked me to call you and let you know that the police have arrested her for *murder*—they say she killed all those old ladies."

"She did not!" I shouted. "How could she have done it?"

"Poisoned them," he said slowly. "Heartlessly."

"That cannot be true," I stated.

"Mrs. Droogie was full of poison. The police have proof it was your *girlfriend* who did it," he said quickly.

"What proof?" I shot back.

"They found 1080 all over the chocolates at Miss Volker's house," he barked. "She must have been giving them to the old ladies."

"She was poisoning the mice in her basement with the chocolates you gave her," I shot right back. "She hated those crummy chocolates. She gave the old ladies Thin Mints."

"Don't be so smart-alecky! They found 1080 in the Thin Mints too," he snarled.

"So what. A lot of people use 1080," I said as calmly as possible. "That doesn't mean anything. You use it. And Mr. Huffer uses it."

"We use it for pests," he said, getting wound up. "Not for people. We don't cook with it or sprinkle it on cookies or serve it on chocolates."

"Maybe it was the Hells Angels," I suggested. "Miss Volker said they brought a curse on the town."

"That phony curse was just a way of covering her tracks in advance of murdering those ladies herself. Believe me, I know how she operates. She says one thing when she means another."

"I guess that means she won't marry you?" I surmised. "Even though she said she would."

"I'm the one asking the questions," he said in a steely voice. "Did you help her? She can't use her hands so she must have had a murder accomplice."

"I didn't do a thing," I said, standing up to him. "I don't even believe she did it."

"Well, the police might want to talk with you next," he said. "So you better get your story straight and tell the truth."

"Then I can tell them that you were the last person to touch the food before serving it to the old ladies," I reminded him. "You probably murdered them."

"I'm a police officer," he said with authority. "I don't think it's a good idea to accuse me of murder."

"You made me buy you the 1080," I said.

"The police were informed that you bought it for Miss Volker," he replied smoothly. "They found it at her house."

"Anything else you lied about?" I asked.

"Only you would know if someone is lying," he boomed out. "The police are with her now. They put her under house arrest and I have to stand guard."

"You better not hurt her," I warned him. "She's old."

"She may be old but she's a cold-blooded killer," he howled, and hung up.

I went back to my room and sulked a little bit as I looked over my collection of obituaries. It seemed impossible for someone like Miss Volker, who loved people, to turn around and hurt them. And I felt pretty rotten for thinking that she might have wanted to kill me too.

After a while Dad walked in and put his hand on my shoulder. "I just heard about Miss Volker," he said, and shook his head at the mystery of it. "And I know you are worried about her, so I'll give you something to take your mind off her. I'm going to fly to Florida in a few days to look for work. I was going to stay and move more empty Norvelt houses to West Virginia, but now the police want to keep them here while they investigate the old-lady deaths, so we can't even sell our house. This is a good time for me to go, and you can keep busy by helping your mom out."

"Am I still grounded?" I asked.

"Once I'm gone she'll need you to run errands and stuff," he said. "I figure she'll let you off the hook."

"Well, what about my flight in the J-3?" I whined. "You promised to take me up."

"I thought you turned that ticket in to go play baseball," he replied.

"I did, but can't we do it in secret?" I begged. "When she's not looking."

"Okay," he figured, "but we'll have to find a time real soon, and we can't take off from the house because she'll spot us and then we'll both get into even more trouble."

"I can sneak away and meet you in a field," I suggested.

He nodded. "Yeah," he said, and smiled secretly at some crazy thought he had. "That'll work for me."

27

Mom reached into the kitchen cabinet and removed a small basket made of twigs. "This is my wild raspberry–picking basket," she said proudly, and inspected it to make sure all the twigs were still woven in place. "I made it in this house when my mother ran the Girl Scout meetings in our basement. I got a badge for the best-made basket."

"Was your mother the judge?" I asked, and looked her in the eye, then looked back at the basket, which looked like it had been woven by a raccoon.

"Don't be a wise guy," she reproached me gently. "Now I'm going out to hunt for raspberries in the woods up behind Fenton's gas station. I'll be back soon because I'm going to make a raspberry tart for Miss

Volker to cheer her up. It's just criminal that she is under house arrest."

"Can you bake a pistol into that tart?" I asked. "She must be going insane down there with that creepy Mr. Spizz as her jailer. Just having to listen to him all day would make me want to take a shot at him."

"Don't you worry about Miss Volker," Mom replied as she headed for the back door. "That machine gun she has for a mouth is more than enough to handle Spizz."

She went off to the woods and I sat at the table and slowly paged through the *Norvelt News*. It was sad that all the Norvelt originals had now died and there were no more obituaries to write except for Mr. Spizz and Miss Volker, and they might just go on living forever as they promised each other. There wasn't much to read about in the paper—in the Chat Line section a pet ferret had gotten stuck in the tailpipe of a car. The owners were asking for tips on how to get it out. Someone suggested that one person hold a butterfly net behind the tailpipe while another person start the car, which would allow the engine exhaust to blast the ferret out into the net. I'd love to witness that. And then I turned to the back page. As usual, I saved This Day In History for last:

August 14, 1935: **United States Social Security Act was passed (supported by our Mrs. Roosevelt), creating a pension system for the retired.**

August 14, 1945: **Japan surrendered, ending World War II.**

I didn't get to the third one because at that moment I heard a rifle shot, followed by my mother hollering, "Jack! Jack!"

I ran out to the back porch. I didn't see her but yelled out anyway, "It wasn't me! I didn't fire the rifle!"

"Come quick!" she shouted. I couldn't see her though her voice was coming from behind the pony pen. I dashed down the steps and had just cleared the pen when suddenly a small deer crashed out of the underbrush and into our backyard. He had been shot in the neck and the blood was running swiftly from that small entry hole and down the golden curve of his fur, where it gathered brightly in the soft thatch of his heaving chest. He must have been dazed by the bullet because once he ran out into the open he just stood still, as if he wasn't hurt at all and was only figuring out a safe place to hide. But there was too much blood for anything good to happen.

From the same path as the deer my mother came

crashing out of the woods. She still clutched the empty basket in her hand as she glanced anxiously back over her shoulder to see what was moving from behind. When she turned her head and saw me she hollered out in a razor-sharp voice I'd never heard before. "Jack," she ordered, "get the rifle and bring it to me. Now!"

I knew she didn't mean my dad's deer rifle, because that was locked up in a special cabinet. She meant the Japanese rifle. I stood there frozen for a second until I could just make out a man in the woods wearing a camouflage hunting outfit and a black ski mask. He stepped from behind a white birch tree and he had a dark rifle held up to his shoulder. It was aimed not at Mom but at the deer. Mom saw it too, and the first thing she did was step into the line of fire between the hunter and the deer, which was still dazed and bleeding and completely motionless except for the steady drops of blood ticking off seconds against the dry summer grass.

"Jack!" Mom shouted at me. "Now!"

In a blind panic I ran for the garage. Dad had the regular door locked, so I cut back around to the half door. It was already open so I ducked down and went inside. I lifted the top of the chest where he kept the war souvenirs. The Japanese flag was balled up and pushed to one side and the rifle was gone. I dug frantically through the other souvenirs, but there was no rifle. Oh God, I thought, don't let that man shoot my mother.

I pulled out the long Japanese sword, and when I scrambled back around the corner of the pen nothing had changed except I was even more afraid. The hunter had moved forward to the edge of the woods and my mom was still standing in front of the deer, and that was when the deer suddenly dropped down onto his front elbows and bent his head forward, as if death were a pool he could dive into. I looked at Mom and then at the deer and back at Mom and I knew she was one shot away from dropping to her knees. I stood paralyzed with fear and willed myself to raise the sword inch by inch above my head as Mom kept her eyes locked on the hunter's eyes.

"Step away from the deer," the man demanded, and slowly shuffled forward. "It's my kill."

I ran up to Mom, panting, and handed her the sword then jumped off to one side, as if leaping from a train. She gripped the sword in her hand and savagely slashed the air back and forth, as if in an instant she could cut that man out of the picture in front of us. "I will use this," she said in a threatening voice. "So just turn around and leave."

"The deer is mine," he said in a firm, menacing voice, and took a step forward. He must have been ten feet from her, with that long rifle barrel pointing directly at her face. Then she took a step forward and with her fully extended arm pointed the tip of the sword right at the center of his masked face. "Turn around and go back where you came from," she said fearlessly, as if bullets would bounce off her.

The deer quietly slumped over onto his side, with his glossy brown eye wide open to the sun and pink foam collecting around his sad, quivering mouth. I dared to slowly walk over to him and knelt down and put my hand on his firm side. He was breathing harder now and I knew he was dying because there was nothing we could do to help him.

"You are trespassing," Mom said harshly. "And what you have done to this deer is criminal."

"Let me get my deer and you'll never see me again," he replied, and inched toward her.

I looked from the deer to the man.

"I wouldn't take another step if I were you," she stated. And then her face switched from being ready for a fight to a look of disbelief. She tilted her head to one side in a puzzled way and took a measured step toward the man, and then another, as if she were one of the British troops marching eye-high into the barrel of the rifle. She was about two feet away when she slowly lowered the sword and said, "Will? Is that you?"

He stepped back and swung his face away from her, then took more back steps into the woods.

"It is you!" she shouted angrily. "Come here!"

He dropped the rifle and ducked down, thrashing his way through the lower branches and summer undergrowth. We listened to the cracking branches in the woods until we couldn't hear him anymore. Then silently we turned and looked at the dead deer. My mother held out the sword. "Take this," she said. I reached for the handle and took it from her. Every move she made was deliberate, as if she had already lived this moment a dozen times and had always done the right thing. She strode forward into the woods, then bent over at the waist and hoisted the rifle off the ground.

It was the Japanese rifle! Uncle Will had taken it from the chest. She opened the chamber to check for a round. There was one in there. She pointed the barrel toward the dirt and fired. It was loud and I flinched. She cocked the rifle and checked the chamber again. Another round had entered and she fired it into the ground. She cocked the rifle again and fired. *Click*. The clip was empty.

"I hate these damn war souvenirs," she said firmly. "They don't care if they kill your enemy or your family." Then she turned and held it out to me. I grabbed it with my right arm, which was stronger.

"Now put that back just how Dad keeps it," she ordered. "Honestly, if he knew my crazy brother took it out to poach deer he'd shoot him."

"I bet Uncle Will was the one who left the bullet in the gun the night I pulled the trigger," I said. "I know I didn't load it and Dad said he didn't either."

"Well, that may be true," she considered. "But we still can't tell your dad."

"But it means that I shouldn't even be grounded," I protested. "It was never my fault."

"My crazy brother did not cut down the corn," she quickly reminded me. "That is the bigger reason why you are grounded."

"Dad made me do that," I cried out to defend myself. "And Dad thinks I put the bullet in the gun. It's not fair and now my whole summer has been ruined."

"It's not ruined," Mom said. "You made a new girlfriend."

"Who?" I asked. I really liked Mertie-Jo but I hadn't told Mom about it.

"Miss Volker," Mom said, teasing. "You go down there all the time and you spend the whole day there. You might be down there kissing all day for all I know."

"Don't say that," I said. "I really don't want to be kissing her. Besides, Mr. Spizz wants to marry her."

"Well, they used to be lovebirds in the old days," Mom remarked. "Now he's got her under house arrest. Who knows, maybe that's what he wanted all along."

"I bet they're arguing all day," I said.

"You know what they say about love," Mom said sagely, "the more you pester someone the more it means you love them."

"Is that true?" I asked.

"It's one of the ten commandments of love," Mom said confidently. "So you can count on it."

"I'm going to put the gun away—and the sword," I said. "Before Dad returns."

"Hey," she said. "Look at me."

I looked at her face, but not directly into her eyes.

"Your nose," she said.

I ran my hand over it.

"Why isn't it bleeding?" she asked.

"I was keeping it a secret," I replied. "But I'll tell you. Miss Volker operated on it and fixed it, and I helped too."

"Oh my God," Mom said in horror. "With *her* hands?"

"You should have seen the veterinarian tools she used on me," I said, wide-eyed. "They were like torture tools from the Spanish Inquisition."

"I've heard enough," she said. "Not another word. This day has been too insane already."

I nodded. "Yep," I said. "How are you going to explain the deer to Dad?"

"I'll tell him it just came out of woods. There have

always been poachers back up that way. He can dress it out and we can use the meat since he's leaving for a while."

Then I took a chance. "Hey, Mom, can we barter for something like the old-fashioned Norvelt way?"

"What are you getting at?" she asked.

I walked over and gave her a big hug, then stepped back. "Now, how about one in return?" I said.

And she stepped forward and wrapped her arms around me. "If you say one word about my brother and the gun, you will be grounded until you turn eighteen no matter what your father says—do you hear me?"

I heard her.

Once she walked off I turned the other way and took a few steps back. I looked directly down at the dead deer, and in its shiny eye I could see myself reflected. But instead of turning away in fear I knelt down and placed my hand over the eye. I loved that deer. It never did anything wrong in its entire life except to be in the wrong place. History could be like that, especially for the innocent.

"I'm sorry," I said, and smoothed his eyelid across his eye and held it there until it stayed. Then I stood up with the rifle and sword and walked away.

28

By the time I woke, Dad had already used the tractor to drag the deer into the garage. He had been a hunter all of his life and he knew what to do. He spent the morning cutting it up, separating the good from the bad and packaging the meat.

I didn't want to watch so I stayed grounded in my room. Slumped was more like it. I was so bored I wished the telephone would ring with Miss Volker calling to tell me Mr. Spizz had dropped over dead and I had to come down and write one last obituary. But that wasn't likely to happen. Still, that didn't mean I had to stop writing obituaries. I figured I could write one about the deer. I tried to get myself worked up like Miss Volker. I swung my arms around and did some deep knee bends, but I didn't have her scratchy old voice and her bottomless well full of words. I just took out a sheet of paper and began to write something that seemed honest.

> The deer, whose name was The Deer, was born about a year or so ago and grew up freely in the woods. He spent his days smelling and hearing and eating and feeling the warm hand of the sun on his back and doing all the things that deer have been doing for thousands of years until one day he was standing still and listening to a shoe snap a twig followed by the sound of a Japanese rifle and felt the bullet strike his neck. He ran but there was no place to hide because his life ran out of him faster than he could run for cover. We thank him for providing food, and even though his death gives us life, it is hard to thank even an animal enough for that.

It was a sad personal history and like Miss Volker taught me, I tried to think of a famous story in history to link to it, but all I could think about was *Bambi* and that wasn't real history. That was just a cartoon story that people cried about, but it didn't stop them from hunting deer. If I was going to take this to Mr. Greene and ask him to print it, I would have to come up with some good history to go along with it.

I was sorting through my books to find something just right when Dad came into my room.

"Hey, I have a little souvenir for you," he said casually, and in one motion he reached into his pocket and tossed me something. I caught it with one hand and when I opened my hand I saw the bullet and felt the weight of it.

"It was still in the neck," he said.

"Thanks," I replied, and smiled only because I knew he would want me to smile.

"I know you didn't load that Jap rifle," he said. "But you did pull the trigger. Promise you'll never do something that stupid again."

"History won't repeat itself," I said. "Promise."

He turned and walked out of the room to prepare for his trip. I stood up and closed my door and sat on the edge of the bed feeling very different from myself. Maybe I felt like a city before it was invaded. Or a ship before it sank. Or happiness before it turned into sadness. I couldn't say exactly. But something was about to change in me.

That change came two days later when the phone rang. I whipped open my door and ran to the kitchen and snatched the receiver and pressed it against my ear.

"Gantos boy!" Spizz hollered into the phone.

"How's Miss Volker?" I asked breathlessly.

"Don't talk. Just listen," he instructed. "Go to her house and down into the basement. She's tied up down there."

"Why don't you go to her yourself?" I asked, confused. "You are the one in her house."

"I'm not," he said. "I've vanished."

"That's impossible," I said. "A grown man can't vanish on a tricycle!"

And then the phone went dead. A feeling of horror came over me and a moment later I was out the door and running full speed down the hill to Miss Volker's house. I yanked open her back door and dashed to the basement door and pulled it open.

"Miss Volker!" I hollered as I hammered my way down the steps.

"Take your time," she advised. "If you fall and kill yourself, I might starve to death all tied up like this."

When I reached the last step I looked at her. She was sitting in a kitchen chair with her arms loosely pulled back behind her. On the floor around her were open heart-shaped boxes of chocolates. A few bold mice were nibbling on them.

"This is how he tortured me," she said. "He knows I don't like rodents."

I kicked at the boxes, which scattered the mice. "I'll wring his neck," I said, stepping behind the chair to untie her.

"Don't hurt ol' Spizz," she said warmly. "Over the last few days I really had a pretty good time with him."

"That's hard to believe," I replied. But maybe he hadn't been so bad—her hands were gently tied up in a floppy bow with the red ribbon from the chocolate boxes.

"Yes," she continued. "Ol' Spizz was very cooperative with me, and it didn't take too much work to get him to confess that he did all the poisoning."

"He killed them?" I shouted.

"Yep," she confirmed. "He even let me dictate his confession while he wrote it down. Honestly, we never did get along so well as when he was telling me how he knocked off all those ladies. It was flattering that he killed them for me. He wanted to get them out of the way so my duty to Mrs. Roosevelt would be over and I would be free to run off with him. Can you imagine that? The two of us on his tricycle! Ha!"

"Did he say anything to you before he left?" I asked. "Like where he was going?"

"All he said was he'd tie me up while he got a six-hour head start out of town," she said. "That's about all."

"I don't think he got far, because his tricycle is in front of your house."

"Oh, he didn't take the tricycle," she remembered, and made a sad face because she knew what I was about to figure out.

"He escaped in my car?" I yelped, and stomped the ground, which sent a few more mice running.

"Yep," she confirmed. "I figured you'd be upset about that."

"Oh cheeze! Well, now I really hope they catch him before he crashes it," I said.

"Me too," she agreed. "But at the moment this is the least of my worries. Now help me stand. I've got to go upstairs and sit on the couch. Sitting in this chair has just about killed my rear end."

I helped her up the stairs and got her onto the couch. "Can I help you with anything? Can I call the police?"

"First I've got to call Mr. Greene and apologize. He was right about the ladies being murdered—though he was wrong that it was me. But I was wrong about them dying of natural causes, so I guess my medical examiner days are over. After we set the record straight we'll call the police and tell them to come get Mr. Spizz's confession." She pointed to the typewriter table where he had typed it and signed it. "Can you believe that he killed them all? D-U-M-B. How stupid can you be?" she asked no one in particular.

I went over to the map and put a red pin in Mrs. Droogie's house—D-21.

"I'm hungry," she said. "And thirsty."

I went into the kitchen and got her a glass of tap water. "Don't eat anything from your house," I warned her. "I'll go up and have Mom cook something for you."

"Okay," she replied. "That would be nice. I suppose because I'm the last original Norvelter in town I should celebrate, but I think I'll just lie down and take a nap."

"Don't you want to call Mr. Greene and the police?" I asked. "We don't want Spizz to get away."

"Just let me have a tiny catnap," she said. "It won't matter how much head start Spizz has. He's too ugly not to be easily spotted."

I plumped up the pillows. And once she was stretched out I pulled her woolen afghan over her.

"One more thing," she asked with her eyes half-closed. "Keeping in mind all those old ladies who have passed on, today is the eve before we honor the first English child born in America—Virginia Dare in 1587. Don't forget your history," she murmured. "Life is a cycle."

Exactly, I thought. Life *is* a cycle, and this is the history part I can add to the deer obituary. I bet Virginia Dare's parents even called her a "little dear."

I waited for a moment until she fell asleep before I leaned over and kissed her on the forehead. Then I went outside and hopped on Mr. Spizz's tricycle and rode up to our house. It was a pretty good ride.

I told Mom everything. She called the county police, then quickly gathered up a basket of food for Miss Volker.

"Do you want me to come?" I asked.

"I think it will be better if I handle this alone," she said. "You've been a big help, but the police are just going to want to speak with adults. Besides, your dad is leaving tonight for Florida and you might want to help him out—and you have a baseball game."

"I'm ungrounded?" I asked.

"As long as you don't do something stupid again," she said.

"Reading all those books has made me a lot smarter," I replied. "It's probably *impossible* for me to do something stupid again."

"Never say never," she advised me, then hurried off.

I found Dad out by the J-3 and told him everything. "Figures it was Spizz," he said. "I should have known that tricycle was a clue to just how demented he was."

"He took my car," I said angrily. "Do you think we can fly around until we spot him?"

"The cops will track him down. But here's our J-3 plan," he said, changing the subject. "I got a flight plan out of Norvelt tonight for Florida."

"But Mom has just allowed me to play baseball tonight," I cried out, and nearly broke into tears. "I'm finally free and I won't get my airplane ride."

"Don't start blubbering," he said. "I've got it all figured out. You'll be playing in the outfield, right?"

"Yep," I said. "Usually center field because we don't have enough players to cover all the positions."

"Well, when you see me come out of the left field lights, run for the right field fence," he said, and winked.

"What else?" I asked.

"You'll figure it out," he replied, and snapped his fingers. "You're a smart boy."

"Do you need me to help with anything?" I asked.

He looked over at the bomb shelter. "Maybe you could start filling that in," he said, and laughed.

"Really? Now?" I asked.

"Not now," he said. "You're free to go."

I ran back to my room to finish my obituary with the Virginia Dare story. Then I ran down to Mr. Greene's office. He was pecking away at a typewriter.

"Another dead old lady!" he shouted when he saw me. "Impossible."

"A deer this time," I said, and passed him my handwritten obit.

"The hunters around here won't like it," he said after reading it through, "but I'll print it."

Then I stuck out my hand. "I won the bet," I said. "Miss Volker didn't kill those ladies."

He smiled, then opened the drawer where he kept the bet money. "Here is your four bucks. I thought I had you when they arrested her but then old Spizz turned out to be the killer. I'm writing up an article on it now," he said, and went back to his typewriter. "Sorry, I have a deadline."

That evening I decided to ride Spizz's tricycle to the game, and when Bunny saw me ride up in my uniform and walk onto the ball field she wanted to know everything about the murders.

"I'll give you all the details after the game," I said. "In full—I know *everything*. The *who*, the *how*, and the *why*!"

"Everything?" she asked.

"Remember how you told me about all the details on that dead Hells Angel?" I reminded her. "Well, I'll tell you all the details about how the ladies died and how Spizz did it—and I bet it will make your nose bleed too."

"It's a deal," she said gleefully, then she slapped me across the butt with her glove. "Good to have you back on the field. Now let's play ball."

When the game began I took the outfield. The sky was just growing dark and I kept looking up into the air as if every batter was hitting me a fly ball. And then I heard the J-3 to my left. I looked up and he was coming in low. He didn't have a lot of room to land and so he was feathering his engine to keep his speed down. I ran as fast as I could to the far fence. By then a few people in the stands had seen him and they began to point. And then I could hear their voices, and then I could only hear the engine of the J-3 as Dad barely cleared the fence and set it down in right field, and then he rolled across center field, and by the time he reached left field he turned the tail rudder and the plane spun around.

At that moment I hopped off the fence and ran as fast as I could along the warning track until I was well past the propeller, then I circled around to the passenger side. Dad leaned over and opened the door and I hopped into the plane.

"Put your seat belt on," he hollered over the engine noise, and then he hit the throttle and the J-3 *hop-hopped* forward and we went speeding across the green outfield grass. For a moment I looked at the infield, and the entire team was just standing as still as painted plastic toys, and then I turned back to look out the windshield just as Dad lifted the nose and we left the ground and rose up over the fence and gained speed as we climbed into the air over Norvelt.

"Take a good look," Dad hollered above the sound of the prop. "They should put a fence around this town."

"Like a Japanese internment camp?" I asked.

"More like a museum," he suggested. "Your mom is right. It's a piece of history. But like a lot of history, it won't last. I mean, it's not like Rome was saved, or Athens. All that is left of them are some stone ruins. And in a few years the wooden Norvelt houses will be hauled off and just the stone basements will be left—and some tombstones. That'll be the end of it. Of course, there will be a historic plaque recording what Norvelt used to be."

"But it's sad that it will be lost," I said. "The whole idea behind why they built it will be gone."

"Things change—that's why they call it *history*," Dad said. "But before this town is gone for good, let's give them one more thing to talk about."

He pulled back on the stick, and when we banked to the left I could see we were headed for the Viking Drive-in.

"Look in the back," Dad hollered above the noise of the engine and airflow. "You'll find a milk crate full of balloons—filled with *red* paint!"

"I thought we were doing *water* balloons?"

"Red should leave a little more history," he said. "Water will evaporate."

"What's playing?" I asked.

"*Sink the Bismarck!*" he replied. "Maybe we can help!"

In a minute we were heading directly for the screen. "Grab a balloon," Dad said. "When I say 'bombs away,' let it go."

Because the sun had just gone down, the black-and-white preview for tonight's movie was still rolling. On the screen the massive German WWII battleship was being launched. Then the picture changed to a worried British captain and a war-room map of the Atlantic Ocean covered with little toy-sized ships.

"Is this okay to do?" I asked Dad, and held my balloon by the window.

"All is fair in love and war," he said. "Bombs away!"

We both let the balloons drop, and Dad pulled back on the stick and we climbed into the sky. "Did we hit anything?" I asked.

"You never know until you go in for a second pass," he said, and laughed like a maniac.

I gave him a balloon and got one for myself, and we turned and headed back toward the screen. Right away I could see that both of us had scored direct hits. Two red blotches had exploded against the black-and-white movie images and the red paint ran like bloody tears down the face of the screen as torpedoes skimmed across the water toward the hull of the *Bismarck*.

Once again Dad went into a dive. "Bombs away!" he shouted. We let go, then quickly climbed up into the air again. There were two more balloons left. "One more time," he said, "and then we better get out of here before they call the air force on us."

He steered the plane around and I could see the red splotches on the screen, but this time I also saw that all the cars had started up and their headlights were on and people were running out the pedestrian gate, and it wasn't funny. Cars were jamming up around the exit and their horns were blowing and a few people were pointing up in the air at us, and I suddenly realized that I was doing it all over again. It was like I was shooting Dad's Japanese rifle at the screen. Only then I had no idea how frightening it would be if I had shot someone or just scared someone. Now I knew exactly what I was doing. The reason you remind yourself of the stupid stuff you've done in the past is so you don't do it again. That was what Miss Volker had been teaching us all these years.

"Dad," I said. "Let's leave. People are scared."

"We aren't hurting anything," he said. "It's a joke."

"Maybe this joke isn't that funny," I said. "Really. I want down."

"On the ball field?" he asked.

"Sure," I said. I knew Bunny would think it was

really funny. And I knew I would laugh about it with her. But it would be a false laugh because I'd probably get into trouble, and later when I got home Mom would already know I had done something wrong, and I knew that being a jerk in the airplane and scaring people was really stupid. And being stupid at that moment would forever be a part of who I was. If Miss Volker was writing about it for her This Day In History column it might read:

> **On the morning of August 17, Jack Gantos was released from being grounded by his parents. But stay tuned because on August 18 he might be grounded all over again—unless he remembers his history!**

'I think my brain is filled with bees.'

Joey is a good kid, maybe even a great kid, but his teachers say he's WIRED . . . they never know what he's going to do next.

He bounces round the kitchen and spins down the school hall. He sharpens his finger in the pencil sharpener and swallows his house key.

He can't sit still for more than a minute . . . Joey is BUZZING!

978 0 440 86433 2

Walker is in a dilemma . . .

Sixteen year old Walker has discovered that two female classmates are having an affair. He knows that to give away their secret would be unforgivable. But when, suddenly, he finds the heat is on him, betrayal seems to be his only way out.

Feel Walker's pain as you are gripped by this powerful, emotional and unputdownable novel.

Unsuitable for younger readers

978 1 849 41744 0